WATCHERS

FAYE KNIGHTLY

Acknowledgments

First and foremost, I would like to thank my family, especially my husband. Writing a book means disappearing into another world for a while, and I absolutely could not do so without the love and understanding of my family. Thank you for knowing sometimes I need to disappear, but I will always come back.

I'm eternally gratefully for my editor, Rachel Mitchell who pushes me to produce the very best work I'm capable of. Thank you for never holding your punches, Watchers is better because of you. You're stuck with me now, Rachel. I'm never letting go. Yeah, that's kind of cute...in a stalkerish kind of way...

A big shoutout to my beta reading team who managed to read Watchers and give me their all important feedback within a week of receiving it. I appreciate every word of support and critical thought into the inner workings of the Breeders universe.

Lastly, I got stuck on the jail scene in this book. REALLY stuck. In my head, I could see it all working fine, but when my editor asked me where Syl's legs were, I blanked. Thank you to Laurae Knight for helping me figure out where the hell Syl's legs were. You're the hero of that scene.

WATCHERS

Dedicated to anyone who's ever felt less than.
To the misfits who know what it's like to sit on your own at lunch and to anyone who's
been cast out for perceived differences and inadequacies.
You're perfect.
This one's for you.

WATCHERS

Trigger Warnings

This book deals with the topic of infertility and reproductive control through forced sterilization. Bullying of the fmc does occur and past child abuse is mentioned. Please protect yourself. If any of these topics are a trigger for you, PUT DOWN THE BOOK! Your mental health is important.

Chapter I

THE WATCHER

The armrests on my shitty chair dug into my bony hips as if whoever had chosen it didn't give a shit that I'd be sitting here for the next twenty-four-plus hours with only brief backroom breaks and a few scheduled naps. This wasn't my first observation, and you'd think I'd be used to the shitty seating, but this one was terrible. That and the dark, cramped room where they put us watchers wasn't something you got used to. My ass sure hadn't.

Fuck me. At least they'd provided a mini fridge with sandwiches and drinks, and I could press a button if I really needed to use the bathroom. Otherwise, I'd be allowed to use the facilities in exactly eight hours from start time.

Leaning back into the poorly padded chair with almost no movement, I studied the monitor in front of me, wondering what sort of girl I'd be watching this time. The last one had been a scrawny thing with enormous eyes and small tits who had squeaked when she came. Fucking squeaked. I'd still rubbed a few out, purely out of boredom. At least the coordinators knew enough to provide an ample supply of lube.

You didn't watch people fuck for days of your life without needing some release. But somebody needed to watch them—to make sure the rules were followed. Masks stayed on. Touching kept to a minimum. No one spoke. Ensure the girl was okay. There was a guard to call if one of the breeding males got out of control, but mostly I was here to watch the women. I've never had to pause a heat before, but it's happened. At thirty hours without water, your body was none too happy.

I wondered if I'd ever have to stop one—rush in there like a hero and unstrap the girl, force her to drink through her lusty moans until she imbibed enough fluid to keep her organs from failing.

Sighing, I stretched my arms over my head, fingertips grazing the walls of this tiny box of a room. I wished, not for the first time, that I was a smaller man, but I was tall with broad shoulders, making this small room comically tight. I unzipped my backpack and carefully took out my charcoal and sketchpad, placing them carefully in the small space in front of the monitor.

At least I could draw in peace.

Or I could have had the monitor not come alive with a flurry of activity. The door opened to reveal a girl, tall and luscious, with a gorgeous golden tan to her skin. Her chin length hair, an unusually light ash-blonde appearing almost white on my monitor, accentuated her high cheekbones.

What a fucking goddess. I would definitely need the lube. My hand moved of its own volition, sketching out the confident smirk twisting at her plump lips. She laughed with the coordinator while she climbed on top of the bed. My hand turned jittery, moving lower to sketch out the curve of her breasts, peeking out through the slip she wore and trying to capture the way her nipples peaked the fabric.

The coordinator put the straps around her ankles, and my jaw clenched. The curve of her legs taunted me, and I longed to feel if they were as smooth as they looked.

I bet they felt like silk, and they'd wrap around her breeding males in a few minutes. A growl rose in my throat, and I self-consciously looked around in case someone heard. Nope, still an empty room.

The woman laughed when the coordinator held out the vile of purple flowers that would induce her. Full on laughed, her eyes twinkling and her face transforming into something even more stunning than before.

Fuck, she was a pretty one, and I'd seen enough to know. The uncomfortable chair was forgotten. The tiny room disregarded.

She took the bottle, swiftly unstopped it, and breathed it in with a confidence that I'd never seen before in a breeder. Usually, they were nervous about the physical trial ahead.

Not her.

She pulled off her shift, and I leaned forward in my seat, trying to get closer to the monitor and see her better. Fucking things were grainy as shit. I couldn't even see her eye colour on the thing, and I felt a tugging in my chest, a pull to know if they were brown or blue. Maybe hazel—the green swirling with brown.

My hand itched to sketch her. I indulged the urge, flipping through the pages of my sketchbook to find a new page where I could draw out the beautiful face of the girl on the monitor. The delicate curve of her neck. Those pert breasts begging to be touched. I couldn't wait to watch her be bred, to watch the breeding males come in and do their thing. Would she squeak when she came? Or maybe she'd scream. Yeah, I bet she was a screamer. She looked like the type.

I was lost in the art, tracing her lips and the curvature of her face over and over in an effort to get it right, when it happened.

My hand paused—the tip of my charcoal poised above the paper. The girl on my monitor was crying.

It was the kind of crying you reserved for time spent alone. Large wet tears dribbling down her crumpled face. No, these tears weren't to impress somebody or to seek comfort, these were for her.

Mouth hanging open, I ripped at the lewd drawing I'd been making. Tearing off the page, I started fresh.

This was her. Scared. Vulnerable. This was what I needed to capture, and my hands skidded across the paper, desperate to preserve the sorrow etched into the beautiful girl's face. The girl who had been laughing a moment ago, smiling so damned big, I'd thought the coordinator was going to make a pass at her.

But that wasn't her. This was her and—fuck.

I wanted to know why she was crying. What had caused the beautiful woman on my screen to feel so utterly broken? Sobs shook her body, and my heart clenched.

A desire unlike any other took hold of my chest and squeezed. I'd seen a dozen girls being bred in the breeding rooms, but this one...

I wanted to know her.

I slammed a fist into the table, rattling the monitor.

Get to know her. Right. That was an impossibility. All I could do was watch, and watch I did, completing my sketch of her tearful face and starting another, determined to catch the glimpse of despair I'd seen in her eyes of an unknown colour.

I watched as her cheeks flushed and her breathing quickened. She leaned back on the bed and fumbled for the remote beside her. Eyes glued to the screen, I watched as she hammered the button, her slight chest rising and falling erratically as the heat took hold. She wiped at her face until there was no trace of tears, though how she had the presence of mind to do so was beyond me.

Normally, girls were so overcome they sometimes forgot to press the button, and the coordinator had been forced to come back in to verbally obtain their consent before sending the first male in.

The first male entered wearing an eagle mask, the fake feathers pressed into rubber. He was rock hard when he stepped forward between her legs. She took him with a gasp, her back arching prettily when he sank to the hilt, and began pounding into her without restraint.

Fuck. The Eagle didn't even let her catch her fucking breath. He went up on his toes, pressing down on her abdomen to get deeper. The crying girl moaned in ecstasy, her voice breaking. She grabbed the rails beside her, panting when he gripped her hips and pulled her back to the edge from where she slid. They should really put some kind of grippy shit on those mattresses.

My hand moved to sketch the look on her face as she neared release. The tension in her features, and the moment they slackened.

Perfection. I grabbed for my hard on, not bothering to pull down my pants, and gave it a few quick strokes before finding my release. I hadn't needed the lube, barely had to touch myself. My body responded to hers when I wasn't even in the same room. She came down, but not completely. The heat didn't allow for that.

The Eagle wiped himself off, leaving the girl to moan in the bed. With the man out of the room, I fumbled with the file on my desk, desperate for more information about the crying girl.

"Sylvia."

I don't know why I spoke her name aloud or why it felt so good to say it, but my tongue caressed each syllable. I wondered if she went by her full name or if she had any cute nicknames. Sylvia's panting on the monitor caught my attention, and my breathing quickened right along with her. My body was desperate to align with a girl I'd never seen in person and could barely make out on the shitty monitor. But she was just in the other room. Close enough, I could bust in there and take her myself.

Only that wasn't my role.

I was a watcher, and so I resumed my vigil. My breath hitched when she leaned back on the bed, helplessly fondling her breasts and moaning in quick little pants.

She was suffering, and I wanted badly to replace her hands with my own. To take my place between her legs and press into her wet heat, fucking her endlessly until the heat released its hold.

The next man entered. This one wore an alligator mask, the snout almost comically long, but the snarl on the rubber mask's face was anything but. He was huge, tall like I was, but thick. His cock looked like it might break my crying girl, my Sylvia. I watched with bated breath as he took up a position between her legs and eased into her entrance.

Sylvia's jaw dropped and she squealed. Straining my ear, I detected no pain in the noise. Shit, what would I have done if she had been in pain? Busted in there like some kind of fucking hero and pried her off The Gator's enormous dick? Not that I could manage to move such a mountain of a man. No, my wasted body was far too weak for that, and my hand tightened into a fist. I was powerless, pathetic, defective.

A watcher.

If Sylvia really was in trouble, I wouldn't be able to protect her, not like this. I'd have to go through the embarrassment of calling our resident guard.

Shit, I need to get it together. Shaking my head, my shaggy blonde hair fell into my eyes. Annoyed, I brushed it away. The Gator was fully seated now, and Sylvia was stretched tight around him, twisting and turning as the heat madness consumed her. He moved gently, rocking his hips, careful not to hurt her, and I said a silent prayer that I didn't need to intervene in some completely embarrassing way.

He came after only a few minutes, releasing inside of her with a guttural growl I could feel in my bones.

A shiver raced down my spine, followed by burning as it traveled its way out from my chest. My clothes were too tight, the cotton of my most comfortable joggers and t-shirt turned itchy against my skin. I wanted to be in there with her—badly. I was hard again by the time The Gator left the room, and I looked down at myself in shock.

This shouldn't be possible, but Sylvia moaned again. Begging to be filled now that The Gator had taken his leave, and I moaned right along with her. Sharing in the experience. Pretending it was me wearing a mask and waiting to enter the room.

Scattering my precious drawings, I stood up, getting as close to the monitor as I could. Feeling every pant. Every tantalizing sound she made.

The next man entered wearing a tiger mask, and I pulled down my soiled pants, taking my cock in hand.

He stepped up to her and pressed inside, moaning at the sensation. I fucked my hand to the rhythm he fucked her, dreaming, wishing it was me in there. The slapping of skin—my own and theirs—echoed all around me, mingling with our moans into a beautiful cacophony I never wanted to end. Only it did with a shudder on Sylvia's part, the smallest thing shaking through her that sent me barreling towards my release. My cum splattered on the monitor, and I angrily wiped it away, pissed that it would dare obstruct my view of the angel on the screen.

An angel. Yes, that's what she was, and she had been sent to me. I watched as The Tiger cleaned himself up and left Sylvia without a backwards glance.

Hours passed in a haze of pleasure, my body helplessly responding to hers until I lost count of how many times I found release.

This wasn't normal.

But it was happening, and I'd become a helpless participant in Sylvia's heat.

My body only slowed when hers did, the telltale agitated movement common to those in heat easing and leaving her laying on the bed, relaxed with a frown puckering her brow. Fuck, what colour were her eyes and why was it so important for me to know?

With a sigh, I looked around at the absolute mess I'd made of the room. Now that Sylvia's heat was over, I felt like a fool. My eyes fell to the floor where I'd shoved my drawings of her, and I angrily bent to retrieve them, brushing a bit of dirt off the one of her sorrow. I stared at the image, wondering what had been going through her head when she'd cried. If it was something I could help with. But she wasn't mine to help. She was one of the elite, and I pulled up my soiled pants over my scrawny hips and sat down hard into the uncomfortable chair I'd barely used. At least my ass wasn't sore, even if the rest of me was.

Grabbing a few tissues, I worked to clean up the sopping mess I'd made of the table. My legs were shaking with fatigue. The way I'd reacted to her was severely fucked up.

It reminded me of a woman I'd observed a few breeders ago. One of her breeding males had been so desperate for her he'd climbed right onto the breeding table to fuck her. She'd been touching him, too, and it had been one of the most beautiful things I'd seen. There'd been something between them, and I'd felt—for the first time—like I was truly intruding on an intimate moment.

I should've reported it, but I didn't. I couldn't. To do so would have been to call that desperate passion wrong. Then they'd come to me and asked about her, that breeder. She'd left with him, her ram. Fucking left. Unprotected into the icy wasteland of the world.

Packless, friendless. I'd hated myself every day since for not speaking up. The poor girl was probably dead by now, and I could've stopped it.

I understood their passion better now. I'd never felt it myself, but my reaction to Sylvia had felt akin to it. With a sigh, I looked up at the monitor, expecting Sylvia to be unstrapped and helping herself to the water. Fuck, I didn't even know how long it had been. Like her, I hadn't used the bathroom, hadn't slept, hadn't drunk water. I checked the clock in the room and was startled to find it had been twenty hours.

Twenty hours lost to this woman, and I'd be happy to lose twenty more.

Only Sylvia wasn't unstrapping herself. She was laying back watching the door expectantly.

What. The. Fuck.

But her heat was over. I'd seen it. I'd *felt* it. I watched, my mouth hanging open, as a man wearing a panda mask entered the room, and Sylvia began wiggling helplessly on the bed. She was acting. Barely a moment before, I'd seen her laying perfectly still and not within the throes of her heat. The masked man didn't care. He took her anyway, positioning himself at her entrance dutifully and sliding into what must be a mess of fluids. He pounded into her, and Sylvia continued her charade, moaning and crying out as though the heat still consumed her.

It didn't, and I couldn't understand why she wouldn't press the button. Why she would make a choice to stay? My body ached after accompanying her in her heat—my legs tremored and my cock was sore. She must feel worse, but she carried on as if her heat hadn't ended for three more masked men.

When the third left, she sat up with a sigh, and I saw it again—the mask of sorrow overtaking her features as she sat up and her hair fell forward. She reached out and pressed the button calmly before moving to undo the straps on her legs.

Frantically, I reached for my paper and charcoal, sketching her. Every detail. Every feature. Every bit I could see trying to recreate the way she'd moved during those countless acts. I was desperate to have something of her to hold on to, and I managed a few more pictures I knew would never do her justice before the coordinator entered the room to check her and declare the breeding party over.

She left the room with him, wearing that smile of hers. The one I knew was an act, a fake. She clung to his arm and disappeared out the door, leaving the room empty. Leaving me empty. I looked down at my papers, happy at least to have something to hold on to.

The experience I'd had here in this room would be one I would remember for a long time, but the way Sylvia had cried, the sorrow on her face, would haunt me forever.

Chapter 2

SYL

Fuck, I was sore. The last man who had taken me—long after my heat had ended—hadn't been gentle about it, and my aching body had protested. I'd barely managed to get through it with him, feigning enjoyment. But then, every deposit counted.

It had to. Because this needed to *work*. Drinking another bottle of water, I eyed the freshen up room with distaste. I hated this place. Everything about it reeked of the control the pack had over my life. Oh, sure, I had a choice. I could choose not to be a Breeder, but if I did, if I threw this role back in their faces and confessed a child was the last thing I wanted, they'd send me there.

The poisoned fields.

A shudder skittered across my skin. A life of hard labour away from the comforts of home. This was my last cycle to try to achieve a pregnancy, and if I failed, they'd deem me with no further purpose to the pack except trying to salvage the dead earth for future generations.

I had a choice, but it was no choice at all.

I would breed or die.

With a sigh, I drained the last of my bottle and snatched another from the table beside my chair. My body was ruined, every bit of energy taken by the heat and its lust-filled mania. I needed to eat and sleep before I could even think about propositioning any of the guys in the house, but the urgency to conceive made me wish I could go again, that I'd been able to take one more man in the breeding room—two more. Any of them might be the one who would end my suffering and make me a pack mother.

I chewed down a protein bar from a basket on the table, wincing at the chalky taste. These things sucked, but at least they'd give me some energy back. Forcing myself to eat another one, I cautiously stood up, pleased when my legs were sturdy beneath me.

Time to head back to Pack Breeders 103C and see what everyone was up to.

The walk to our front door was a familiar one, and I didn't even need to look down for the arrows. With a yawn, I pulled open the door, not at all surprised to see everyone drinking and partying.

"Hey, Syl!" Carter raised a bottle to me, and I smiled in greeting.

"Think you have a baby brewing yet, babe?" His grin was friendly enough, but I still wanted to punch him in his stupidly handsome face. Maybe rip out a few hairs.

"Oh yeah, definitely." I grinned at him, giving a chuckle like he'd made a fabulous joke instead of driving a needle right into my heart. There was no use in making enemies here. I was The Party Girl. Always up for whatever with whoever, and I had to be if I ever wanted to get out of this place.

That dream. Now that put a smile on my face, made the grin I wore as I squeezed between a couple of guys drinking beers all the more true. I'd get pregnant, go have the babies—or baby—pass them off to the aunties, and never come back again.

I wanted nothing more than to go to my room, to sleep until my body recovered from how depleted I felt, but The Party Girl didn't do that. No, The Party Girl took every opportunity to socialize, to engage with others, hoping to increase her chances of a pregnancy.

So, I sat down on the soft couch next to Carter. He gestured towards the kitchen and gave me an eyebrow waggle. A smile was the only reply I could manage in my drained state, but he understood and went to get me a beer. He returned with it a moment later, slinging an arm across my shoulder. If I had someone here I was regularly with, it was

Carter. A bulky guy with an athlete's stamina, he never told me no. Plus, he was pretty to look at, with chestnut brown hair hanging nearly into his green eyes.

He could have anyone here, but I made sure he wanted me most. The paddles he liked to use put the other girls off, but not me. It didn't turn me on, but I was used to pain and could suffer through it better than most. I still remembered telling the aunties about the way my mother would test my skin and hit me across the back when she thought no one was looking. She'd never explained herself, but there had been a malevolence in her eyes when she'd done it. Why she'd singled me out amongst my siblings, I'd never know, but maybe she'd been preparing me for Carter.

The aunties had laughed when I'd told them. Sure, they'd checked me over, but I'd healed too quickly for any of my mother's abuses to leave a mark. She'd made sure of it.

Smiling, I took the offered beer from Carter and twisted off the lid like my hands hadn't been cramping from grabbing those railings just an hour ago. They were stiff. I needed sleep, but I'd manage one beer before slipping away.

One beer to prove nothing fazed me.

One beer to prove I was strong.

But I couldn't stop myself from drinking it faster than normal, nearly choking on the bubbles, and laughing cheerily when Carter told me about a bottle cap flipping game they'd been playing.

Finishing the beer, I set it down on the coffee table. Carter leaned in, the arm around my shoulders tightening. He kissed my cheek, his hand snaking forward to fondle my breast like he owned it.

With a sharp inhale, I gripped his hand. My breasts were incredibly tender from the heat cycle, but Carter didn't care. I saw a familiar glimmer of lust in his eyes as he gauged my reaction.

Fuck.

"I have to use the ladies' room, baby." Carefully, I slipped out of his arms, watching with satisfaction when I saw his drunken grin.

"Yeah, you go for it." Relieved, I made my way down the long hallway and into my room. I knew Carter would give up and go find someone else to fuck tonight.

Which meant I could rest for a bit. I took off the tight clothes I'd packed to wear back to the dorms and riffled through the drawers until I found a simple, white cotton nightgown. My favourite. Nobody knew I wore this—I kept it hidden at the back of the drawer. Certainly, when I had company, I had more alluring nightwear, but for tonight, I would be comfortable and lose myself to the sleep my body desperately needed.

As I tucked myself into bed, I knew I wouldn't dream. The exhaustion took hold, and I welcomed it, slipping into the darkness and glad to have my bed to myself.

THE WATCHER

What did those chosen for the breeding program have that I didn't? My records mocked me as I skimmed them over for the fourth time. I had the height, the potential, but with a severe case of asthma that may or may not be genetic, the words "unsuitable for the breeding program" had been written in the administrator's notes. I'd found them when I'd become a watcher and sneaked a peek at my file.

How neatly he'd printed those words, as though they didn't affect him. He'd signed away my ability to contribute to the next generation with a painful amount of ease. Defectives, they called us. Oh sure, we were all serving the pack and were equal under the alpha. No one was supposed to use the term, but they still did.

I looked down at myself. I was as tall as any of them at six feet, but scrawny with hip bones jutting out more than they should. Once I'd been assigned my pack role as a watcher, there had been little point in keeping myself in shape, in bothering to take care of my body. Not when it, and I, was *unsuitable*.

But now I had a reason, and I pulled out the paper of my crying girl, Sylvia. Carefully unfolding it and putting it on the table. The file room stank of mildew, and I sniffed, hoping it wouldn't irritate my lungs and bring on an attack. My medicine was within reach, but fuck if I had time to deal with it right now.

A couple of Syl's breeding males had been part of a successful pregnancy with another breeding female, which meant she'd be getting some new ones this cycle. Thank fuck. It provided the perfect opportunity for me to slip in unnoticed. All I needed was someone I could pass as.

I pulled file after file, searching through face after face in the breeding program until I found one that was passable, one who looked enough like me, one who was set to be called during Sylvia's next cycle.

Height, six foot one. Close enough, but the weight—this guy was a solid two hundred pounds with zero body fat, and I was one-eighty with my bulkiest clothes on. With a sigh, I looked over at the picture of Sylvia.

Why are you crying, baby?

Fuck, I wanted to know, to be a part of her world where I could touch her and talk to her. Everything I was doing was to that end. So, I scribbled down the details of the man I was planning to impersonate, taking a moment to double check no one else from his squad or surrounding squads would be present. Nope, he would be a lone wolf in Pack Breeders 103C, and now, so was I.

Reverently, I folded my drawing of Sylvia and put it in my pocket, along with my scribbled notes, and replaced the file in the cabinet. I wasn't ready to change things yet.

There was work to do.

"Yeah, baby, yeah." Carter came, and I felt like I was going to puke. My ass still stung from where he'd used the rod. My body still sore and my energy spent from the heat. But every single drop counted, so I stayed laying down on his bed, smiling up at him like he was the fucking sun rising.

"You going on the run today?" Carter smirked, his eyes roving my body like he owned it.

I really shouldn't. What I should do was take a few days off to make sure I recovered my energy, but I was close enough to my fertile period that I didn't dare waste an opportunity.

"Yeah, of course." I showed him my teeth, tonguing the gap beside my incisor. "I fucking love the runs."

"Of course you do. Well, I'm going to go grab some food. Later, Syl." He tugged up his sporty black sweats and walked out without a backwards glance, like he hadn't been inside of me less than a minute ago.

I gave myself some time to relax, pissed I'd been forced to use Carter again, but with only a few queasy hungover guys to choose from, he'd been the only sure thing.

At least he'd brought his own bedding, a comfortable red duvet that felt like I was lying on pillows. It was the only thing I liked about him, and I appreciated the softness on the sensitive skin of my abused ass.

Eyes on the prize, Syl. This would be the cycle. I knew it because it had to be. There was no other alternative. I just had to do this for a few more weeks, and I'd never have to look at another man again.

With a bit of difficulty, courtesy of my achy muscles, I pulled myself up and exited Carter's room, closing it carefully behind me. Somebody pinched my ass, and I jumped with a squeal.

"Where you going, baby?" Sam eyed me hungrily, his dark eyes lingering on the curve of my breasts peeking out through the top of my shirt. He was another sure thing. Smoothly, I closed the distance between us until our faces were inches apart.

"Wherever you are, sexy."

Sam's thin lips curled up in a smirk, and his heavy brows knitted.

"I was thinking I might like a run if you want to step outside."

Two runs in one day, I knew I couldn't do. "How about a shower?"

"How about we do what I say, or I won't fuck you?" *Shit*, now he was annoyed, his lips twisting. I hated how the guys knew I was desperate after three months of being here. Was it that painfully obvious?

I smoothed my shirt down over my taut abdomen.

Incensed, Sam slammed me against the wall, his palm landing beside my face, effectively caging me in. I didn't flinch, just gave him my best sultry smile. "You like to tell me what to do?"

"We'll go to my room. You're mine for today." I relaxed beneath his grip, letting him know I would submit to him, that there was no need for a display of strength.

"No problem."

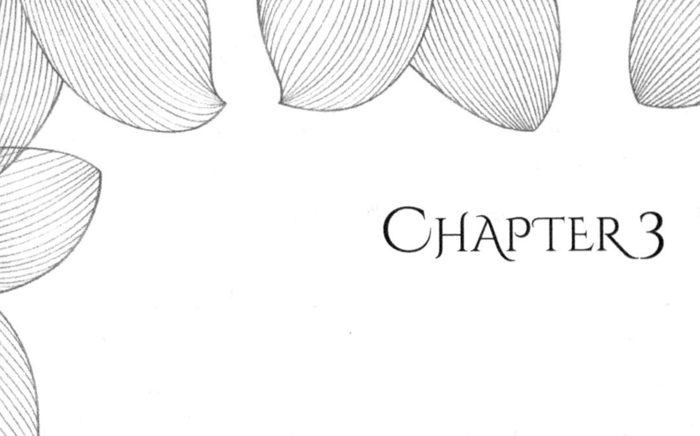

Chapter 3

THE WATCHER

My muscles screamed as I pulled up the totes full of large cans and started another set. Staring at Sylvia's picture made it easier, and I'd pasted every sketch I'd drawn of her on my wall to remind me why I was doing this. I swear I could feel the muscles tearing, but each tear, each rep brought me closer to her, and I counted on my lycan healing to get me there fast. A dangerous practice forbidden in the guard program and one that left my body throbbing with pain and filled with an alarming weakness, while my system worked to stitch itself back together.

But I needed to look the part, and with only four weeks left to go before Sylvia went into heat again, time was running out. That was assuming she didn't get pregnant this cycle and that she'd remain for at least one more. If I were religious, I would have prayed to the Moon Goddess for this one chance, for everything I was doing to be worth it.

Or maybe just to meet her.

Anxiety clouded my mind, turning every thought into one with sharp edges. If anyone caught me, there'd be no coming back to my current, albeit miserable, existence. They might forgive a guard, but no one would think twice about reassigning or exiling a watcher.

Oh sure, they told us we were just as important as everyone else. Each pack member had their role, but they'd already deemed me unsuitable for the hard labour in the fields. There wasn't much respect to be had for supervising the breeding progress. Just a bitter sort of jealousy that had poisoned my mind and body for the past three years, leaving me a husk of a person with no real prospects for life. Until Sylvia had appeared on my screen and made my body her willing puppet.

But if I was being honest with myself, something I was typically brutal about, it had happened long before Sylvia pulled me into her heat. It had started when she'd cried.

Just a few tears, a simple thing, but the crumbling of that beautiful face and the way she'd hid it from the coordinator had struck a chord deep inside of my chest, had revived something within me I'd thought was long dead. A spark of interest.

What reason would a beautiful girl chosen as a pack mother have to be so heartbreakingly sad?

Her place in this pack was secured. She was to be honoured and given every privilege, so why the tears?

Fascinated, I pulled the sketches of her crying from the wall and held them under my desk light.

Beautiful. Her face, touched by sorrow, was so much more real than the joy I'd seen there a few minutes prior. That wasn't Sylvia, this was.

And I could help her. Whatever was bothering her, I would meet her and find out what it was so I could play the hero. I didn't care what happened to me, and the realization hit me with a jolt. My life had been nothing but going through the motions since I'd been assigned as a watcher. I'd resigned to it, but I wouldn't call it a living. If sneaking into the breeding program to meet Sylvia meant my life was forfeit, well, I didn't have much of a life to forfeit in the first place.

With a smile, I brushed the charcoal tear off her cheek as though it were real, and I could touch her. There was a promise in the movement. I might only have my drawings of her for now, but one day soon, I would meet her and see if she reacted to me the way I reacted to her.

"Hey, are you in there?"

Reg. Shit. His booming voice would not be ignored, and he pounded on the thin door to my tiny room hard enough to leave it trembling. *Fuck.* "Um, yeah, just one sec." Hurriedly, I gathered up the drawings of Sylvia and tenderly tucked them into the drawer of my single tall dresser. Moving aside the folded up pants, I dropped them back in place to obscure the precious papers. "Yes?" I pulled open the door, catching the man outside in mid knock. Reg, my would-be best friend. At least on his end. I'd done absolutely nothing to encourage him, and all my attempts at dismissal had failed.

A friendship between us didn't make sense. His abrasive personality had rubbed me the wrong way since we'd met and we had nothing in common. Physically, he was my polar opposite, beefy where I was thin and squat where I was tall, with a thick neck and a buzz cut that only served to emphasize how fleshy he was. With a grin perfectly showcasing his wide mouth, he retracted his outstretched hand.

"Time to get to work, Buddy. Everything's got to be spic-and-span for tomorrow's breeding party."

Right. Fuck. I only hoped my trembling arms could complete the task.

The microfiber cloth slid easily over the gleaming, thick plastic of a stag mask. Its horns twisted majestically above its head. Cleaning up the rooms wasn't bad. Cleaning the masks they deemed us unworthy to wear? Now, that was a stab in the gut, and a cruel reminder we weren't suited to wear the mask.

I decided right then and there that I would play The Stag when I entered Sylvia's room. I would come to her for our first meeting not as a watcher, but as a breeding male.

"Fuck, man, it's clean. Now come help me with these. They want to get started within an hour and everything needs to be disinfected and dry or they'll be pissed," Reg grumbled, moved past me and bumping me with his shoulder.

With a parting look at the stag mask, I placed it carefully on the table, wondering who would wear it this night. I turned back to Reg, who was fumbling clumsily with a stack of masks, his meaty hands unable to work the delicate creases.

Taking half to myself, I lifted my bucket of disinfectant, wincing as the movement pulled at torn shoulder muscles. Those muscles would be stronger tomorrow.

I would be stronger.

We worked in silence. When I noticed Reg getting particularly frustrated with the grooved beak of a hawk mask, I took it from him, wondering which mask he would have chosen if he had been selected for the breeding program. I didn't dare ask. It was bad enough I'd be leaving him and everyone else behind. I couldn't arouse their suspicions, or I'd risk the whole plan.

Instead, I turned to a different line of conversation.

A safe one.

"I'm almost finished restoring a new comic."

Reg's blue eyes lit up like I knew they would. Rolling my eyes, I pretended I'd said something as uninteresting as washing a dish. I didn't particularly like comics myself, but it passed the time, and it was a good skill for trades.

"Oh, man." Reg's gaze turned hopeful. "Please, just tell me if Chaosman survives."

The comic I was restoring for him had left the hero trapped in a cage at the bottom of the sea and rapidly running out of air. The nearly indecipherable image had been a challenge, but I'd discovered gill lines on his neck and used my imagination to fill in the rest.

"You got extra jerky for me?" I asked. Reg knew someone in the building's kitchens. With all the muscle I was tearing up, I needed a lot more meat than we were given.

"Yeah, yeah. Though I don't get why you want so much all of a sudden."

"Chaosman has gills," I blurted.

The distraction worked, and I watched in satisfaction as he smiled, eyes twinkling. He gave a knowing nod. "I fucking knew he was a child of Atlantis. You know Caleb said I was crazy when I told him my theory, but I know my shit. Yes." His fist shot up into the air so fast, I was at risk of being struck, and I took a step back with my hands raised defensively.

"Whoa, easy there." I held up a hand to block any further wayward limbs.

Reg smiled sheepishly. "Sorry, and yeah, I've got you two trays of beef jerky. You're my hero, man."

I didn't want to be Reg's hero. I'd much rather be Sylvia's.

The invasion startled me, but I quickly regained my calm, letting my muscles relax as Carter pushed past the first ring of muscle. He used enough lube that the anal wasn't as painful as it could be, but tears still leaked from the corners of my eyes.

I couldn't wait for it to be over. His deep grunts warned me that he was near to finishing, and if he came there...Well, this entire act with him would've been a waste. But The Party Girl didn't complain, so I cooed and leaned back into him. The last thing I wanted was to make it seem like I was only eager for their cum.

Even though I was.

Positioned at the edge of the bed, on my hands and knees, I curled my fingers into the soft, white bedding. He was close, and I couldn't stop myself from gasping when he stepped onto the bed and slammed his way in with one stroke.

Damn, I'd be sore tomorrow.

He gripped me about the waist, pulling me towards him and ramming himself into me with a guttural growl. His tense bicep was an iron band across my abdomen as he ravaged my ass.

He came a moment later, and a swell of frustration took me when his release shuddered through him. What a wasted opportunity. I could've chosen any of the guys huddled around the counter eating breakfast, and instead I'd let Carter intercept me. I didn't even know he liked butt stuff.

His arm still around my waist, I gasped when he flipped me over in one, swift movement. Grinning in my face, his teeth gleamed.

"Your turn, baby."

Oh fuck, now he was going to concern himself with my pleasure.

It was the last thing I wanted, but The Party Girl—she was insatiable.

I gave him a coy smile as he pulled my nipple into his mouth. He trailed kisses down my body, spreading me with both hands.

He sucked on my clit, and I arched back off the bed. But I knew by the clumsy movements of his tongue that it was likely to be an ineffective attempt.

"Baby, I could really go for some wings or something spicy," I interrupted. He looked up at me, his mouth wet.

"Yeah? Cool, I'll go put some on for us."

My muscle tension eased, and I relaxed back into the bed, watching as Carter jumped nimbly back onto his feet and went to retrieve his pants from the other side of the bed. *Fucking butt stuff. What a waste of my time.* Carter was only too happy to get out of his pussy-eating duties and go prepare something to eat for us.

So much for aftercare.

I used some tissues on his nightstand to clean myself up and quickly dressed in my miniskirt and tank top combo. There was nothing stylish about my outfit and I hated it, but this place wasn't about what I liked or wanted. It was about being someone different until my future could be secured.

Tugging the top down to make sure the swell of my breasts was visible, I headed out to the main area. Three guys sat at the counter, laughing and digging into cereal bowls, the milk spraying from their mouths as they talk and ate. Maybe wings for breakfast were a bit weird, but I spotted Carter whistling while putting them in the oven. At least it had been believable enough to fool him.

"Hey, guys." I sidled up to Casey at the end. The conversation stopped abruptly, and all three men turned to me.

"Oh uh. Hey, Syl."

I pushed my lips out into a pout, draping an arm across his shoulder.

"What are you guys doing before the run?"

Casey cleared his throat and looked over at Carter, where he was fussing with the oven.

"Yeah, well, we're actually going to go hunting beforehand and see if we can catch some fresh meat." His eyes slid back to mine, and I nodded, turning with a huff.

Carter had warned them off. Good old butt fucking asshole. I was pissed, but The Party Girl wouldn't be. What would she do? I kissed my teeth in thought before turning back to Casey.

"Oh cool, I love hunting. I'll go get ready and join you guys in ten, okay?" I grinned, knowing the little gap beside my incisor was showing. Why guys thought it was cute, I didn't know, but I was happy to use it to my advantage. Turning back to my room before Casey could answer, I left him with his mouth hanging open and his hand still in the air, but it was Carter's voice that gave me pause.

"Hey, Syl, wings are ready in twenty."

I pretended not to hear him.

If I planned it right, I'd be getting gangbanged by the guys on the counter by then, and I swear to fuck, if any of them went for my ass, they'd learn what happened when you pissed The Party Girl off.

CHAPTER 4

THE WATCHER

The sounds coming from my current breeder were just sad. I'd been curious if my body would react to her heat the way it had to Sylvia's, and I'd come prepared to give myself over to it, but watching her didn't even get me hot.

My interest was curiously absent. So, I set the three pictures of Sylvia I'd smuggled into the room against the monitor, partially obscuring the screen. I still needed to watch and ensure the breeder's safety, but no one said I needed to see the floor of the room at the bottom of the screen.

Sylvia was much better to look at.

I pulled over my black duffel bag. It was packed full with cans, and I strained as I hauled it into the right position to work the muscles I was targeting. Since I started lifting, I found I could amp up the weight without triggering an asthma attack.

My eyes fixed on Syl's crumpled face, at the tears pouring down her cheeks. I remembered how it had felt to watch her, to feel the pain of her sobs. The mystery of it kept me doing rep after rep until my breathing became wheezy, and I was forced to stop.

By the fifteen-hour mark, I could tell this breeding session would be a long one. The breeder's movements were too slow. She wasn't anywhere near the frantic peak state that should have consumed her by now. Looked like we were in for at least a twenty-four-hour session. Good thing I'd packed myself an ample amount of beef jerky to support my healing.

I'd tear apart every muscle in my body if it meant getting one step closer to being in that room with Sylvia.

By the time it was done and the girl sat up to press the button, I was in so much pain I could barely walk. But being back in this room had been good for me. It was a reminder of everything I was working for—to see Sylvia, to touch her, to become her breeder. To learn her body and her mind, both of which threatened to consume me with curiosity.

The fresh air of the hallway was a welcome change from the small stuffy room. The heat had lasted nineteen hours, and I'd spent almost every minute repeatedly destroying my body so it could be remade stronger. I should've been exhausted.

But an idea had come to me while I'd been in there, and now I needed to see it through.

I went down the hallway and rapped my knuckles on the observation room door.

"Yes?"

I opened the door to reveal Jerry, a small, mousy guy with glasses so thick they magnified his otherwise beady eyes.

"Hey, man, I'm sick of this breeding party shit. Want to trade the next one?"

Jerry's eyes lit up, and I saw hunger in the way he pressed his lips together and considered my offer. Jerry watched the dorms. There was no guarantee of anything interesting happening on the main room cameras, while the breeding party watchers got to see some action. It wasn't unheard of for us to switch assignments.

I just hoped he wouldn't figure out my reasons.

"Well, when's the next one?"

I thought back to the schedule they'd posted on the wall, trying to make the image in my head make sense.

"Uh, three days from now."

The grin on Jerry's face was sickening, and I almost wanted to rescind my offer, but then I saw her on the monitor behind him, and my heart nearly beat its way out of my chest.

Beautiful. She was just as beautiful as I remembered from her breeding party. Only the lighting was better in the common room, the image not as grainy. Jerry noticed the way I stared, turning in his swivel chair to search the monitor.

"What? What'd you see?" He panned the camera around nervously.

"Nothing, man. I thought I saw a dead pixel on the screen, but you're good."

Jerry relaxed in his chair, turning back to look at me with furrowed brows.

"Don't scare me like that," he snarled.

Holding my hands out in a placating gesture, I reached into my duffel. My fingers closed around a sealed pack of jerky.

"Sorry, man, I have some extra of these if you want a few?"

Jerry gave a quick nod, and I handed over a couple of sticks. I could've just taken out the sticks, but I wanted him to see I had an entire pack. It was helpful for him to know in order to ease future transactions. He tore into the first pack, taking a big bite of the salty meat.

"So, I'll see you in three days?"

Jerry glared up at me, the meat visible in his mouth as he chewed.

"Yes, yes, in three days. Let me know the hour so we can switch places a bit before, and don't think you're getting out of cleanup duties. These breeders are a real pack of slobs."

Cleanup duty. His words hit home, and I nodded quickly, turning so he wouldn't see the wide smile stretching across my face. Of course, the watchers for Pack 103C would also be responsible for cleaning the place, which meant—

Shit, it was almost too much. She wouldn't be there when I went into the dorm—they didn't allow anyone to remain during the monthly deep clean—but with any luck, I'd be

able to sneak into her room and have a window, at last, into the mind I desperately wanted
to know.

Each set brought me closer to Sylvia. I barely felt the aches and pains I was putting my
body through. A towel wrapped around my flimsy door at the dead of night allowed me to
do pull-ups just as well as any bar or piece of equipment the guards used to train. Because
that was who I was now—a guard. Or at least, who I needed to appear to be if I was going
to slip into the breeding program unnoticed.

My hair was a shaggy mess, and as annoying as it was to get the occasional sweat-soaked
strand stuck square in the eye, I was waiting to cut it until it was time to put my plan into
place. It'd be soon. I was almost ready.

The request was put in for family leave. In the three years I'd been a watcher for the
program, I'd never requested one and wasn't surprised when they put through my request
for two months of leave.

Two months, such a long time, but also so short. I had no actual plans beyond taking
my place in the program and getting to know her in the dorms, but what if—?

No, the way my body had responded to her heat was unusual, but it didn't need to
mean that. The thought of her responding in kind was an impossibility I refused to
consider.

Only a few more weeks now. Weeks of exquisite agony as I trained my body to resemble
something worthy of the breeding program. I dropped to the floor, my lungs screaming
for air I couldn't suck in fast enough. Snatching the towel from atop the door, I shut it as
quietly as I could, stumbling over to my dresser and ripping the drawer open hard enough
to strain the mechanism.

Every breath burned, and I could feel it worsening, as it always did during an attack.
While I used to panic each time my breathing became strained, it had long become a

source of annoyance. With a frustrated growl, I grabbed my blue inhaler, flipped off the plastic cap with my thumb, and brought it to my lips in one quick motion.

My heart was still pounding even as I sucked in the first bitter breath of medicine, holding it in my lungs as I'd been taught to do since childhood by my irritable mother. Fuck, I'd need to go there if only briefly to complete the illusion of my taking leave, which meant I'd need to see her and my sister. The thought of sitting down to meal with them, wearing the sour expressions they reserved for my presence, did not appeal to me. But I'd have to. It was just another one of my trials on the long road to Sylvia.

I took an extra puff of my medication, though my airways were mostly clear. I'd pushed myself too hard by hanging off the door frame for an extra second, trying to maximize the movement's impact, and I'd paid for it. It was a foolish mistake I wouldn't make again.

Every part of me ached by the time I stumbled into bed. My arms were sore from the different positions I'd been put in, and my ass was in pure agony. Luckily, I knew it would all fade after a solid night's sleep. In total, I'd taken five guys today, and that had to be good enough.

It just had to be because I needed to rest.

I awoke to the sound of a bird bumping against my window, its claws fighting for purchase on the ledgeless brick. Curious, I approached the brown bird. The poor thing was agitated, and it pulled at my heartstrings. My mind still clouded from sleep, I opened the window and watched as it perched on the edge, breathing hard. The red feathers on its chest pumped in and out violently.

It didn't move to come in, just cocked its head from side to side for a few moments. After recovering, it flew off, headed straight for the line of pines across the field.

Why or how it had come into such a predicament baffled me, but I'd been able to help it. My heart swelled at helping an innocent creature. It had been so long since I'd felt anything but fear that I stood an extra moment at the window, watching until the bird was out of sight. It tilted at the last minute when it reached the tree line, and I saw another brown bird come up to meet it. Together they swooped down, disappearing beneath the thick pine.

The life of a bird. Such simple dumb animals, but it looked a lot better than my life right now. Depending on yourself, doing your own thing, making your own choices. It was a dream I couldn't fathom, but having someone to share it with? Well, that wasn't something I bothered to hope for.

But the animals did it. As someone who had always had to safeguard herself, it seemed nice to have someone to swoop with beneath the trees.

I stared into the treeline where the birds had disappeared.

One week left before I'd know if I'd been successful this cycle.

One week until they decided whether to send me home or keep me on. It'd happened for girls before. Even if I'd failed to get pregnant, this didn't have to be my last cycle.

Exceptions were made, I reminded myself, rubbing my bare arms against the chill and moving to close the window now that my little friend was gone.

Rarely. But they were made for the right genetic combination.

They hadn't made one for my sister. A shiver traveled up my spine. Elise had failed to conceive for her four cycles and been sent to the fields. I didn't know if she'd asked to stay or begged them—as I was planning to—but they'd dismissed her as infertile and determined a different path forward for her.

A path I had no intention of treading.

This was the week when I'd bleed or test, and a quick squeeze of my breasts for pregnancy symptoms didn't tell me much. Were they sore from Carter squeezing them mercilessly, or had I achieved a pregnancy?

Fuck, I hated the mind games, but with the end of my cycle in sight, at least I didn't have to bother engaging with the guys. I could finally put The Party Girl aside and just be Syl for a while. With a sigh, I fell back on the bed with my arms outstretched, staring at the popcorn ceiling. Who was I anymore if not this desperate, fearful thing I'd become?

There was one thing I still had. One thing they couldn't take from me. One thing that was just Syl. I sat up to search through my nightstand and carefully pulled out my precious magazines. The faded ghostly faces of former celebrities and beauty queens stared back at me. Their souls were frozen in cheerful smiles, but I didn't care who they were or who they'd been.

This one had a round face with broader shoulders, and the designer had paired her with a stunning lace v-neck, open to her waist and draped across her generous breasts. Not a distraction from her shoulders, but a redirection of the eye. I loved it. I'd read these magazines a hundred times, and some pages were so badly worn I couldn't make out much about the clothes or the women wearing them. My mind was hungry to understand how it worked, and how I might use the art of clothing design to draft my own pieces.

If I was designing for someone else, I'd do something with the collar to draw attention differently. For myself, my delicate shoulders were a feature. I took out my sketchbook and a pencil, clumsily sketching my figure onto the page. It looked nothing like me, but the shape was right. Sketching a long dress, I left the neckline bare. The neckline was key. The rest of the dress would be fitted—a luxurious black dress with velvet cutouts in a pleated skirt.

I paused with my fingers poised over the blank neckline. Lace, yes. Instead of leaving the neck open as they'd done, I gave the drawing a high collar, taking the sleeves off so the dress cut in and emphasized the shoulders. It was good, but heavy. A slit between the breasts with a flash of skin would break it up. I drew in a small diamond there.

Sitting back on my knees, I admired my work.

It was beautiful, or it would be beautiful if I had any of the materials to make it. I'd love to go foraging in one of the abandoned human cities, just once. They might be ravaged by the nuclear bombs, but maybe there was something I could use. The clothes we had from those times were so picked over it was hard to find anything that would suit a dress like this.

Still, a girl had to try. I moved to my closet and found the bundle of precious scraps in the corner. Carefully taking out my needle and thread, I prepared to make yet another beautiful dress The Party Girl would never wear.

CHAPTER 5

THE WATCHER

My hands were slippery with sweat, and I'd combed my hair for the first time in ages. As if I were about to meet Sylvia in person instead of hoping to spy on her hanging out in the common room.

Jerry opened the door to his observation room with a toothy grin, standing up to meet me. The dude came up to just past the belt of my jeans, and I eyed the room behind him warily. It was definitely smaller than the breeding party observation rooms, and inwardly, I winced at the thought of being confined in such a small space.

Fuck, sometimes I hated being tall.

"You know the routine? Just keep an eye out for anybody acting weird or any danger. You know the rules. It's pretty close to the end of the cycle, so don't expect to see all that much of interest." Jerry's grin widened, and his eyes twinkled as he turned to leave. He meant I wouldn't be watching anybody fucking while he'd be doing nothing but. Like he'd gotten the better end of the deal by planning our trade at such a low point.

Inwardly, I chuckled, happy I wouldn't have to watch Sylvia getting fucked by other guys. Not sure it wouldn't send me into a rage and straight into the dorm, eager to test out my new muscles. No, I wasn't here for that.

I just wanted to see her.

Turning my eyes downcast, Jerry sneered. Like he'd suspected watching the breeders fucking in their dorm was all I was interested in.

Sorry, Jerry.

With a nod, the smaller man sidled around me, clapping me on the back.

"Cleanup is tomorrow afternoon when the breeders go home for family visits. Don't forget to bring a scrub brush. That shit gets really caked on." With a cackle at his own joke, Jerry headed down the hallway towards the breeding party observation rooms.

Shaking with eagerness, I stepped into the room. Something told me they'd chosen this room especially for someone with a small stature like Jerry. No way my long legs would fit comfortably under the desk. My body would be crammed into it like an extra sardine shoved into a full tin.

But I wouldn't be alone. Once I'd folded myself into place and adjusted the rolling chair to its pathetically inadequate height, I turned to the monitor, my heart hammering against my ribs. I'd see her today, watch the way she walked, talked. I couldn't be part of her world yet, but the thought of knowing her a bit better made me jittery. Three monitors, all pointing inward, were on a curved desk. Each had a different view of the common space. No cameras in their rooms, though, that was private. As if nobody got naked in the common room. I rolled my eyes, searching the space for any sign of Sylvia.

But the girl of my dreams was nowhere in sight. I got a glimpse of everyone's face using the three camera angles and not one of them was her. I didn't even need to see her face. I'd recognize her just from the way she stood or maybe her gait.

Convinced she wasn't about to sprint up on the monitor, I took out my drawing supplies. I'd brought ample sheets of paper and a few other mediums, pencil, and coloured wax, expecting to see her. But this was just the start. I had set Jerry up for the next three days, and Sylvia had to come out at some point.

She didn't.

I kept watch long past midnight when all the other breeders had cleared the space and only one couple making out on the couch in the dark remained. What were the odds she'd come out for a midnight snack? I didn't know, but fuck if I was going to miss it. Pulling out my duffel, I unzipped it to be hit in the face with the rich aroma of coffee beans. Fucking heaven. Chocolate-covered coffee beans would be enough to keep me alert. The handful of beans I tossed into my mouth were probably too many, but I crunched them with relish, savouring the sweet chocolate and its bitter undertones. I'd rather be exhausted than miss this opportunity of seeing Sylvia again.

At some point in the night I did nod off, waking to find I drool on the smooth amber wood of Jerry's desk, the moisture pulling up at the laminate.

Shit, well, it wasn't like we were best buds. Jerry was probably messing up my desk with his own fluids right now, anyway. Shaking the image of Jerry coming all over the desk and leaving it for me to clean up out of my head, I searched the monitor but again found no sight of Sylvia. They were supposed to be going home for family time today. She was probably getting ready to go. She had to be. That would explain her absence.

Good thing I was a patient man. With a shoulder popping stretch, I reached my hands into the air and stood up to get some blood flow back into my legs. There were two weeks left to get myself into shape for the program. I figured I might as well use this time to break myself a little more. The floor space wasn't long enough for pushups, but I was able to position my body under Jerry's desk and wheel the chair back far enough that I could use the edge for pullups. My eyes scanned the monitor with each pull until my trembling muscles gave way, and I could do no more.

Breathing strained, I climbed back into the chair, searching the monitors again as if I'd missed her in the minute it had taken me to reemerge.

Fucking nope.

So, I started drawing. Her face. Her body. Her in different poses—as if adding a personality to the images would make the woman herself appear before me.

Then, I glanced up, and like magic, she was there.

I paused, my pencil poised over the image I'd been drawing of her.

She slipped smoothly into the room with that big, beautiful smile on her face. The same one she'd worn for the coordinator.

None of the drawings I'd done did her justice.

Blue. Her eyes were blue, just like mine. My heart clenched, and I reached for the colour. Shoving the stupid cartoon I'd been drawing out of the way, I watched as she went up to a guy at the counter and took a seat. I switched to stare at the rightmost monitor where her face was on full display, the camera on that side positioned lower.

Beautiful. Every line a lesson to the artist inside me. Every stroke a challenge to duplicate such perfection. Her face was round with a pointed chin complimented perfectly by the chin-length cut of her sandy blonde hair.

She laughed, and I swear I could hear her clearly through the crackling audio. Though only the loudest sounds made it to my ears. What was her voice really like? When she talked normally, would it be low and husky like in my dreams, or soft and lilting? Only the thought of joining her soon kept me from punching the piece of garbage monitor for keeping her from me.

My clumsy fingers sketched her face, heart stuttering as she tucked a strand of hair behind one delicate ear and chewed on her lip. I pushed the paper out of the way and started a new drawing, trying to capture that exact expression. Was that nervousness? Nervousness about what? Seeing her family? Did she not get along with them?

I thought of my own impending visit, and I could well understand any trepidation she might be feeling. But her records had shown she had eight siblings. Surely she must get along with at least one of them?

Fuck, it was a mystery and not one I was likely to solve until I was on the inside. For now, all I could do was draw pictures of the girl on my screen. Useless scraps of paper that could never do her justice, but were the only connection I had to the girl who was both so close and so far away.

She laughed, throwing back her head in a way that made her breasts bounce, and my cock stiffen. I hadn't gotten off since I'd watched her breeding party, though I'd observed three parties since then, and now I knew why.

None of those women could hold a candle to her. She wasn't in the same room as me, wasn't strapped to a bed. It was her simple laugh and the way her delicate shoulders shrugged. Her plump bottom lip jutting out in a mock pout grabbed a hold of me like she was in the room, whispering words in my ears and stroking my cock.

Shrugging off the needs of my body, I focused on drawing her, knowing I'd have an opportunity to relieve myself later. Sylvia would be called soon to head home. Just my luck. She wasn't out in the common room for five minutes when she was called to the door, her hips swaying seductively as she sauntered out of the room. Fuck, the confidence to be so unhurried when I could see the coordinator tapping her foot and waiting at the door. It did things to me.

But then she was gone, and I had to watch the rest of the room slowly clear out. When the door shut from the last Breeder, I scrubbed my hands over my face and stood, wincing at the tightness in my legs from having fallen asleep in a contorted position.

Time to clean. With a spring in my step, I went straight for the stairwell, going down to the first floor where the dorms were and seeking out Pack 103C.

Across from the door was a general cleaning closet, and I lined up behind the other cleaners, keeping my eyes down and my shoulders stiff to avoid unwanted conversation. A fair number of the coordinators were women. Something about putting the breeders at ease. All the watchers were male, which made my cleaning group composed of a bunch of guys I'd never met and wanted to actively avoid getting to know.

I took a bucket and a few pumps of soap along with a heavy-duty cleaning cloth and headed into the dorm. Everyone seemed to be starting with the common room, which worked out perfectly for me. I tried to piece together where the cameras were located based on my experience in the observation room. Moving to the wall behind a foosball table, I was sure the angle on the couch matched it. And sure enough, my scan of the opposite wall revealed a framed piece of art featuring a vibrant splash of oranges and blues with a small camera jammed into the corner of the frame. The black lens blended seamlessly into the design. I wondered if someone had designed the art with a camera in mind, or if they'd salvaged it from some old human home and placed the camera to fit it.

Continuing to explore the room while cleaning, I located the other two cameras in the room. One was set into an art piece just like the oranges and blues, but this one was a portrait of some colourful flat-faced cat that annoyed me just to look at it. The other was more skillfully placed in the crack of a kitchen cabinet, aligned with the hinge and peeking out the other side, hidden in shadow. Well, not unless you knew the exact angle it recorded and went searching for it. With a smirk, I cleaned the fridge next to the cabinet, frowning like I'd seen something worth washing.

Everyone avoided the couch at all costs, cleaning the table, wiping the TV, but never the couch. Not until a tall skinny guy with pale skin and a shaved head shoved a short, bespectacled ginger guy towards it.

"We saved the couch for you, Cam." The asshole laughed as the ginger eyed the couch warily and adjusted his glasses.

Pissed off at the sight of the shover smirking and demanding the ginger do his bidding like he was any better than any of us when he'd been assigned the same role, I went straight to the couch, glaring at the shover and thinking that his buzzed head and pasty skin made him look like the giant dick he was. The guy just shrugged his shoulders, still wearing that annoying smirk before moving off and heading back towards the kitchen.

Silently, I moved to help the ginger. He peered up into my face in surprise. I tried not to look as I slid the soapy cloth across the smooth brown pleather, and fuck if I was going into the cracks of the cushions.

"Hey, thanks, man. Everybody hates the couch."

I chuckled. "The people who live here sure seem to like it."

He laughed, the sound jarringly nasal. "Yeah, that's why we hate it."

He winked at me, the freckles covering his skin standing out, and I decided I liked the guy. There were worse things than being assigned a watcher. At least I was big enough that I didn't get hassled.

"The name's Cam," he said.

I nodded, making a point of not offering mine. As much as I might like to make a friend today, any connection to the people watching these rooms wasn't a great idea. Knowing where the cameras were placed would help, but the more familiar with me the Pack 103C Watchers were, the more likely they'd be to recognize my face.

So, I cleaned the couch by his side, giving the occasional non-committal grunt when he tried to engage me in conversation. No, he hadn't seen me before. No, I wouldn't be coming back. The poor kid seemed desperate for a friend, and it made me feel like shit about rejecting his advances, but I had to—for Sylvia.

"I've got to take a piss," I muttered, heading for the bathroom I knew was at the end of the long hall off the common room. The guys were still busy scrubbing down the kitchen, which meant I'd have a few minutes to explore.

Breeders were tasked with cleaning their own rooms. We weren't supposed to enter their private spaces, but I just couldn't help myself. The desire to get closer to Sylvia hurried my steps as I scanned the nameplates on each door for hers.

Nope. No fucking Sylvias, but I knew she lived here. What the fuck?

And that's when I realized.

Sylvia was here, but none of the doors had her name hanging on their front.

Shit, she didn't go by that name. I turned back to a door I had dismissed.

"Syl." I said the name out loud, testing it on my tongue. She went by Syl. I'd been calling her Sylvia this whole time, imagining her as Sylvia, but that wasn't her name at all. I felt like shit, realizing even that small bit of knowledge I had about her was wrong.

But now that I'd figured it out, I turned the brass knob slowly, as though she was inside and not off visiting with her family like all the others.

The bed inside was empty, and I found myself staring around, drinking in every detail about Syl. A music box sat on her tall standard-issue dresser. She'd made some kind of cute circlet to place around her bedside lamp, and I saw another in matching blues and greens on the top of her dresser. As if she cared about how things looked. Well, of fucking course she did.

I imagined her as the kind of girl who took care of things, who knew where every article of clothing was, and it was true. Her clothes hung neatly in the closet, and a quick check showed them folded carefully in her dresser.

Eager for her scent, I opened the top drawer and found her underwear.

"Mm," I grunted my approval, pulling out a pink thong and picturing Syl wearing it. Clearing my throat, I adjusted my pants from where they were snagging on my rapidly hardening cock.

This was her room. Her private space, and I was invading it, pressing myself inside and exploring. Everything about being in here gave me a thrill, and I clenched the pink thong in my hand, tugging my pants down and bracing myself against the dresser.

Smooth as silk. That was the only way to describe the delicate material of Syl's thong. I gripped my cock with the fabric wrapped around my hands and moaned at how good it felt, and how much better it would feel if Syl was in front of me wearing it.

This was her bed. She'd been sleeping here just a few hours ago. I stared at the pale pink of her coverlet, imagining her splayed out before me, and gave another tug. Panting, I yanked hard.

Syl, not Sylvia, Syl. I could see her in my mind. She smiled at me. Opening her legs, she laid back on the bed. She wore her pink thong for me. Just for me. Only for me. With a growl, I moved to the bed, lying down and burying my face in her pillow, trying to scent her on the freshly washed sheets.

Fuck, why did she need to be so tidy? The silky fabric of the thong took my thrusts as I rammed myself into the bed, imagining her beneath me. She moaned, just like she'd done in the breeding room. Sweet little panting breaths tickled my ear as I buried myself in her wet heat like I'd watched the others do.

I'm coming, don't stop.

I wouldn't stop. I would give her what she needed. I would give her every last drop.

With a roar I trusted would be muffled by the room's soundproofing, my release took me, and I moved against her mattress as I came back down.

The mess I'd made of her thong and sheets should've bothered me, but I couldn't bring myself to feel bad. Syl was mine, even if she didn't know it yet, and some animalistic part of me wanted her to walk back into the room and find I'd defiled it.

It'd be a message and a warning.

I was coming for her.

I was already hot at the idea of her sleeping in the cum-soaked bed.

The thong was another story, and I looked at it, realizing there was no way to hide how I'd used it in such a satisfying way. I tucked it in my pocket, knowing this moment would be the stuff of my dreams until I could have her for real.

Satisfied and languid, and safe in the knowledge that I'd be visiting this room again soon, I looked around the room for any other signs of Syl. Any other clues as to the woman I'd only seen on my monitor.

Her nightstand drawer was ajar, and I frowned down in surprise. Everything else in here seemed intentional, but the drawer was cracked open enough to see the darkness within, as if she'd slammed it in a hurry and it had bounced back. Smiling as the scenario played out in my mind, filling me with more insight into the beauty who was to be mine, I pulled the drawer open to see what she'd been in a hurry to hide.

What?

Inside was a thick stack of what appeared to be human magazines from before the bombs. The woman on the cover wore an enormous flower larger than her head on the side of an extravagant dress. Syl liked this?

Curious, I pulled the first magazine from the stack, being careful with the brittle pages as I opened it for any clue for why Syl would have amassed such a collection.

Notes. There were messages in the margins on many of the pages inside, details and thoughts on the outfits the smiling women wore.

Scooped neck, not V would be better.

Draped here to follow the flow of her leg.

All the comments were much the same—minor adjustments to the clothing within the book and the deepest thoughts of the woman I was desperate to know.

Greedily, I continued looking through the magazine, eager for more, when I came across a page ripped in half. There were no comments on this page. Not a word from Syl's scratchy handwriting, and I could see why. The tear cut straight down the middle, leaving half the dress to the viewer's imagination.

Or a watcher's. I smiled to myself. This was exactly like Reg's comic books—a piece of patchwork for me to unravel. I could see how the lines would continue and match them to the other side. Fortunately, I always carried a few folded up pieces of paper and a pencil in my pocket in case I came across something to sketch. Not charcoal. Shit was messy, but a pencil would do if the inspiration struck, and it would certainly do for this.

Sitting down on Syl's bed with a creak, I sketched out the figure, imagining her missing hand placed elegantly on her hip. The outfit was tricky. I could match it to the other side, but some designs Syl seemed particularly fond of were asymmetrical. Once I'd matched the way the dress hugged the woman's figure to flare out at the bottom, I added one of the enormous flowers Syl seemed fond of on the missing side.

Pleased, I made a few final adjustments and slipped the paper in behind the figure so it nearly lined up perfectly. Half the woman was in faded colour, her navy dress standing out against pale skin, and the other was a pencil sketch, making her look like a patchwork human. Half real, half fake. I liked it, and it gave me an idea for a project I was working on. Syl was by far the most beautiful woman I'd ever seen, but she was also complicated. There was a depth to her she let few others see. I wanted to show that, to paint her unique beauty in a way that would do her justice.

A thud came from somewhere outside the door. The soundproofing in here was probably too powerful to hear voices. Shit, I'd stayed too long.

Slipping the magazine back on the top of Syl's stack, I closed the drawer, leaving it open a crack the way I'd found it. Smiling as I imagined her opening the magazine and my quick sketch falling out, I stood and went back to the cleaning crew.

I had a feeling the fucking bathrooms were next.

CHAPTER 6

SYL

"Welcome home, Sweetheart."

I winced at the sickly sweet way my mother spoke, and the warm hug she enfolded me in. I was taller than her now, stronger, but I knew that wouldn't stop her.

"Hey, Mom, where's Elise?"

My mother pulled back to stare up at me angrily. Her cheeks flushed and brown eyes blazed. I hated the bits of myself I saw in her—her pouty lips, so like mine. The same straight nose. I suppose I got my fiery temper from her, but unlike her, I'd never direct it at those I loved.

Her shoulder-length blonde hair flying, she took a step towards me, and I stiffened.

"I'm saying hello to you, and you're asking after your sister?" she hissed, her fingers traveling to my side and digging into the flesh at my waist.

My mouth went dry, and I whimpered, knowing she would twist the skin hard enough to leave a bruise if I didn't answer her right.

"Sorry, Mama. I missed you." Was that enough?

Her fingers stayed where they were an extra moment before withdrawing.

"That's fine, dear. Your sister is down enjoying herself in the games room."

With a sigh of relief, the stiffness in my shoulders eased, and I smiled at her now cheerful expression.

"I'll come back soon, Mama." Against my own instincts, I forced myself to lean forward and plant a kiss on her offered cheek.

Then I was out of there, the reminder of her mood swings and abuses enough to make me wish I could move out of our family space and into my own space. But that would only be granted to me once I was pregnant and confirmed as a pack mother.

Once I moved out, I'd make a point of avoiding this hallway, of never visiting the woman who had made my life a living hell.

The corridors leading around 14F were busy, and I smiled, nodding at all the aunties and kids I passed. The games room was on the other side of our kitchen, and quite the trek from where my mother's house was tucked in at the end of a hall. When I reached it, I was surprised to find it relatively empty.

I guess most people visiting for family day spent time with their family and not engaging in recreation, but my family was more complicated than most. It was there that I found my sister Elise.

She was playing some kind of dungeon crawler, and I planted myself beside her on the low squashy couch designed for kids. My knees were bent awkwardly, but there was enough nostalgia in the old couch to make it seem comfortable, even if it wasn't.

"Hey." She didn't even look at me. Her vacant brown eyes fixed on the screen, frizzy brown hair sticking out at all angles. She'd lost weight again, and I noticed her colour was off. Not drastically, but it wasn't as rich as it had been, like working the poisoned fields had leached it out of her somehow. "I said, hey." No reaction. I cleared my throat and passed a hand in front of her eyes, disturbing the screen. "Elise? Hello?"

That did it, and I almost wished it hadn't. Elise jumped, nearly dropping her controller in her lap, and turned. There was no expression, no warmth, and for one terrible moment, no recognition when she turned her honey brown eyes on me.

"Oh, Syl. Hi. Sorry, I guess I got lost in the game."

The fuck she did. I could see the horror behind her soft smile, the way it did nothing to change the ever present sadness in her eyes.

No, not sadness. Despair.

"Are you okay?"

Her grin widened, stretching across her face like puppets pulled the strings. "Yeah, for sure. I'm great. Do you know how important working the fields is for the pack? I actually really love it. I'm doing so much good for the future generations, Syl. It's such important work." Her voice dripped with a contentedness that failed to match the lack of expression in her eyes.

I eyed her quizzically.

My sister had gone kicking and screaming to the fields. Each time she came back, she was more resigned to her fate, and I saw less of the sister I had once known and loved. The one I'd trailed after, joining her in whatever she happened to be doing. Just wanting to be near her, to learn from her, to be strong like her. I took Elise's hands in mine, intending to find the spark she'd been known for, but she yelped, pulling them to her chest.

Startled, I eyed her hands. "What? What's the matter?"

She buried her hands in her lap, her eyes turning downcast and tears springing to her eyes. Panic flared in my chest.

"Elise, what's the matter? What's happened to your hands?" When she didn't answer again, I gave a desperate grab for her hands.

"No, Syl, please. I don't want you to see."

But it was too late. I pulled her hands roughly free, panicking anew at how little she was able to resist me.

She used to play the piano. Her long delicate fingers flying across the keys to the delight of everyone in the building, but not anymore.

No fingernails.

Not a one.

My mouth hung open as I looked over the ruins of her hands—inflamed pink, fleshy nubs on her delicate fingers.

She wasn't Elise anymore—trusted, loved, and once celebrated for her talents and kindness.

She'd failed to become a pack mother and her future had been taken from her. I turned her hands over, noting the burnt flesh on her palms. Elise quietly sobbed while I did so, though I moved too gently for it to have pained her. How bad had these burns been that they would linger so cruelly?

The message was obvious.

I was staring at my future.

It was either breed or burn.

I forced myself through the rest of the visit, chewing down a meal of rolled oats with Elise, all the while eager to get back to the dorms. Elise's mangled hands haunted my steps on the way back to Pack Breeders 103C. Only a few more days before I would find out if I'd been successful this cycle. I'd either bleed or they would test me to see if I'd conceived. If I hadn't, I'd have to beg for one more chance, and they'd be within their power to say no.

Elise. She was so beautiful, and so much kinder than I was. My favourite of all my siblings. She was the one who had brushed my hair out, who had listened to me when I'd said mama was pinching me while no one was looking. Now she'd been cast aside and tossed like meat to the hungry wolves because her body wouldn't do what she—what they—wanted.

Not me. No fucking way. If I didn't conceive this cycle, I'd make my case and make absolutely sure I conceived the next cycle. I knew it wouldn't count for much to have sex so close to my cycle's end, but I needed to keep playing The Party Girl. Keep the guys thinking I was a maniac for sex, even if the thought of it didn't interest me at all. It was a game I needed to play if I wanted to keep my fingernails.

I curled my hands into my palm, feeling the comforting press of my nails on the soft skin.

No way would I end up like Elise.

I burst into the dorm, banging the door against the wall loud enough to attract every eye in the room.

"Hey, guys, did you miss me?"

A sea of delighted eyes met mine and a few beers were raised. Carter came rushing over, and I smiled at him like the thought of him taking me outside of my fertile period did anything but turn my stomach.

"Hey, babe, I've got a cold one for you." An icy beer, still wet with condensation, was shoved into my hands.

I winked. "Yeah sure. You want to play some foosball?"

I didn't bother to take a minute for myself to change or unwind from the emotional upheaval of seeing Elise in such a state. There was no time for it.

Placing the beer on a floating shelf beside the foosball table, I set up across from Carter, gripping the handles on either side and flashing him a flirty grin. But the moment Carter's faded out soccer player kicked the ball towards mine, someone slipped in behind me and pressed their hard-on into my back, gripping my hips and pulling me up against them.

I hissed in surprise, molding myself back against them, not caring who it was.

"Come on, man, we were just about to play a game." Carter spun a handle and launched the little white ball into my goal, easily slipping past my defenses.

"Yeah, well, I have a better one in mind."

I arched backwards into the husky voiced man who held me prisoner.

"Okay, but I get her ass. She's tight as fuck."

I let myself sink into the sensation. This place wasn't all bad, and if I had to do this—had to be here—I might as well find some enjoyment in it. There was something about them taking dibs on my body parts that turned me on. A hand gripped my throat, my pulse hammering against his fingers, and I moaned as a bolt of arousal went straight to my core. At least my body had its head in the game, even if my mind was still swirling with images of Elise's burnt hands.

THE WATCHER

She'd just returned from family day. I didn't know what I was expecting, but Syl getting ready to be double-teamed was not it. I stared at the screen, eyes bugging out, my gaze shifting from monitor to monitor as I tried to take in all angles of her at once.

Breathy moans escaped her plump lips, and my heart hurt to know they were true sounds of arousal, mirroring her heat. Fuck, I wanted to be in there. My hand curled into a fist, and I slammed it down on Jerry's desk. She might enjoy what these guys were doing to her, but I knew instinctively that I could do better. That her body would respond to me the way mine did to hers.

I wanted to mark her, claim her. Walk into the dorm and point a finger at her in front of everyone there.

Mine. This one is mine. Fucking hands off.

It was all I could do to keep my legs crammed under Jerry's desk, my fists helplessly clenched as I watched the second guy come around to the other side of the foosball table. He pushed the first guy out of the way, and rage flowed in my blood like fire at the way he moved in front of Syl possessively. But nothing could compare to the icy chill when he slapped her and pushed her back hard enough into the foosball table that she was forced to brace herself.

What the fuck? I leaned forward in my chair, focusing on the central monitor. He ripped up her shirt and bra, taking a nipple between his fingers and pinching hard. Syl cried out, and I knew it was a genuine cry of pain. Her face twisted, and the arousal from a few moments ago was gone, replaced with the tiniest hint of hatred. Some women liked pain. I knew this. I'd watched enough breeders moan their approval when their males twisted a nipple, but I also knew the sound women made when they liked what was being done to them, and that was not it.

Pain was not Syl's thing. Her yelps held no notes of arousal. But the fucking asshole just kept up, taking her other nipple and twisting it cruelly.

Syl kept her arms pressed against the pool table, crying out as the man mercilessly manhandled her breasts, but making no move to stop him.

No. Just no. No way would I allow her to suffer at the hands of this sadistic bastard. I burst out of my chair, sending it screeching on tired wheels across the room, and dashed out into the hallway.

Where was it?

Yes, down the hall and around the corner was a fire alarm. I broke the glass with my elbow and pulled the handle without hesitation. The alarm blared, and I raced back to Jerry's room and shut myself inside, hoping no one had seen me pull it.

Anxiously, I turned to the monitor. The bastard had taken his hands off Syl, and they were all crowding around the door, getting ready to leave and escape the supposed fire.

Breathing a sigh of relief, I stayed to make sure she was out before leaving Jerry's room to join the other watchers assembled in the hall.

Administrator Sampson's usually blotchy face was beat red as he stared us down.

"I want to know who pulled the fire alarm, and why. You will tell me, or there will be dire consequences."

I'd never seen him so pissed. His tie was pulled loose and the white sleeves of his shirt were rolled up like he was ready to hit somebody.

Fuck.

We were all lined up in the watchers hallway near the fire alarm. If I'd have thought this through, maybe I could've come up with a way to excuse what I'd done. Maybe started a small fire in Jerry's office or something. But I had acted on pure desperation, and now my mind was blank as I stared down at the raging bull before me.

I was in Jerry's area, not my own, and the only watcher present who didn't belong. Cam stood beside me, and I was disturbed to find him watching my face. I kept my features schooled as he examined me, the shorter man at my side looking curiously calm in the face of the administrator's ire.

"I demand an answer." Administrator Sampson pulled out the digital timer the breeders used in their freshenup rooms and waved it around. "I'm setting this for five minutes and leaving the area. When I come back, somebody had better fucking fess up or all of you will pay, and trust me boys, it will *not* be pretty."

Swallowing my fear, I watched him set the timer and walk away.

Shit. I just needed my brain to work out what to do, but with everyone angrily talking around me, it was no simple task.

"Why'd you do it?"

Cam's whispered words grabbed my attention. Turning to him, I tried to force a lie to my lips, but the way he looked up at me—not angry, not scared—the lie wouldn't come.

He seemed curious of all things. I cursed myself, and Cam waited patiently, studying my face.

"For a girl. They were—they were—" What could I say? Doing something she was pretending to like, but I knew she didn't? That I knew without a doubt she was being abused, even though it looked like some kinky sex shit to anyone else watching those monitors? "Hurting her."

Cam's eyes cleared, and he smiled sadly. "Yeah, I get it."

Nothing else. No anger. No further questions. Just—*I get it*. In his situation, I would've been pissed as hell, but not Cam.

With the timer's shrill beeping, a blanket of quiet came over those assembled, and Administrator Sampson came stomping back down the hall towards us.

"Well?" His eyes scanned each man in the line, pausing just long enough to make them sweat before moving on.

"It was me."

No.

The quiet confession came from the man at my side, and I looked down in horror at Cam. He gave me a wry smile.

"I was smoking in my office, and I accidentally started a fire in the wastebasket. I freaked out and pressed the fire alarm, but I was able to put it out on my own and clean up."

My mouth fell open. It was the answer my brain couldn't come up with.

Administrator Sampson stepped up to Cam, looking down his barrel chest at him.

"And why didn't you say something sooner?" he said through gritted cheeks. The vein on Administrator Sampson's head was set to bursting.

"I-I didn't want to get in trouble, sir. I apologize for disturbing everyone." A simple apology, but I saw some guys behind Cam cracking their knuckles and glaring in his direction.

"Oh, you're in a fucking shit load of trouble" Administrator Sampson gripped Cam by the back of the neck, and he yelped pitifully.

Administrator Sampson effortlessly marched him down the hall towards his office, and I gritted my teeth at the sight.

As far as I was concerned, Cam was a fucking hero, and I was determined to repay him.

I felt the tension in my shoulders loosen. Syl was safe for the moment.

Until I could get in there myself and make her mine.

My nipples still ached from Carter twisting them. By the time we came back to the dorm, I made a beeline for my room, not answering the calls of my name. Now I knew why they gave us locks, and I twisted mine into place a heartbeat before falling to my knees beside the bed and sobbing into the coverlet.

I hated him. Hated this place. Hated this world where, to be safe, I had to become a mother, or sent to the fields until every ounce of who I was and what I loved was ripped from me. Deemed worthless.

Sobbing so hard my shoulders ached, I let loose all the emotions I'd been bottling up. The interaction with my mother and the way she still controlled me with fear. My sister's pitiful state. The way I'd thought I might get to enjoy sex for once before Carter came and ripped that possibility away from me. The pure relief I'd felt when the fire alarm had sounded, and I'd had an excuse to escape Carter's clutches.

I cried for my sister, for myself, and for all the other party girls here who were just doing what they had to do to survive. Tear after tear fell until my eyes were dry and puffy. Crawling up onto the bed, I meant to tuck myself under the covers when I noticed a darker spot in the middle of my coverlet.

Shocked, I leaned in and sniffed it, wrinkling my nose when I realized what it was.

"Sick fucks!" I shrieked, tossing the coverlet onto the floor before searching the sheets for any other stains. Convinced there was none, I climbed under the thin sheet and pulled it tightly around myself, dreaming of the day I could leave Pack Breeders 103C behind and The Party Girl with it.

The emotions poured out of me in streaks of cleansing tears. I was tired, but too agitated to sleep. Fumbling with my nightstand drawer, I grabbed the magazine on top and moved onto my back, intending to take comfort in the pages I'd pored over a hundred times before.

The women inside these magazines—the glorious, elegant beings with their fabulous dresses and perfect hair—had always felt like old friends from another world. Like if I wished hard enough, I could go back to the place and time when they'd existed and join them. Wear a beautiful dress I'd have to be stitched into. Have my hair and makeup done and go mingle among them. A perfectly acceptable addition to their circles.

Only, they were from another time, and this was all I had left of them and their world. But I could dream, and I carefully flipped through the pages. Eyes roving over every inch of fancy fabric, as I tried to learn how these designs had been dreamt up.

Something slid loose, and I cursed, a fresh set of tears threatening to spring free. These magazines were ancient and found within the rubble of human civilization. They were bound to start falling apart. But when I looked at the loose paper, it wasn't a torn page from the magazine at all.

Sitting on the edge of the bed, I found myself staring down at a pencil sketch of a woman who looked familiar. Squinting down at the drawing, I traced the curve of her dress with a finger before the answer came to me.

Page thirty-two.

I flipped to the page, my mouth hanging open when I found I was right. Navy blue dress, sweetheart neckline, a tight bodice, and fabric draping by her feet, but the woman was ripped in half. The other side of her dress's design a mystery. Only it wasn't.

Not anymore. I took the paper and fit it behind the ripped up page, marveling at how well the two halves of the woman matched.

Someone had finished it. More tears sprung to my eyes, and I laughed, looking down at the perfectly matched other half of my favourite dress in the magazine. Whoever had done this had added a flower to the missing side. I chuckled, knowing exactly where my mystery artist had seen the flower—page five. How I'd drawn in a flower on the peach-coloured babydoll dress and made note of how it added the right touch. It'd been a phase, but whoever had done this hadn't known that.

Someone had looked through my most private things without my permission, and while that left a bitter taste in my mouth, they'd also liked what they'd found enough to make this sketch. They might've fouled my coverlet, but the picture was sweet—in a stalkerish way.

CHAPTER 7

One line.

A timer beeped somewhere outside of my stall.

Fifteen minutes. It'd been fifteen minutes, and no second line had appeared.

Just that single damning line. My legs wobbled, and I dropped to the floor. Pain flared through my knees as I hit the tile, lost in the swell of emotions.

I'd failed.

Everything I'd done—enduring Carter's fetishes, doing whatever anybody wanted no matter how tired or disinterested I was—none of it mattered. My fingers clenched on the cheap plastic as rage quickly replaced sadness. With a roar, I chucked the test against the wall and dropped my head into my hands, trying to breathe through the tears that distorted my vision and tightened my chest.

This was my last chance. Unless I could convince Administrator Sampson that I should be given more time, they'd send me. They'd send me.

No, I couldn't even think about it. I wouldn't let it consume me. Instead, I smoothed my hair back and bent over the toilet to retrieve the test.

There was no fucking way I was going to the fields.

Straightening my back, I left the stall to an empty bathroom. I'd been the only girl whose period hadn't arrived, the only one to test this cycle.

Each day it hadn't come, I'd been so hopeful. Scared to be a mother, but hopeful that I'd succeed this cycle, and I could end this charade. Go home to 14F and make a life for myself.

That hope was gone now. Dashed.

Clearing my throat, I looked myself over in the mirror. Red face, puffy eyes from crying.

Shit.

I scooped some cold water up in my cupped hand and carefully bathed each eye, hoping to soothe any evidence of my weakness.

I am not going to the fields, I promised myself, pursing my lips at my reflection and giving it a wink.

This would not defeat me.

Giving my reflection a toothy grin, I left the bathroom to walk down the long hall, knowing a roomful of breeders was waiting for me at the other end.

Today I'd worn pants and a short-sleeve shirt with a ruffled neck to outline my dainty collarbone. It was flattering, but very different from my usual revealing garb. I'd been so sure I'd gotten pregnant this cycle, that I wouldn't need to dress up for the guys anymore.

Stepping out into the open common area, I could feel all the eyes on me. Silence filled the bustling room. Everyone stilled, studying my face. Women who had failed to conceive, waiting to see if they'd have to bite back the tears to hug and congratulate me or share in my frustration. Men waiting to see if they'd become fathers and return to their squads.

With a twist of my wrist, I held up the test forward-facing so they could see the single line. That fucking line.

"Sorry, boys, I guess you're stuck with me for another cycle."

The room exploded with a mix of groans and whoops.

"Good morning, Sylvia. You've now completed four cycles with the breeding program, and I'm told you're requesting an extension?" Administrator Sampson seemed almost bored, like the decision he was about to half-heartedly make didn't determine the course of my life. He tapped a ballpoint pen on the paperwork laid out across his richly stained oak desk and raised an eyebrow at me.

Clearing my throat, I folded my hands neatly in my lap, and met his eyes with steely resolve.

"Being a pack mother is everything to me," I lied. "I can't imagine my life without children in it."

I couldn't imagine my life working the poisoned fields. Giving the rotten ground every last part of myself until it eventually took my life. All for the good of future generations I would never see.

He studied my face, and I was sick of his scrutiny. Done with the games. Sitting up in my chair, I stared him down.

"I need this." Letting some of the desperation come through in my voice was a risky move, but a calculated one. I'd lick his shiny black shoes if I had to.

With a sigh and a nod, Administrator Sampson sat back in his chair with a squeak and began marking up the paper in front of him.

Worriedly, I tried to see what he was writing, but the angle was wrong for it. I could only wait in the silence to see what he penned with bold strokes.

"I will give you an extension for two cycles."

My breath whooshed out. I felt deflated. After not sleeping the previous night and worrying about how this would go, I'd somehow done it.

Or I'd been too valuable to lose. Elise hadn't been. They'd cut her from the program as soon as she had completed her four cycles without a pregnancy.

Who exactly was my father that my genes were so much more desired?

Fuck if I cared, so long as my records kept me in the program long enough to conceive a child.

"Thank you." My voice squeaked, and I tried to clear my throat again—to clear away the emotion clogging it and force my words back to a normal pitch. "I appreciate it."

"Two additional cycles, Sylvia. That is all you are permitted. Make them count."

With a nod and a weak smile, I stood and left the room.

His words followed me all the way down the hall and through the stairwell leading back to the breeder dorms.

Make them count.

CHAPTER 8

THE WATCHER

"Dude, you've got to push yourself until it hurts. Bad."

I watched with frustration as Cam did a few easy reps with a can of peaches I'd traded a runner a couple of doodles for. He just didn't seem to get it.

"The point is to push yourself," I continued, but he just stared at me with confusion swirling in his bright green eyes.

Cam frowned down at the can. "I don't see how this is going to help."

Glaring at him, I snatched the can out of his hand.

"Oh, it'll help when you get some meat on your bones, and the other guys realize you're not such a fucking easy target."

Why was I so pissed? This was Cam's life. It was his decision to take control of it and learn how to defend himself or not. But some small part of me knew that if I hadn't had my height these past years, I would've been Cam. Not caring about my appearance or strength. Resigned to a life I didn't want because it was the only one I was likely to get.

Fuck that.

"This is too easy for you." I tossed the peaches onto my bed and began loading cans of various sizes into the black duffel at my feet, pausing occasionally to test the weight. "I've learned a few things this past month, and you're going to learn them, too, or I'll be the one kicking your ass."

Cam grinned in a lopsided way that emphasized his oversized teeth. Watchers had to be at least twenty, but I had a feeling—given Cam's size—he still had some growing to do. It was like his body was just waiting to catch up to everyone else. If all I could do was help him get even a fraction stronger than he was, at least I would know I was on my way to repaying my debt.

"How's your back?"

Cam winced, rubbing his arm. "It's okay. They gave me some extra rations and helped me ice it after."

I nodded, not expecting much more after the public lashing we'd been forced to watch. It was hard to hear him talk about it, but I needed to hear this. Needed to know the cost of my idiocy. Sure, I'd protected Syl, but Cam had gotten hurt on my account, and I didn't like it. Not one fucking bit.

Why he'd taken the blame for the fire alarm was still beyond me. I'd have happily taken the lashes for Syl, but owning up to what I'd done so publicly would have meant a lot of attention. The exact sort of attention I wanted to avoid.

If I had any hope in hell of my plan succeeding, I needed to continue to be an easily ignored cog in the machine. So long as the machine kept running, you didn't look too closely at the cog, and you certainly wouldn't notice if it went missing.

At least Cam had agreed to come back to my room to train. I'd be lying if I said it wasn't kind of nice to have some company for a change. Even if my goal was to alienate everyone and everything from my sorry excuse for a life.

"Try this." I shoved the bag into Cam's arms, wincing when the air whooshed out of him on impact. "Sorry."

"That's okay. I can take a hit."

Sadly, I felt that was true, so I gentled my tone. "Hold the strap right in the middle with both hands facing up and pull it to your chin."

Cam did as I instructed, struggling to lift the weighted duffel. He looked at me for help, but I shook my head.

He struggled, but after a minute, he got the strap up to his chin and let it drop. Huffing, his face nearly as red as his hair, Cam set the bag down on his feet.

"Okay, are we done now?"

I grinned, retrieving the bag from the ground and handing it back to him. Reluctantly, he took it, bringing his eyes up to meet mine.

"We're just getting started, my man."

Cam came every day for two hours over the next week. After the fire alarm scare, I'd switched back to my usual shift watching the breeding parties, not willing to take a chance and arouse suspicion by hanging out in the dorm watcher's area.

That, and it was better if the guys there weren't too familiar with my face.

With muscles large enough to strain my previously baggy shirts, I was about ready to set my plan in motion. There were a few loose ends.

Like getting Jerry fired.

I almost felt bad sneaking into his office when he was asleep in his room, but then I remembered what a horny asshole Jerry was. Maybe I was doing the breeders of Pack 103C a service by getting him moved elsewhere.

I tucked the stolen breeding female's file between a desk leg and the wall, so it wasn't immediately visible. No one would think to look there. At least, they wouldn't until my anonymous tip reached Administrator Sampson.

When they located the file, they'd find a picture of the cherubic brunette circled by a red heart, with Jerry and Shelly scribbled beside it. It was the kind of immature shit you'd see from a childish crush, but it was the exact thing Administrator Sampson would crack down on.

We were observers.

Meant to watch.

Never to involve ourselves emotionally with our charges.

The irony of Jerry being an honest watcher while I was the one obsessed with Syl was not lost on me, and maybe that was why I was so certain this would get him reassigned.

A watcher becoming obsessed with someone on the screen wasn't unheard of, and Jerry was highly intelligent, if creepy. He'd be okay. They'd find another place for him.

Whereas, if they found out I planned to infiltrate the breeding program, I had no idea what they'd do, but the precedent it would set for the other watchers would not be tolerated.

Closing Jerry's door quietly behind me, I headed down the hallway and slipped an envelope into the brass mail slot set into Administrator Sampson's door. Inside held the details of where they could find the stolen file. Signed by a concerned pack member.

Since watching that asshole hurt Syl, it'd been torture keeping myself out of the dorm watcher's area, but I couldn't guarantee I wouldn't do something stupid again. Not if I saw her on screen with him. She'd survived this long. I just needed to trust that she would survive a little longer.

The sigh of relief I'd breathed when her name appeared on my breeding schedule had been enough to snuff out a sea of candles.

Not pregnant. She wasn't pregnant, which meant she wasn't going home. It was nearly time for the final phase of my plan.

I didn't have the heart to get Cam moved, nor did I feel I could tell him what I was about to do. I just had to hope my intended transformation and knowledge of the dorm's camera positions would be enough to escape his notice.

After all, who would believe a watcher would mix seamlessly into a breeding program?

With a grin curving my lips, I went next to the records office to rifle through the file cabinet until I found the next cycle's set of breeders coming into Pack 103C.

There he was—the breeder I was to replace. Thank fuck one of the new guys looked enough like me that it'd be passable. Tall with sandy blonde hair and blue eyes. Even his nose was similar to mine. We could've had the same father, and hell, maybe we did.

But there were a few things that needed changing.

First, I studied his haircut, preparing to replicate it on my own. Short on the sides and slightly longer on top, brushed forward across his forehead. Ideally, I'd use a shaver, but the scissors I'd gotten from Reg would have to do. Next, I pulled the black ink pen from my pocket and carefully adjusted a few of his numbers. He was six feet, but I was taller. Drawing a two after the six to give him the extra inches, I mimicked the printed font as best I could. Perfect.

Despite all my efforts, my weight was less than his, and at one-seventy-five, I was still skinny for my height. That one would have to go unchanged. At two hundred pounds, the man from the file's weight was out of my reach in the short time I had left.

Fuck it. I'd double up on shirts or something.

Convinced I'd done everything to the breeder's file to set me up for success, and taking one last look at the man whose identity I was about to assume, I slipped the file back into place and headed back to my room.

There was one more detail I needed to take care of, and I pulled out the letter I'd been working on. Thank fuck I'd gotten a good look at Administrator Sampson's signature on more than one occasion.

I finished the note with his signature, leaning into the end of the n to produce the darker splotch I'd seen him make, and finished with his customary flourish. Sitting back in my chair, I looked the note over, ensuring the handwriting was a good match for the Administrator's. Sebastian would be surprised to learn he wouldn't be needed for the breeding program after all, especially so close to when he was supposed to start, but he'd get over it. I wondered if my "brother" had been looking forward to his stint as a breeder or if he'd been dreading it.

Well, fuck him. He'd have another opportunity.

I wouldn't.

Good thing I knew a runner who would deliver my letter, no questions asked. Liam was a good kid. Recently separated from the family compound but too young to be assigned a role, he always lit up like a damned light bulb when I had a new assignment for him. I'd never known what it was to be a runner, not the sickly asthmatic boy, but it seemed like a good way to keep busy—delivering messages, earning a few extra tips along the way.

Liam would make a good guard—a role I'd never been considered for.

This was it. Everything was set in motion. There was no turning back. There was a spring in my step, and a thrill creeping up my spine as I headed back to my room.

In just one week, I'd be donning a mask.

CHAPTER 9

SYL

I was straddling Jessie on the couch, his thick cock buried inside me, when Kevin came up on his knees behind me and placed an eager sweaty hand on my back.

"I'm sure we can both fit, just—pass the lube."

He was sure.

Kevin was sure he could fit inside my body even with Jessie's thick cock stretching me until it was a painfully tight squeeze.

I whimpered when he butted against my entrance, trying to make a space that didn't exist.

"Sorry, baby, you'll have to wait your turn," I told him with a touch of satisfaction.

With a frustrated huff, Kevin came around in front of the couch.

"The fuck I will." His voice was thick with lust, the veins on his hard cock standing out. Grabbing a fistful of my hair, he pulled me forward against his length. I gagged when he hit the back of my throat. When he groaned with appreciation, I fought to swallow it down and press him deeper. At Kevin's groan of satisfaction, Jessie stirred beneath me, gripping my hips and working me up and down.

Except for the three of us, the common room was quiet, our standard nightly party having wrapped about an hour ago. They were all in their beds. Sound asleep as Jessie fucked me while I sucked Kevin's massive cock, the width of it straining my jaw as he mercilessly thrust into my face.

But none of them were desperate the way I was, and every chance I could get, I would be out here.

Make them count. Two cycles, just two more opportunities, and if I failed...

Fleshy stumps where fingernails used to be. Hair tied up to mask the fact that it was thinning. Dark haunted eyes. My sister's fate awaited me, and I rejected it.

The reminder had me sucking harder on Kevin's cock, pulling him deeper as my jaw adjusted and barely gasping for breath. I wouldn't pass out and ruin this chance. Jessie worked my hips, finding his rhythm, and it wasn't long before he stiffened beneath me and groaned his release.

I waited until he was quiet beneath me before climbing off and pulling myself up on my knees in front of Kevin with my pussy pressed in Jessie's face. He licked it, his face getting covered in his own release and my fluids. Some guys might balk at a pussy soaked in their own cum, but I knew Jessie wouldn't. He loved that shit.

Kevin's handsome face was twisted with tension, his face flushed. Mercilessly, I pushed him back on the couch and straddled him. I'd gotten him close. He didn't fight me. Didn't say a word as I straddled him and seated him deep within my body. I skated my fingernails down his torso, catching on the grooves of his abs.

I leaned forward.

"Come for me, Kevin," I whispered, lifting myself up and slamming down on him hard. Kevin's eyes bugged out. I did it again, not letting him think, not letting him react or try to take control of me. I set the pace, and it was designed to drive him over the edge.

Kevin's eyes rolled back, and his hands hovered over my hips as I bounced up and down on his cock. He let out a guttural groan, gripping my hips as he found the release I'd built in him within my mouth. I gave him a moment to come down before climbing carefully off, trying not to dislodge his precious seed.

If they weren't here, I'd have gone to my room and propped my legs up in bed for as long as I could stand. Anything to get their seed to take root, but that would be a turnoff, so I smiled and went to retrieve my miniskirt and tube top.

"Syl, has anybody ever told you that you're a fucking goddess in bed? Cause, shit. That thing you do with your hips." Kevin stared at me with wide-eyed awe as he spoke, and I gave him an answering wink.

"More than a few times, yes." I laughed, and it was genuine.

Four cycles I'd had to perfect my technique. When I'd first arrived at Pack Breeders 103C, I was sure I'd been total garbage at sex, but I'd picked up a few things while here for months on end.

What a sweet, shy child I'd been. Sleeping with the occasional guy in the comfort of their room or mine. Drinking a bit with everyone, but not really participating in the parties. A surge of anger swelled within my chest at how foolish I'd been to waste so many opportunities to get pregnant and get out. Angrily, I squeezed myself into my tube top, hating the shapeless bit of stretchy fabric that had no style to it, no class.

"Goodnight, boys." I winked and blew them a kiss, tugging on my miniskirt and heading back towards my room.

I needed to lie down as soon as possible, let their seed soak in. Maybe this would be the time I got pregnant.

Please let it be the time.

THE WATCHER

"You really want to take a whole two months off to visit with your family?" Cam's confused expression would have echoed my own if I hadn't been lying about the visit.

"Yeah, it's been three years since I've seen my mom and sister. I figure it's about time."

I'd been entitled to two weeks a year with regular overnights, but I hadn't used a single day. I hadn't wanted to go back to that shithole once, and it wasn't just the crushing depression and hopelessness of my life that had driven me away.

No, there were worse things. Like my mother and sister.

Cam studied my face, and I cleared my throat to ease the tension. We'd gotten close, but I hadn't been able to tell him about my plan. Better he didn't know in case they questioned him. If he knew and didn't tell on me, what good would it be?

The work we'd put in these past few weeks was already showing, and I eyed Cam's biceps with satisfaction when he crossed his arms in front of me.

"You're hiding something."

Fuck you, Cam. Why did I have to make an actual friend now? But I knew the answer. Before Syl, I'd been a husk of a person.

My body had moved. My mouth had formed words. I'd eaten, slept, done my duties as a watcher, but no part of me had wanted to do more. It had taken every ounce of energy in me to keep doing the bare minimum. The old me wouldn't have stepped in when Cam was being bullied, nor would he have offered to train another person and have them be involved in his life. It would've been too much for him, too heavy a burden.

But Syl had changed all that. She'd brought the husk to life, and awakened my mind as much as my body when she'd pulled me into her heat. There was a fire in my chest now—a spark of hope. Though what my obsession with her would accomplish, I didn't know.

I only knew this was the way to meet her. Maybe then I'd know what to do next.

Smiling, I clapped a hand on Cam's shoulder hard enough to shake him.

"We're all hiding something, my friend. Worry about yourself. You've got the plan I gave you, yeah?"

Reluctantly, Cam reached into his pocket and retrieved a paper, waving it at me in annoyance. I might've asked him already. *Fuck.*

But the paper was important. The last thing I wanted to do was to abandon Cam to the literal wolves. I needed to know he'd be okay. So, I was giving him my home exercise equipment and a much gentler schedule than the grueling one I'd put myself through.

Cam didn't need to become strong to wheedle his way into the breeding program and impress some girl. He needed to be strong to protect himself. To find the spark of life they'd denied us by assigning our lives away to this role with no care for what we might want to do.

"Good. You'll be okay, man. Just stick to the schedule, and stay the fuck away from everyone until you're ready to push back." I held his eye, wishing I could stay longer to make sure Cam was safe, but I couldn't.

Syl was waiting for me. As much as Cam needed me here, Syl needed me more. I still had nightmares about that asshole hurting her and her taking it.

She needed me, and I needed her.

"I'll see you later?"

A question. Why a question? I studied Cam's face and decided he was just joking. I laughed it off, knowing it didn't sound exactly right. No matter what happened with Syl, I didn't expect to be back.

"Yeah, man. I'll see you later."

The building was just as I remembered it. A monstrosity of brown brick with a few pathetically small windows pressed into the side. Even the sight of it made me pause, but everything about my leave needed to appear legit. So, I stepped up to the heavy door and pulled it open.

Thank fuck I wouldn't be going back to the old compartment I shared with my mom and sister. They were too keen to keep men and women separate to allow it. Instead, I veered right and skirted the wall on the narrow path most people would've missed if you hadn't been looking for it.

The family visiting area was little more than a small strip of crummy compartments with threadbare curtains and a few worn out chairs within, but they worked. My note had said IC9, and I looked up at the plates at the top of each dangling curtain for the right one. But I didn't need to. I would've recognized my mother's shrill voice anywhere.

Clearing my throat, I pulled back the ratty blue cloth serving as a curtain and looked down into two identical startled faces. Well, they would've been identical if there wasn't a sizable age gap between them. In my mind, my mom and sister had long ago merged into the same person.

"Hi." My greeting hung in the air, but no one returned it.

There were no welcoming hugs or signs of happiness at being reunited after three long years. I hadn't expected there to be. Navigating the small space with my large frame was tricky, requiring me to bend under the pole holding our curtain in place and awkwardly slip between my mother and sister to locate the third chair. My mother tsked when I brushed past her.

Awkwardly, I took a seat in the circular black chair, too small for a man of my size. With a side eye, I noticed my sister's chair was much roomier than the one they'd left for me. I was sure she'd done it on purpose, but I wouldn't fall for her games. These people were behind me now. I only met with them out of necessity, I reminded myself.

"So, how's life been going for you two?"

My mother's lips curled up cruelly. "We've been managing just fine."

Without you.

I heard the last two unspoken words. Every word out of that woman's mouth was designed to hurt, and it had hurt, for far too many years. But I had Syl to look forward to now—a shining star waiting for the sun to set, so she could peek out.

"Yeah, me too. I love being a watcher," I lied.

The look of disgust on my mother's face was worth it. But then my sister had to pipe up because, of fucking course, she did.

"Yeah, I bet you love watching people fucking when you've never done it yourself."

I'd forgotten how much of a joy she was. Of course, she'd find a way to cut me as deeply as possible, as concisely as she could manage. I wasn't worth wasting extra words on, after all.

What a fucking gem of a sister. How fucking lucky I was to have a twin.

"No, I love doing my duty to the pack, and watching people fuck is a lot closer than you've ever come."

The shock and horror on her face was something I would cherish. Fuck her. She sputtered in rage, her heart-shaped face contorting into something monstrous.

"Only because of you. It's all because of you. Mama and I have suffered because of your pathetic existence." She said the last with a snarl, but I was beyond being affected by her shit words.

"Mmm, yeah, I'm sure you would've been chosen for the breeding program if not for me. All your problems are my fault, right?" Who knows if she would have been or not? Only the revered keepers who spent their days poring over our genealogy and selecting the most advantageous matches knew. Maybe an asthmatic twin automatically disqualified her, but there was no telling she'd have been chosen if I'd never existed, and I was sick of her shit.

My sister sat there sputtering, trying to form words through the anger when my mother intervened.

"Yes, she would have been chosen as I was chosen. Only they'd never take me back again after you were born. Must've been something in my genes to produce such a pathetic excuse for a wolf. Care to go for a run and prove me wrong?" Her lip twisted up. "No? I thought not. Can't protect the pack. Can't do shit but sit and watch as real wolves do their duty to the next generation."

Hands curled into fists, I stood and glared down at the woman who'd birthed me. Who must've been happy to have a sweet little boy at one point, but who had tried so hard to poison me with her hate when I'd developed breathing problems, and they'd pulled her from the breeding program. She and my sister blamed me for their exclusion, like I'd asked to be born this way.

I hated them for it. For all the poisoned words they'd poured down my throat. Now that I had a goal, a plan, I saw them for what they were—two pathetic, desperate women who had made their problems mine. The old me would've been cowed by my mother's words. Would've let the guilt of their situation wear him down until he was small.

Not anymore.

"You've tried so hard to beat me down—both of you. Well, fuck you. I won't be beaten down, not anymore. I'm not your dog to whip when you're feeling sorry for yourself. Excuse me, *my family* visit is over. Three years wasn't nearly long enough." Stiff with tension, I pushed past them, glancing over my shoulder to see their faces wore identical expressions of shock. Mouths agape and eyes wide as they tried to process the way I'd rose to meet their cruelty instead of absorbing it like a self-hating sponge.

Each step away from the visiting compartment felt lighter, and when I burst through the door to breathe my first breath of piney air, I knew I would never let myself be treated like shit by them again.

I couldn't wait to thank the woman responsible.

I just hoped my cabin was ready. They accounted for family visits of at least a few hours, not a traumatizing five minutes. Huffing out a breath, I wondered what it would be like to have a family I actually wanted to talk to for more than five minutes.

Probably oppressive and shitty. I grinned to myself, navigating the path through the trees carefully. At least my family was such incredible shit that it would not hold me back, and I knew the look of shock on my mother's and sister's faces were already helping to heal the years of hatred they'd force fed me.

At least the aunties had been kind, if overly sympathetic. I'd always felt it was because they hadn't lost anything due to my defects while my mother had been ousted from the breeding program, and my sister had never been considered for it.

Following a wooden sign with the directions carved into it, I turned right at the fork. It took two more forks before I reached the solitary cabin I was supposedly going to call home for the next two months. Only, I wasn't. With a chuckle, I approached the rough-hewn log cabin with its thatched roof. There'd be a generator for electricity, but I'd only need it for a short time.

The inside was just as plain, with a bed and a kitchenette dominating the one room. A small chest of wooden doors with silver knobs blended into the room.

No bathroom. Well shit. Good thing I'd brought a mirror.

Anyone could book a cabin like this when they wanted some solitude. We might be pack animals, but these cabins existed for a reason. Everyone needed their space sometimes.

I dropped my black duffel on the ground and took a seat on the bed.

Tonight. Syl's breeding party was set for tonight. Just a few more hours and I'd be meeting her in person—touching her, hearing her voice properly. Just the thought of donning the stag mask and entering that room to find Syl waiting for me was giving me a hard-on. A hard-on I refused to do anything about. I was saving it for Syl. Ready to give her everything in me. My soul, my heart, whatever she wanted or needed. I just needed to figure out what that was.

There was no time to rest, so I hauled my ass off the bed, grabbed my duffel, and plopped it on the pink speckled kitchen counter. Inside was everything I owned or wanted to take with me—the duffel busting at the seams. I carefully unpacked a few folded up shirts and pants to reveal the shaver I'd bartered for. Turns out the barber wanted extra rations just like everybody else.

The little pocket mirror I'd brought would have to do, and I set it up on the windowsill behind the kitchen counter. With my height, it was a challenge to position it so I could see anything, but whatever. It was good enough, and I got to work. Grabbing a plastic piece to set my length, I shaved off my chin-length, sandy blonde hair into strips that fell into my face.

Annoyed, I swept them out of the way. It was a long and annoying process to make the first pass, and then I still had to do the sides. I only prayed the haircut was passable.

The haircut took me a lot longer than expected, but by the time I was through with it, I was pleased. Longer on the top, with neatly trimmed sides. That's what my counterpart had, and I looked even more like him now. It'd been a long time since I'd seen my face without hair falling across it, and I grinned at my healthy reflection. This past month of exercise had done wonders for my complexion, giving my face a healthy glow that would help me fit in with the other breeders.

As much as I'd tried to step outside more in the past few weeks, I'd still be a pale, sickly colour next to them, but whatever. Some guys were naturally pale, their skin preferring to burn than to tan. Would mine have tanned if I'd spent my life outdoors like the guards did? I had no idea.

Shaking my head, I reached deep within the duffel along the left side to find my bundle of papers. Reverently, I pulled out my portraits of Syl—her face, her body, a hundred different expressions and positions. It was past time to find out what this thing with her meant, and I was already late.

After cleaning up the hair, I walked out of the cabin as a different person.

The defective watcher was gone.

In his place stood a breeder.

Chapter 10

You'd think I'd be used to this by now—that it'd be easy. It wasn't. I smiled cheerily at the young coordinator who read me the rules and explained the breeding party like this wasn't my fifth time doing it.

No touching, no kissing, do not remove the mask. When your heat is done, push the button twice.

I could've read it back to her from memory. The familiarity of the cozy room and waterproof mattress made me sick. Four times I'd been here. Four times they'd forced a heat on me, so I could be ravaged again and again in the hopes of achieving a pregnancy. Four times—and I was about to do it again. Only this would be my last shot.

The coordinator blushed prettily as she stumbled over her words. Soft brown hair fell past her shoulders, framing a long stately face. What gave them the right to deny her access to the breeding program? As she wrapped up her speech, I smiled reassuringly at her.

Her answering smile was nervous, and she turned to her clipboard, holding it in front of her like a shield.

"Okay, next you'll breathe in the contents of this vial"—she reached into the pocket of her lab coat and pulled out a familiar glass vial. I noted the pocket—"holding it in your lungs for as long as possible. This is what will start your heat. Then I'll leave the room, and it'll start in about five minutes. When you feel ready to receive your first breeder, you can press the button there three times."

I pretended to listen intently and nodded my head like she wanted.

Smiling patiently at me, she said, "Are you ready?"

"Thank you. You've been so nice to me." With a watery smile, I reached out and hugged the coordinator, catching her by surprise, and she nervously moved into my embrace. I waited until she hugged me back before deftly slipping a hand into her coat pocket and retrieving one of the vials.

The coordinator stiffened and gave me an awkward pat on the back. This was too easy. We broke apart, and I gave an enormous sigh of relief at being nearly done. The coordinator held the vial out to me.

I took the stoppered glass vial with the purple flowers inside and opened it, holding it under my nose and filling my lungs with its flowery scent. At least this shit smelled better than the air fresheners back in our dorms, and its effects were near instant—a soothing sense of relaxation softening the tension in my muscles.

"Good luck," the girl said almost gleefully as she headed out of the room, leaving me naked and strapped to the hospital bed.

After she left, those damnable tears creeped into my eyes. Why did this have to be so hard? Why couldn't I just get pregnant on my first cycle and maintain my dignity instead of having to go through this again and again?

My shoulders shook with the force of my sobs even as the arousal kicked in. Then I was angrily shaking out my shoulders and swiping at the tears on my face. I hadn't come here to cry. Administrator Sampson had told me to make this one count, and I fucking would.

The heat was starting, a burning fire spreading through my core, and I leaned over to press the button exactly three times.

THE WATCHER

Undressing in a hurry and tucking a towel around my waist, I fought to steady my nerves. My hands were shaking. This was it. I thought I'd be late, that I'd walk in and have to choose whatever shit mask was left, but I was wrong.

Instead, I found one other nervous guy with short brown hair leaning forward on his knees, naked, with a towel across his legs. His foot bounced, nearly revealing what he hid beneath the towel, and he looked up at me with a watery smile.

"First time?" I asked him, and he nodded, not volunteering any more information.

That was fine with me.

The mask he held wasn't the stag, so I stepped up to the table in the center of the room. A variety of animal faces were placed proudly on display. Some were brushed with gold paint, while others were a matte black that seemed to absorb any surrounding light.

Taking in the array of masks, I pretended to peruse the selection while searching for the one I had already selected for myself. There were more masks than there were breeders and I wondered about that, but as I hadn't been briefed on this part of the process before, I dared not ask the other first timer lest I give myself away.

I found my mask at the end of the row; the gold shining off its antlers drawing me in. Its perfectly regal face outshining all the rest.

Tonight, I would be Syl's stag.

Glancing nervously behind me to see if any new guys had entered the room, I grabbed the mask off the table and tucked it under my arm and went to sit on the bench across from the other man. I'd worn my towel tucked around my waist, assuming that was how they wanted it, but seeing the other first timer and noting the clean paper running along the wooden bench, I removed the towel to sit on the paper and laid the towel across my legs.

I placed the mask on my lap, staring into the hollow eyes of the stag and wondering what Syl would see at our first meeting. How good it would feel to press into her and relieve the heat consuming her body, mind and soul. Getting to know her would come later.

First, I would make her mine. My body would own hers. I didn't care what the other breeders looked like or who they were. I knew there was something between Syl and me, and I couldn't wait to see it revealed.

A man with shaggy blonde hair burst his way into the room, breathing hard and clutching a hawk's mask to his chest. Even in my state of agitation, I thought it strange he'd chosen to bring his own mask when others were set out for our use. I watched as the man sat down a few feet away from me on the bench, tipping his head back with a sigh.

The rest of the breeders came in as a rowdy group of beefy men who walked past my position without looking, heading straight for the masks. I recognized the asshole who had hurt Syl, and my hand tightened painfully on my knee.

"Yeah man, well, it's not like we can't fuck her whenever and wherever we want, anyway. Breeding parties aren't very exciting when the girl gives it away every chance she gets." His laughter didn't reach me, the sound disconnected from the rage pounding in my head.

This fucking asshole thinks he's so superior to her.

I couldn't wait to show him he wasn't. When I'd watched Syl on the screen, I thought the guy manhandling her body had made a mistake. That he'd assumed she liked it because she didn't stop him.

I was wrong.

The smirk he wore and the way he reached back to grab whatever mask, without even looking at it, were proof of his apathy.

He didn't give a shit about Syl or this process. He didn't care about anything but himself, and I would see him pay for the way he disregarded her.

But not now. Not when Syl was so close, and I needed to lie low. So, I swallowed hard enough to hurt, and looked back down at my mask, trying not to hear the disgusting words spewed about her. Syl—who had only ever given them her beautiful body.

"Yeah man, I swear she likes it in the ass and with spikes. The way she squealed. Music. Fucking musical, I'm telling you guys. Too bad they won't let us do that shit in here."

Syl, Syl, Syl.

Close. I was so close to seeing her. If I broke this asshole's nose, lost control and slammed his head into the wall until he stopped laughing, I wouldn't get to see Syl. I might even be discovered. My fist clenched, turning white with tension and longing to be let loose right at this asshole's face.

My control began to slip when the bastard laughed with his friends. Laughed like Syl was nothing but a *thing* meant for his enjoyment. With effort, I worked to rein myself in, the cramping pain in my tight fist barely noticeable as rage threatened to consume me.

But then I heard that fucker laugh and every muscle in my body locked as I fought for control. *How fucking dare he.*

Just when I thought I might lose it, the door banged open and a russet haired youth wearing a lab coat and holding a clipboard peered in.

"The induction has been administered to your breeding female, which means you have five minutes to um"—the poor kid's face turned beet red—"prepare yourselves."

A couple of the guys laughed at his discomfort because, of course, those assholes liked to see somebody suffering.

"It is now time to put on your masks, and I will hand out your personal lubrication packets. Your breeder should be lubricated enough when you enter, but if you find she isn't, there are additional packets on the nightstand where the waters are set up. Your role here is simple—go into the room ready, engage with your breeder, touching her as little as possible, clean off with a tissue and help yourself to water before leaving." The boy cleared his throat, flipping the page. "Any and all talking is forbidden, as is touching not required by the act. You are permitted to reposition your breeder if needed, but the goal is to go through as many of you as possible, so please be quick and courteous."

I snorted, unable to help myself.

Quick and courteous. The idea was completely at odds with the very many things I wanted to do with Syl. The weight of eyes on me was suffocating, and I looked up to find the other first timer watching me carefully, his eyes darting between me and the exit like I was about to explode and he needed to know where to run.

Shit. How long had he been watching me? Hopefully not long enough to know how the chatter of our fellow breeders had sent me into a rage I was still recovering from. It was better now that everyone was putting on their rubber masks. The boy went around to ensure they were secure and no pieces of hair jutted out.

Better now I couldn't see the asshole's face, and everyone was too busy getting ready to brag about the different ways they'd had Syl. I put on my mask, surprised at how comfortable it was, and how lightly it sat on my face. I'd cleaned masks often enough, but never tried one on. Before Syl, the idea of even pretending to be a breeder for a moment hadn't occurred to me.

The coordinator checked my mask, handed me a plastic packet with a tearaway piece, and stood in front of the room once more.

"You can now prepare yourselves. Once she's pressed the buttons, I'll return to take the first of you in to complete your duty."

I looked across and found the other first timer wearing a black wolf's mask. A little on the nose, but whatever.

I had no idea which mask the asshole had chosen, but I scanned the other men, trying to pick him out. My hand clenching and unclenching, eager for the fight I never got to have.

The sounds of tearing packets filled the room, and hands disappeared beneath towels. I barely needed any attention. Thinking about Syl all day had left me painfully hard, and I only needed to imagine her splayed out before me to feel ready to "perform my duty."

Wanting to fit in, my hand slipped beneath the towel, and I lightly stroked my aching cock. But I didn't open my lubrication pack like the others. No, I wanted all my lubrication to come from her. My head dropped back with a thud against the tiled wall as I pictured her getting ready for me.

This was happening. I was really here and just down the hall from me, my angel, my muse, would soon be waiting for me to satisfy her body's needs.

Shuddering, I ran my hand up and down my straining length, imagining what she would feel like to touch. Then I thought of my replacement watcher. There was just the one camera angle, and I'd be masked, but it was strange to realize there would be someone on the other end of the camera watching while Syl and I came together at last.

This time, I wasn't here to watch the party. I would be a participant.

Waiting for my false name to be called was an eternity. Eyes squeezed shut, I gave myself the occasional tug, vaguely aware of men disappearing around me as their turn came. When at last I heard my new name ring out, I opened my eyes to find I was one of the last in the room.

On shaky legs, I stood to follow the coordinator, my heart pounding. I'd been waiting for this moment for so long. Every pull-up, every bicep curl, every ripped muscle and torn ligament had been for this, for her. I followed him down the hall and the boy gestured to the door in front of me.

Gulping, I turned the handle and pushed my way in.

There she was. Perfection. Every inch of her body glistened with sweat. Her blonde hair plastered to her face in thick strands I longed to brush away. She was suffering, clinging to the bed rails so tightly the tendons in her wrists stood out.

"Shhh." I couldn't help it. I knew we weren't allowed to talk, but the soothing sounds came from me without thought or intention. Pitched low and deep into my chest, creating a vibrating purr.

Syl's erratic movements paused, and she looked up at me. Her eyes were wild like she wasn't seeing me, and I remembered the stupid mask I wore.

Fuck. I wanted to tear it off, to show her my real face and take her, but that wasn't why I was here.

I stepped up between her legs, that indistinct sound still coming from me, and she eased back down. Her hands loosening up on the railing, legs still splayed apart like she knew me, and trusted I could ease her suffering.

I would. Stepping between her legs, I positioned my tip at her entrance, smoothing my hands across her trembling thighs. Her pouty lip trembled and her body tensed. My purr intensified, and she whimpered, settling back down. The effect it had on her was remarkable. I'd never heard of anything like it, but the thought that I could calm her, soothe her, and satisfy her thrilled me deep down, and I pressed into her wet heat with a groan.

Syl was packed with other men's cum and her own juices, and big as I was, I slid in the first few inches with ease. The sensation was unlike anything I'd ever known, and my head dropped back as I adjusted to the ecstasy of her grip on my cock.

A helpless mewling sound pulled me out of my daze, and I was shocked to find Syl trying to pull herself down, trying to impale herself on me more fully.

Fuck. Now I was the asshole, fucking this up and not giving her what she needed.

I slammed home, and she squealed beneath me. Her sound of pure pleasure took hold of something feral within me and drew it out.

I ripped away, slamming back in. She cried out, and I thrusted forward. Panting, I gripped her hips, pulling out and leaning forward, and used my height to gain extra leverage and pressed. Deeper. The word wasn't right. Now that I was here, inside of her, I wanted to split her apart.

Syl's hand reached out to rub at a glistening red bud on her pussy, and I understood it was a part of her body that made her feel good. Shoving her hand aside, I went to work on the red nub, keeping still inside her and watching her face as I circled it with my thumb, committing to memory what happened when I experimented with different movements.

When I understood better how it worked, I circled it eagerly, marveling at my power. Syl cried out, her hips trying to work me, and I knew what to do. With one hand, I pressed on her, leaning forward to drive deeper as I rubbed and pressed on her nub. She screamed, her eyes wide and back arching. Then I moved, rolling my hips as I moved into her. Deeper, rubbing her more frantically as the feral beast inside of me crested. I panted. The friction. Her sounds. All of it bringing me closer to release.

Then her hands joined mine, and I looked up to find her eyes wide and her mouth open.

"It's you," she whispered. The sound of her voice contained a gravelly edge that was pure animal.

The combination of her touching me, of her talking to me for the first time, was too much. I pounded into her, watching with satisfaction as her eyes rolled back and she arched backward onto the bed. Mercilessly, I pulled her hips closer to the edge, pinning her onto her back as I impaled her on my cock.

Syl screamed again, gripping the bed rails like they had any chance of saving her from the orgasm shaking through her body. Her pussy gripped me, and I was lost, spilling inside of her and giving her every last drop of myself. Everything I had.

But she wasn't through. Her heat rose, and she cried. Real tears leaking from her beautiful blue eyes in an expression of desire and pain I knew I would draw later. She was never full, never finished until the heat was over, and I'd given her everything I could.

Only something in me rose to meet her desire.

I was becoming hard again. Just like when I'd watched her, my body responded to her needs—determined to satisfy her insatiable appetite in a way that shouldn't be possible. With a shudder as she pulled me into her heat, I became hard again, my cock twitching to life inside of her. The friction bringing a new deeper aching pleasure I'd been missing when I'd fucked my hand in the watcher's room.

I hadn't expected this. Somehow, I'd expected this encounter to be like any other breeding party. The mask, a quick and courteous deposit, and I'd be done. But the thing between Syl and me rose up to declare itself, driving me frantically into her body once more.

Gasping, I pulled her back to me, but something prevented me from pulling out all the way, and my thrusts were shallow. Need consumed me. This wasn't enough. I had to touch more of her, to press my body against hers, so the strange sound I was making and my newly hardened cock could calm her erratic energy.

I made use of every bit of friction I could manage, working her harder. Faster. Until I couldn't stand the sensation anymore. I worked her nub. Press. Circle. Twist. Oh, she liked that. Her face was shining bright with pleasure. My release came more quickly this time, and I pulled back my hands, some sick part of me liking the handprints I'd left on her thighs when I'd spread her as far as she could go.

Syl calmed, her body limp beneath mine. She turned her head, and her hair fell across her eyes, shielding her face. Fuck, I wanted to brush it away, to cup her cheek and tell her I was here now. No matter what happened. But I couldn't, and something about that moment made me remember where I was.

Someone was watching. With a renewed fear, I tried to work myself out of her. It was like I was stuck. With concentration, I was able to get whatever it was to ease enough that I could pull myself loose, marveling at the extra thickness at the base of my cock before coughing and going to grab a tissue. I wanted to bring her a tissue, to talk to her about what had just happened between us. Her head remained twisted to the side, her face covered, and with someone watching, I didn't dare speak a word.

I left the way I'd come, wordlessly opening the door and closing it.

I left forever changed and more determined than ever.

Chapter II

SYL

What even was that? I'd meant to continue on, pulling in more breeders after my heat ended, but after that man, I was so shaken it was all I could do to press the button and wait for someone to come get me.

A desire to move, to act, pounded in my veins, and I undid the straps, sitting up on the bed despite my exhausted state. But to act on what? I had nowhere to direct my energy, so I just perched on the edge of the bed like a good little breeder, waiting for the coordinator to come take me to the freshenup room.

He'd finished. I'd felt it shudder through his body, the tension and release of it. I'd been prepared for him to leave, for the terrible emptiness when he pulled himself from me, but he hadn't and when my heat had risen again, he'd grown hard like his body was made for mine. Like he lived to slake my need. A shiver raced across my sweat-soaked skin, the room no longer feeling warm and cozy.

Idiot that I was, I'd spoken to him, and what was worse, he hadn't spoken back. He'd pushed me down onto my back and fucked me until I couldn't have said another word if I'd wanted to. To speak through my heat—it wasn't something that should've been possible, but the words had been pulled from me, like I'd been compelled by the sheer magic of the moment.

And that was him restrained, held in check by the restrictions of the breeding room. He must be new. Must be. No way was he someone I'd met before. The way he'd been so adorably hesitant at first warmed something in my chest. Like he was nervous and didn't know what he was doing but was determined to do it well. He'd figured it out, and damn had he done so, bringing me to my release with an ease even the heat shouldn't have made possible.

What was I doing? I should be focused on the goal, on the pregnancy I needed to secure my place, not fawning after some hot guy who may or may not have come twice.

By the time the coordinator arrived, my heart rate had slowed and my breathing had evened out. I was feeling much more myself, and I smiled at the same brown-haired girl who had set me up. The vial I'd swiped secured in my palm. Smiling at the girl, I went to ease myself off the bed when she held up a hand.

"Not so fast, Sylvia. I still need to check you."

I frowned. How could I have forgotten the standard procedure? Knowing what to expect was something I prided myself on. Angrily, I lay back down on the bed, spreading my legs and averting my eyes when I heard the coordinator's gloves snapping into place.

She must've assumed my mood was directed at her because the coordinator remained quiet throughout her task, gently squelching a finger into place. Removing it, she took off her gloves with another sharp snap and wrote a note on her clipboard.

"Let's get you to the freshenup room," she said with a false cheeriness. I let her help me up and escort me to the freshenup room, its flowered wallpaper welcoming me after a job well done. But that last bit with The Stag hadn't felt like a job. I'd dare say I'd enjoyed every second of that man's company.

Swallowing the strange sense of excitement gripping my chest, I smiled my thanks at the coordinator and set to freshening up.

I wanted to look my best when I met The Stag without his mask.

THE WATCHER

After Syl, everything around me held so much less substance, and I walked into Pack 103C Breeders on shaky limbs, going up to the group of guys crowded at the counter.

A guy with slicked back hair and a jean jacket cleared a space, but nobody stopped talking. That was perfect for me. It had always been my goal to slip in amongst them, to hide in plain sight. I grabbed an unopened beer in the center, popped the top with a fizz and laughed right the fuck along with everyone else, no matter how stupid the joke.

"Man, who had the blonde? Her screams are such a turnoff. I don't think I can even look at her in the dorms, but I did my pack duty."

Ouch, that hurt, and I looked up to find the other newcomer. His eyes were wide and his hair mussed. He wore a white terry robe. Standing at the other end of the counter as he was, I shouldn't have been able to hear him so clearly, but my ears had perked up when I'd realized who he was referring to.

The asshole who had hurt Syl clapped him on the back.

"Oh, you get used to it, and that one will let you do whatever the fuck you want with her, and I mean whatever." A chorus of laughter followed his comment, and I forced out a barking laugh of my own.

Once I'd introduced myself and chugged another beer, trying my best to keep names and faces straight, I excused myself to go find my room.

I followed the familiar long hallway, searching the nameplates up and down the length of it twice before I remembered I was looking for my new false name, Sebastian. Chuckling at my stupidity for thinking my watcher name would ever grace these doors, I quickly found Sebastian's door.

If Syl could shorten her name, why couldn't I? I decided right away to go by Bash.

This name—this new name from a different person—should have felt strange, but there was something empowering about taking on a fresh name for this new start in life, and I embraced it.

The room was nondescript, just a larger than needed double bed, a pristine dark brown dresser, and one nightstand bordering the bed. A window looked out onto a field below.

My old room didn't have a window. I guess they didn't give much of a shit if us watchers had a view, but the breeders? Oh, they needed the sunlight. As if going for daily runs and spending the majority of their time outside wasn't enough.

Runs. Yes, the breeders went for shifted runs through the woods behind the breeder dorms, and I'd be expected to go with them. I shifted regularly, as was required, but it'd been years since I'd pushed my lungs to a run, and I only hoped I wouldn't have an attack somewhere out in the brush with my inhaler back in the dorms.

Shit, that could really be dangerous.

But it wasn't something I would let myself think of now, not when Syl would be cleaning up from her heat and on her way back any minute. Running a hand through my now strangely short hair, I went to leave the room and head down to the bathroom when I paused with my hand on the knob.

Huh. The thing was busted up. Dented. I peered more closely at the brass globe to see someone had tried to hammer it straight, but whatever damage had been done was extensive enough that they couldn't get it quite right.

Pleased that not everything here was fucking perfect, I turned my banged up knob and headed down the hall to the bathroom. I'd have put on a show of seeking it out, like I hadn't been here scrubbing their piss off the floor, but the hallway was empty.

The whitewashed bathroom was perfect, everything in its place, and I approached one of the oval mirrors to check on my hair. Shit, I hadn't done as great a job as I'd thought. This was my first proper look at it, and while it was mostly even, I discovered a few longer bits at the back when I turned my head. Searching the shelves and drawers of the white vanities bordering the entrance, I found a pair of scissors. Getting to work, I cleaned up as much as I could before I heard a commotion loud enough to reach me down the hall.

Someone was back—it might be Syl.

I snipped, accidentally cutting a piece near my forehead too short and nicking myself in the process. With a hiss, I yanked the scissors away and pressed a hand to the minor cut. With any hope, it'd heal by the time I walked out there.

Jamming the scissors back amongst the other extra toiletries, I wiped my forehead and headed down the hall.

I'd been right. The timing was correct for just one breeder to be making her way through the front door. Syl stood in the door frame, her eyes twinkling merrily as the guys who had been objectifying her earlier crowded around to pat her on the shoulder as if thanking her for a good time. The sight made me sick.

Syl came into the room proper, going to the kitchen and grabbing a couple of water bottles from the fridge. The asshole from earlier put his hand on the exposed skin of her back. I'd love to call it a shirt, I really would, but the strip of fabric barely covering her breasts didn't fit the description. Then he pushed his way in front of her, dominating her attention.

I wanted to push my way past them—growl, and kick, and bite—until I was the only one standing before her, but I refused to meet her that way. Instead, I leaned on the wall at the mouth of the room, watching.

Once a watcher, always a watcher. But I wasn't here to watch, not anymore.

Chapter 12

SYL

A familiar hand skated across the sensitive skin of my back, and I tensed. Anyone but Carter. Please anyone.

I turned to find Carter regarding me with a smirk curving his lips. What would he do to me tonight? He'd talked about burning the last time he'd taken me. The thought of having to smell my own seared flesh made me sick, but The Party Girl was up for anything. I forced a watery smile to my face, dreading where this was going and still weak from the heat, when someone bumped Carter from behind. His hand jostled free of my shoulder.

Holy shit. The man who bumped into Carter was enormous. Taller than any of the guys in the dorms, and he stared down at Carter, looking every bit like a giant of lore.

"Sorry, man. Water bottles in the fridge? I'm parched." The man was big enough to squash Carter, and I felt him stiffen beside me.

"Yeah, we've got lots. Excuse me, I was just talking with my girl here."

A smile curved the giant's lips, and he swung a hand out, gesturing at me.

"Your girl?" The man gave a laugh filled with the confidence of someone who had drank too much. "Aren't none of them *our* girls? Isn't that the point of this place?"

Carter didn't have an answer, just stood there staring in surprise.

"Yeah, well, I mean. Yes, that's true."

Watching Carter's normal composure shatter gave me all kinds of joy, and I coughed to hide my smile at watching him be so clearly outwitted.

The man waited a moment, the silence palpable before clearing his throat and nodding his head at the fridge.

"Still gonna need that water."

"Right, right. You go ahead." Whether because he didn't know a way out of the conversation without losing face, or because he recognized just how much bigger the man was, Carter moved to the other side of me. I thought he would leave, but the next second, I felt a sharp tug on my hair.

"See you later, Sy." His whispered words were more a threat than a promise, and I shook my shoulders to rid myself of his unwelcome presence once he was at a safe distance away.

"Why do you let him treat you like that?" There was an accusation in the tone, but his voice was clear of the drunken candor it'd held when he was speaking to Carter a moment ago. Tilting my chin up, I met the man's eyes for the first time. His eyes—

Blue, such a beautiful colour. Not light like mine but a deep blue like the water at night. He wore a collared polo shirt that fit snugly across his broad chest and strained across his biceps.

He was definitely new, and I studied him, trying to understand his game by asking me such a loaded question.

"I—" I tried to think of a lie, something believable that would get him off my back, but nothing came to mind. I shocked myself by speaking the truth. "He's the only one who will have me. He scares off the others."

He laughed—the sound bold and deep—and I swear it vibrated in my bones. A strange excitement took hold of my system in his presence. He reached past me to grab a water bottle, and I felt the brush of his warmth. Swallowing hard, I tried to pretend that it hadn't affected me, like I wasn't thinking dirty, nasty things five minutes out of my heat, but I was.

He was new here, and I didn't need to see the others to know who he was. Retrieving the bottle, he turned to me, his eyes twinkling merrily and smiling in a way that brought out his chiseled jawline and sent a fresh rush of arousal to my core.

Grinning, he held his bottle up in a mock cheers, looking fucking delicious while doing so. "Good thing I don't scare easily. The name's Bash. See you around."

Bash headed back over to where a couple of other guys were playing foosball, holding up a beer to one and muttering something before being given a turn at the table.

I felt certain I'd just met The Stag, and now flustered in addition to wrung out, I made my way straight to bed.

Bash. His name was Bash.

While I'd been too emotionally and physically exhausted to engage with him, I'd woken up with his name on my lips. I dressed quickly, barely looking at what I was putting on. For once not caring if I showcased enough flesh to be appetizing to the sea of hungry wolves waiting out in the common room.

Not today. I only cared about appealing to one man, and he'd barely scanned my body. Shit, that sexy curl of his lips got me flustered. I smoothed down my hair, curling the ends with my fingertips, so they better tucked under my chin, the sandy blonde strands reluctantly cooperating.

I blew out a calming breath.

The Party Girl was never worked up. Never overexcited for one man. She belonged to everyone, and she was always ready for a good time with whoever would take her.

Only this party girl wanted one very specific man to take her, to awaken her.

It was time. He'd be waiting.

How I knew he'd be waiting was a mystery, but I felt it. When I walked down the hallway and emerged into the common room, I found him seated at the table with a half-eaten sandwich, his eyes already fixed on mine. The intensity of his stare was too much, and I broke eye contact, feeling the loss of our connection immediately.

What was this man doing to me? I was here to get pregnant and get out.

He could help me with that.

A slow, tantalizing smile spread across his face as he gestured to the empty chair beside him. A promise that he could do just that.

I slipped into the chair, our knees accidentally brushing where his long legs were folded uncomfortably under the table. This guy needed some kind of special chair to be comfortable, and pity swelled inside of me at the thought. How annoying must it be to never have furniture you could use comfortably?

"What's up, sleepyhead?" His eyes twinkled, and he took another bite of his sandwich with a crunch.

I eyed the sandwich critically. The word sandwich was almost inaccurate. The brown bread was loaded with generous amounts of meat, and he'd put those strange white sprouts I'd seen in the fridge, but never dared to try. It looked more like he was having meat for breakfast with a side of bread and some vegetables for garnish.

"Just waking up. Looking forward to the run later." Breeders were required to rest on the day of their induction, and I'd missed the power of shifting and racing through the woods. I'd expected this to be a safe topic of conversation and for him to agree. Instead, he looked away like I'd said something troubling when all I'd really been thinking about was what kind of beautiful animal his wolf was. "You okay?"

He didn't answer right away, but the frown marring his face while he stared down at his meat-thing surprised me.

"Yeah, I've always-always loved going for runs." The way he looked up at me was wistful, and I studied him closely, knowing there was more to the story. "So, what does everyone do all day here?"

Good fucking question. The Party Girl knew this was an opening, that I should sidle up close to him and tell him exactly what I wanted to do with him, but I could feel that brutal honesty coming out of me again. Damn him.

"Everyone fucks and plays foosball. Drinks. It gets boring after a while."

Now it was his turn to study me, and I didn't realize a tear had slipped out until he brushed it away with his thumb. I looked up to find his brow crinkled with concern.

"Well, what did you like to do back home?"

Home. I might've had to tread carefully around my mother, but I was free to be myself there. While I should be lying to him—saying I loved it here, loved to fuck and drink all day—I simply couldn't.

"Oh, I designed clothes. Pretty much all day, every day. It's taken me years, but I've amassed quite the collection of magazines from what it was like before. Some of them are in shit condition, but they give me ideas." I rubbed my arms self consciously, looking down to realize I'd thrown on some jogging pants and a white short-sleeved shirt—the kind of thing I'd wear when I was alone in my room, not in front of the guys. I wasn't exactly showcasing my fashion prowess.

"That's great." His enthusiasm caught me off guard, and I looked up to find him sporting an enormous grin.

"Oh, I mean, it's okay. I guess."

He rolled his eyes.

"All right then, what do you do in the off hours back home?" I asked.

He stared straight ahead at nothing, and I could feel that same honesty being pulled from him, like he wanted to lie but couldn't.

"I draw."

"You draw. But what do you draw?"

He looked back at me, his eyes skimming my body. An artist studying his subject.

"Anything and everything. Always have. Always will."

That was kind of beautiful, and I felt a smile creeping onto my face. I was about to ask for more details when a beefy hand dropped to my shoulder.

"Hey, Syl, a couple of the guys and I are going to take a shower if you'd like to join."

My mouth hung open, and I looked up into Gale's eager face. I froze. The Party Girl always said yes. A couple of guys. That meant plenty of opportunity for pregnancy, and not with Carter—who'd been curiously absent after Bash's challenge.

I always said yes.

This was what I was here to do.

My eyes drifted to Bash, and I found him watching me carefully. Not saying anything, just waiting for me to respond.

Make it count. Administrator Sampson's words hammered through my mind. *Make it count, make it count, make it count.*

As much as I was enjoying talking to Bash, talking wasn't what I needed. After coming back from the heat too drained to engage with anyone, I couldn't miss this opportunity.

"Sure, I'll be right there." With a coy smile, I placed my hand on Gale's and let him lead me towards the hallway. "I'll see you later, Bash."

"Count on it." He spoke quietly enough that I almost didn't hear him over the pounding in my ears. I kept my body turned towards him even as Gale tugged me further down the hall, clearly eager to get started. Carter hadn't dominated my time completely, but he'd made it harder for anyone else to get me alone, so I would depend completely on him.

"What kind of panties have you got on, baby?" Gale's lust-filled voice had a rough edge of desperation to it, and my palms grew sweaty in his hands.

"A black thong today." I didn't usually wear panties out around the guys, but I'd fallen asleep in it and been so eager to come out and meet Bash properly that I'd left the lacey little number on.

Gale groaned, his head dropping back.

At this time of day, the showers were often occupied, and I wasn't surprised to find Chloe pressed up against the wall being fucked hard. So many other women had come and gone since I'd first been entered in the breeding program that I didn't bother to learn their names anymore, but Chloe liked it when guys called out her name while they fucked her and I'd had an earful. Chloe's doe-like eyes were wide and her lips parted as a guy with a buzz cut hammered into her. A lineup of guys rubbing their cocks waited behind them.

No wonder Gale had wanted me to join. One girl for all of them meant a lot more waiting and a lot less fucking. Gale moved behind me and pressed his hard length into my back, his lips skimming along the shell of my ear.

"Now let's see those panties." He tugged my pants down and got on his knees behind me, squeezing my ass cheeks together. "Mm-hmm." His appreciative sounds were fucking hot, and I couldn't help but moan when he traced the seam with a thick finger to discover my wetness.

It wasn't for him. As much as I'd been engaged in conversation with Bash about perfectly normal, non-sexual things, his very presence had affected me.

"You were just waiting for me to take you in here, weren't you, Syl? You like being fucked by a pack of wolves."

Swallowing, I nodded shakily as he began massaging my ass.

He stood up behind me, and I gave a groan of protest at the loss of his touch, but then he was wrapping an arm around me and squeezing a breast gently.

"Strip." The whispered words were warm in my ear, and the scent of sex filled the bathroom along with Chloe's moans. The same man pounded into her, grabbing her long brown hair in his fist and arching her back to get deeper.

I took off everything and heard Gale doing the same at my back. His belt hit the ceramic tile with a clang. Then he urged me forward with a palm on my back, into the shower area, where the lineup of men watched me with hungry eyes.

"Right here, baby." Gale pushed me to the wall a few feet from where Chloe was being fucked. My nipples tightened painfully in anticipation as he pressed me against the wall with a forearm. "Now that Carter's backed the fuck off, you can join the party for real. You like that, baby?"

"Yes." The lust was thick in my throat, and I could hear deep chuckles at my back as if what Gale had said was funny. As if they were going to fucking destroy me.

I wanted them to, and I moaned, arching my back the way Chloe had done and moving my pussy closer to where Gale stood at my back.

"Mmm." His growl was all the warning I got before he slammed home, his forearm pressing me into the wet tile of the bathroom wall. Gasping, I planted my palms as he fucked me. I'd been wet, eager, aroused, but now that he was taking me, it wasn't what I wanted. I whimpered, realizing I wouldn't find a release with him. My body was wound tightly from Gale's ministrations and Chloe's desperation as she was fucked by a new man with a cock so thick it must've hurt going in.

Gale finished, his hand moving to the back of my head and pressing my cheek into the tile as he worked through his release. It hadn't taken him long. I felt the absence of his warmth at my back before another replaced it, grabbing my hips and hammering into me at a jarring pace that left me smacking into the tile.

The bathroom door swung open with a bang.

I looked up to find Bash's eyes on me, and I felt ashamed for the first time since entering this place. Like he'd caught me doing something wrong instead of doing my pack duty and working to be a pack mother.

His eyes never leaving mine, he pushed his way through the lineup of men waiting to fuck me. He brushed them aside like they were nothing. His eyes burned into mine—a mix of hunger, lust, and rage that had me gulping back air like each gasp would be my last.

Then he stood before me. I wanted to look at his body, to really look at it without the heat fogging up my senses, but I couldn't break his gaze. Couldn't speak. Couldn't do anything but be captivated by the spell he had me under.

He reached out and gripped my hair, and I gasped at the tug on my roots, moving instinctively into his palm so I was pressing my mouth against his wrist.

Fuck. I could come just like this, with him watching me like that and his firm hand wrapped up in my hair. Instead, I pressed a kiss to his wrist. My eyes rolled up when he crashed down upon me, his warmth pinning me to the wall with his hand still in my hair.

"You don't go with them," he growled and the warmth of his breath on my other cheek was heaven. I wanted to live in this moment. "If I'm free, you go with me." His breath traveled across my cheek, and I waited. Wanting his mouth on me. Wanting him to bite me. Mark me, consume me in some way I couldn't make sense of. "Do you understand?"

There was only one thing I could say. One word that would solidify the strange connection we shared. I was already at his mercy, a helpless bit of moldable clay beneath his hands, and he only had to squeeze to shape me to his will.

His hand twisted in my hair, and the sensation went straight to my core, drawing a desperate moan from my lips.

"Yes." I was dripping, the wetness between my legs combining with Gale's cum to soak my thighs. Squirming in his grasp, I tried to bring my body closer to his, but he held me fast, his eyes searching mine.

Then the hand in my hair released, caressing my cheek almost reverently. His thumb traced the curves and his eyes following it like he was memorizing me.

Fuck, it was hot, and I took a tentative step towards him when he crashed into me. His hot breath was on my neck, and I shivered at the contrast between rough and tender. Then he lifted me under the arms, pulling our chests flush before pressing me against the wall and sank himself deep into my pussy. I gasped at the stretch, remembering how I'd felt it even in my heat state, but after I'd adjusted and took another inch and then another, it began to feel good. Right. Exactly what I'd been missing from Gale with his perfectly average cock.

The realization hit me the moment he bottomed out. He groaned, the sound of him ricocheting off something deep inside of me and demanding a response. He pressed forward, and it was too much. The fullness, the feel of him, his sheer presence seemed designed to turn me on and strip away my defenses. I shuddered—not sure I wouldn't come with the slightest amount of friction between us.

I looked down to see where we were connected, and my breathing strained at the sight of him stretching my pussy. His hand dropped between us, finding my nub and cautiously circling it with his thumb. Hissing in a breath, my head fell back to smack into the tile behind me. His other arm went under my ass, and he lifted me, dragging my pussy against his cock.

Scrambling for his shoulders, I hoisted myself up, taking control of the maddening friction and setting a pace that left him moaning into my neck. He shuddered and took hold of my hips with a growl, slamming me into the shower wall. He tilted my hips as he thrust into me impossibly deeper and hitting a spot deep inside that left me squealing with coiled tension. Still, he rubbed. Harder. Faster. His grip on my hips tightening painfully as he worked me so hard I forgot to breathe. I cried, tears dripping down my cheeks as I fought to find a release I could taste.

He lifted me back into his arms, his mouth at my neck. His teeth skated across the delicate skin. I groaned at the loss of fullness when he slipped nearly all the way out. But then he was slamming me down against him with a growl. He lifted me and dropped me back onto him, using every bit of my body weight to dig his way deeper inside of me. I clutched his neck, pressing my face into his chest, trying to work through the myriad of sensations competing for my attention.

There was no shower anymore, no more room, no more other men. Chloe's moans, so loud and demanding, were lost to the music of Bash's growls and the vibration of the chest I leaned into.

He pressed me back into the wall, pinning me with his chest and planting his palms on either side of my head. Pulling out fully only to crash back into place, I was a helpless participant again, barreling uncontrollably forward.

Release. Pure bliss overtook me, and I shuddered as the tremors of pleasure worked their way through my body. He found his with a bone-rattling roar loud enough to shake my bones a minute before they melted under the most explosive release I'd ever experienced. My legs scrambled against his, fighting to hold him in place as my body trembled and shuddered through blissful release. Something gushed from me in time with the orgasms ravaging my body. They kept coming, just as Bash stayed hard within me. Moving slowly, the friction was just enough that the explosions of pleasure within me intensified, and I was sure this was how I died. On this cock. In this place. The Party Girl taken down by a runaway orgasm.

But the waves of dizzying pleasure eased. I sagged with relief against him, expecting him to pull away and welcome the next man to take my pussy. Only I didn't think my legs could support me. Now I would need to do the very embarrassing thing of asking him to please deposit me in a chair. Maybe the guys wouldn't mind if I was seated.

The Party Girl was always up for a good time. But I was groggy, not thinking straight, and I was shocked when a deep relaxation made its way through me, leaving my limbs floppy and sleep peeking at the edges of my vision. I couldn't explain what was happening. It was a sense of safety, like I needn't be afraid of anyone harming me ever again.

Bash's hand stroked up my back, and he scooped me up, holding me more firmly against his chest.

"The ch-chair," I sputtered out. There was a bath seat in the shower area, meant to be used for different positions, and I gestured weakly at it behind his back.

"Syl, there's nowhere you're going right now except to my bed."

I smiled into his neck. He'd sounded possessive before when he came in to confront me, but I hadn't really thought he would claim my attention in this way. With my bones turned to mush and the vibration of his chest spreading to mine, the only thing I wanted was to be held until I slept.

My eyes drifted shut. I didn't care to look and see if any of the other men watched or what they thought. I only cared that I was with The Stag.

Beautiful. Perfect. Only those words didn't describe it. Couldn't describe her. After tucking Syl carefully into my bed, cause fuck if she was going anywhere else, I took out my sketching paper and a piece of cardboard I'd swiped from the kitchen. With no desk or surface, I needed something at least semi rigid to provide a backing for my sketches, and the cardboard was decent for now.

Only it frustrated the shit out of me not to have a table as I worked to sketch out the way Syl's eyes had burned into mine.

When I'd finally followed her to the shower and made my intentions known to the others, not one of them had said a word. Oh, I'd dared them to. As I'd taken Syl the fuck out of there, I stared down the guys who had lined up to fuck my girl. But they'd broken off, forming a line behind the other women in the shower who seemed more than willing to satisfy everyone present.

Syl slept. It was midmorning, but she was exhausted, and I was fully prepared to give her whatever she needed. Even if it meant letting sleep steal her away from me. I was more than happy to process the beauty of each shared moment with her since I'd arrived. My hand flew across the page, working through the explosion of beauty and inspiration that now had a name.

Syl.

We'd barely spoken, but that connection I'd felt when I'd first seen her on my monitor was there, and her body reacted to mine like we'd been handcrafted for each other by a mad scientist who had aligned our systems, so we were never alone.

Never alone. That was it. This connection with Syl was unlike anything I'd felt with another person. Between my mother and bitch sister, there hadn't been room for connection. Not even with all the other kids, the kind ones with their pitying looks at my damaged condition. Then when I'd joined the other watchers and finally been among other men who got it—who had been classified as inferior from a young age just like me—I hadn't had the strength or interest in trying to connect with them.

But that was before Syl.

I frowned down angrily at the curve of her leg I was drawing, sure it wasn't right. No. It was shit. So far from the right delicate shape of Syl's actual leg, it was almost an insult. I lifted the infuriating cheap computer paper I'd been stockpiling for years, swiping a few sheets here and there, ready to crumple it. But paper was precious, and I had a whole other side. I just needed to take a peek. Just one little look and I'd know how to draw it.

My eyes fell on the sleeping angel in my bed. Her tousled ash-blonde hair obscured everything but lush lips still sporting the ruby red lipstick I'd only been so happy to smear. Hands peeking out to curl around the edge of the blanket, she slept peacefully. Deeply. I reached out to tug at the end of the coverlet, slowly lifting it with my eyes on her face to make sure I didn't disturb her.

Oh, I was such an asshole.

Chapter 13

SYL

I woke with a shiver, opening my eyes to find the thick coverlet I'd been wrapped in pulled to the side. Grumbling, I blinked blearily around the room and found Bash sitting in what appeared to be a chair from the dining room. One leg folded across his lap, he had some raggedy bit of cardboard balanced on his legs and a piece of something black in his hand that he was urgently moving across it.

His eyes glanced up at me occasionally. Wait. Not me. At my leg. I looked down at the way he'd exposed just my leg, tucking the blanket around me to prevent any air from going under the covers.

What was he doing?

His lanky form stayed hunched over the cardboard, not even noticing I'd woken up. I took the opportunity to drink in his body, knowing that once his eyes captured mine, the intensity would pull me in, and I'd be drawn helplessly towards him. That attraction left little time for proper appreciation.

Mmmm. There was something beautiful about the way he worked on whatever he was doing. I was clearly the subject of his attention, his blue eyes darting up to look at my leg and then back down to his work.

Lanky but muscular. A deadly build. He looked like he could have taken on every wolf in the shower with ease. Like he'd challenge them in a fight and leave without a mark.

They must love him in the guard, and he must be a guard. Most every man here was, and I couldn't see him being one of the intelligence personnel they sometimes deemed worthy of breeding. No, those blue eyes had watched me with intelligence, but I was sure he was a guard. And the need to know was starting to burn.

I wanted to ask him, to blurt out a million questions at once until every single detail of this man was known, stored, cherished. But the desire was torn with fascination at the way he studied me. His posture and every bit of his attention focused on whatever was on the torn up piece of cardboard he was using as some kind of derelict lap desk.

I waited until I couldn't stand it anymore. Until the words burned inside me, leaving me tense under the cover's softness. Bash's coverlet was thicker than mine, and I was starting to think I had gotten a shit deal. I moved the leg he was fascinated by, watching confusion freeze him for a moment, before he looked up and found me awake and watching him.

Scrubbing a hand across his head, he cleared his throat and averted his gaze guiltily.

"Oh, you're up. Sorry, I-I—" He struggled for the words, this great big man red-faced like I'd caught him stealing from the alpha's chambers.

"What are you doing there?" I asked, sitting up in the same breath to perch on the edge of the bed.

Mouth agape, he watched me. Sometime since he'd carried me back here, he'd thrown on a black shirt and grey joggers, the shirt ill-fitting across his broad chest. While I'd remained naked, and I made no effort to cover myself now.

The Party Girl would never cover up, and for once, Syl agreed. Watching Bash studying my body so intently, almost worshipfully, filled me with confidence.

No one had ever looked at me the way he did. Like he was seeing more than my pert breasts and elegant neck. I was used to the lust I saw swirling in his eyes, but there was so much more wrapped up in the way he studied me. His eyes fixed on my face, but darted across my body at every opportunity.

"What are you doing?" I asked again, bouncing up on the mattress to catch a glimpse of what was hidden behind the cardboard, but Bash pulled it towards him protectively, his mouth opening and closing as he tried to speak.

Was this really the same man who had busted his way into the shower and taken me in front of a literal wolf pack?

But I knew it was, and his adorable shyness was just another facet of the man I couldn't wait to know better.

"It's nothing, just-just." He was trying to think up a lie, his eyes careening around the room like he'd find the answer somewhere in the thin set of drapes covering his window or the thick door sealing us away from the world. No fucking way.

"I want to see what you're doing. You don't ever cover up from me, and you're wearing way too many fucking clothes," I growled, standing and closing the distance between us.

Bash sat up, pressing his back into the chair and sucking in a breath.

How fucking adorable. The way he was acting reminded me of how he'd entered my breeding party, surprised to find my clit and eager to learn how touching it made me react. He was so innocent, so unsure of himself, except when he was lost in the act. Almost like—

"I was your first," I stated. When Bash's brows knitted together in confusion, I sighed. "The first woman you ever had."

Realization brought a new light to his eyes, and I studied the colour, wondering how they could be such a dark blue with the hues still perfectly visible. A myriad of shades I could spend all day studying.

With a soft chuckle, I pushed his legs apart with a foot and straddled his knee.

"It's okay. I can't wait to teach you everything," I purred, watching in satisfaction as his lip curled up. "Now, what have you got there?" I reached out a hand to rest on a jagged corner of the ripped up cardboard, giving it a gentle tug. He let me pull it loose, sighing and wrapping an arm around me as he turned it fully my way.

A paper lay in the middle of the cardboard and on it were nearly a dozen sketches of my leg, curved and at different angles. The sketches were wonderful, and I reached out to snatch it from his hand, holding the paper closer to my face as if that would help me see them better. He winced.

"You don't like them. I'm sorry to move the blanket. I just couldn't remember a few details and wanted to—"

"Stop," I cut him off, my eyes roving over a full figure of myself with my leg kicked up and one eye peeking over a shoulder. "Do you have more of these?" My breath caught, and I pried my eyes away from the paper, lowering it to meet Bash's wide-eyed stare.

"Yes." His reply was a quiet admittance that made me wonder just how many sketches of me he had made. We'd only known each other for such a short time and yet, him doing this spoke of the connection between us. I couldn't help the grin spreading across my face.

Rubbing myself against his leg, I moaned at the friction against his joggers. "I want to see everything. But first..."

Bash smiled back at me, setting the cardboard on the ground beside him. "Whatever you need."

This man was going to kill me.

Bash's joggers bunched up when I rubbed myself against his hard thigh. I tilted my hips, using the bump in the fabric to hit my nub. My hands braced on his leg. I didn't even look at him as I rode his leg, letting my hair fall back as I arched my back and feeling his eyes on me as I ground myself against him.

He hissed in a breath, and his large hands settled on my thighs, rubbing the sensitive skin in encouraging circles. I cracked an eye and saw the way he was fixated on me—his nostrils flaring, his breath heavy.

Something in him snapped. The dark blue of his eyes sharpened to steely resolve as he gripped my hips and lifted me easily onto his lap proper. My legs wrapped around him, and thank fuck these chairs didn't have arm rests, because I wanted him inside of me, and the open sides meant I could wrap my legs around him more easily.

The length of him pressed in front of me, and I ran my hands up it, teasing him through the thick fabric. But not for long. With a groan, he yanked the pants down, a hand on my back to keep from displacing me. I plucked at the bottom edge of his soft terry shirt, pulling it up. He lifted his arms and discarded the shirt in a crumple beside the chair.

Staring at the wide expanse of his chest, I hissed in a breath, savouring the ability to drink him in. To have him—The Stag—hot and ready beneath me, at my mercy.

I knew what he could do, knew I was toying with fire when I ran a hand up the definition of his abs to lay my palm flat across his chest. He panted beneath me like an animal, his gaze drinking me in, but I didn't meet it. I wanted to take him in without the intensity of his stare. If I met his eyes, he would pull me in until I couldn't think, couldn't breathe, unless it was in sync with him.

"Syl." My name on his lips came out in a guttural groan that vibrated through his chest and into my palm. I shivered at the raw power of it, wanting a taste. I leaned forward, tilting my head up, knowing I was poking the beast, and only wanting to do it harder.

He brushed a thumb across my cheek, studying me. His eyes roved over my face just as hungrily as they roved over my body. Oh. I could lose myself here, with this man, in this place. Where our surroundings didn't matter, our goals, any of it. He leaned forward to kiss me, the gesture heartbreakingly tender, and his tongue traced gently along the seam of my mouth, begging for admittance.

Fuck.

I opened for him. The heat between us built higher at the connection. We hadn't kissed in the shower or the breeding room, and I knew now what I'd been missing. My arms came around to clutch his neck as I held on for dear life. Every part of me consumed by his taste, his presence.

Without breaking contact, his hands glided across my hips to cup my ass, lifting me and positioning his tip at my entrance. I gasped into his mouth, but he only rubbed a soothing circle on my lower back as I took inch after inch of him. My arousal helped the largeness of him to ease into place until we were joined. He nipped and sucked at my bottom lip as I adjusted to the fullness. The sensation was almost too much, and I cried out.

"Bash?" I could barely recognize my voice. The Party Girl was gone. This was all Syl. I couldn't have maintained control if I'd tried, and fuck, I didn't want to try.

I wanted this man. Truly. Everyone I'd slept with here had been a means to an end, but not now. I wasn't thinking about pregnancy, the fields, my sister—none of it. Every fiber of my being was fixated on the man seated inside me. When he began to roll his hips, I clung to him, curling up to his chest, wanting his neck but unable to reach.

Whatever question I'd thought to ask when I'd spoken his name, he answered with his body. Taking hold of my ass, he tilted it up and down, sliding in and out of me and creating a friction that sent me spiraling.

"Bash. Bash. Bash." His name was the only word I had, and I scrabbled helplessly against his chest, heedless of the damage my nails caused him. He drew a sharp breath of lust mixed with pain and worked me harder until his name became a cry on my lips.

He felt amazing, but I wanted more. Wanted him deeper. Wanted him to lose control like he'd done in the shower. Sitting back, I gripped his cock at the base, and used his thighs to ride him, setting the fast rhythm I'd been craving. His hands went slack on my hips.

I watched as his head tilted back, revealing a deliciously thick Adam's apple and corded neck as he fought the tension coiling within his body.

He lost it, just like I'd hoped, and stood in a rush with his hands cupping my ass, stepping out of his joggers, and taking the two steps to the bed. He laid me down almost reverently, breaking the contact between us, and all I could do was stare up at him with wide, trusting eyes.

His lips fell urgently to mine, our tongues ending in a viscous tangle until I was drunk on him. Then his mouth moved to nip along my jaw, following a path down my neck and between my breasts but not touching them. Fuck, they cried out to be touched, and I groaned as he sank lower without giving them his attention.

Unphased, he trailed his tongue along my flat abdomen, and the wet heat of it left me wriggling beneath him, demanding more. I knew he would give it, but the tension was wound so tightly within me I didn't know if I could stand the wait. His mouth reached my pussy, a tongue darting out to flick across my nub, and I saw stars.

This powerful man lowered himself to taste me. His tongue glided through my slick, and he shivered in delight. My legs clenched around his head, locking him in place as I rose higher. Just as I was arching off the bed, arms splayed out, he stopped. Standing, he looked down at me with that permanently stunned expression he wore so effortlessly in my presence, like he had to remind himself where he was.

Fuck it.

I stood up on the bed, taking his face in my hands, and kissing him the same tender way he'd kissed me, wanting to knock that expression of surprise off his face and replace it with something deeper. I had no words for why I felt it was important, or why this fucking perfect male specimen would be anything other than confident, but I kissed him. Letting the fire of it consume us both until his arms came up to hold me back, and he lifted me into his chest, my legs wrapping around him.

He laid me back down before him and came up on his knees. His gaze was steady. Lust swirled beneath the surface, but also an uncertainty. As if he needed to pause at every step to make sure he was doing it right.

"Yes." *What was I saying yes to? Him?*

I was pretty sure he knew my answer was yes. The Party Girl never said no. She said yes to everyone here whenever they'd asked or wanted or showed the slightest bit of interest, but for him—it wasn't just a yes. A yes where he was concerned was a pleasure, and I wasn't above begging.

He hitched my leg over his shoulder and kept his eyes on my face as he sank in with a groan. His steely grip on my thigh with one hand and my hip with the other, he worked himself in. I gasped as my body struggled to adapt—the pain of the stretch turning into something deeper and more satisfying.

"Shh."

I only realized I was making frantic animal sounds when he shushed me, and I snapped my mouth shut. He sank the last inch, his thumb circling my nub. He started out slow, barely moving within me, but it was too much. I cried out. So close to tumbling over the edge that I put a hand over his to stop the assault of sensation.

But he was relentless, and my reaction made him feral. His hand tightened into a bruising grip around my thigh, and he pulled out more to slam into me. Flesh smashing against flesh was all that I could hear and feel.

My eyes rolled back, and I was helpless. My hand went limp against his. His thumb stopped its movements, and I cried out, my hand tightening on his once more in a silent plea to resume, but he didn't. Instead, he blocked me from touching myself as he hammered into me, his face a mask of concentration.

All of it was too much. I needed release. Now.

I tried to sit up, to take control, but he pushed me back down. All I could do was arch my back and make pathetic noises of frustration as the tension grew within me. Tears leaked from my eyes, and I barely noticed when he scooped me back up into his arms and I lay against his chest without losing contact.

Arms wrapped tightly around my back, he lifted me up and down against his length. The weight of my body drove him deeper, and only then did his hand snake around to the space between us to find my nub, mercilessly circling it with the pad of his thumb.

His grunts filled my ears, my head, vibrated through my very bones as I came. I felt a familiar gush of fluid as the waves of pleasure consumed me completely. Screaming through the release, helplessly along for the ride, I clawed at his chest, not caring for the damage I was leaving behind.

He rode out his own release, his heart pounding against mine as he emptied himself deep inside of me with a final few spasms.

This, now fucking *this*, could get me pregnant, and I sighed, sagging into his chest. His arms must be tired from holding me up, but I knew he wouldn't drop me. There was a strange trust between us I couldn't understand.

But I was quickly finding reason was not something that had a place where Bash was concerned. We came back down, still connected, and I waited for him to move me off of him and start cleaning up. To busy himself with his clothes and turn to me like a friendly stranger.

Thanks for the sex. Catch you later, Syl.

Only, he held me. Both hands wrapped around my back, his thumbs rubbing gentle circles against skin still sensitive from release.

"Can I draw you?" His voice was quiet and innocent. Pulling back to see his face, I found it completely earnest—a sheepishness creeping into the crinkle of his eyes.

"Draw me?" My incredulous tone forced his eyes away from mine, and he looked over my left shoulder.

"Well, yeah, while it's still fresh, you know?"

Draw me. After all that, he wanted to *draw me*? The idea was ludicrous. After an experience like that, with our bodies still connected, the thing he most wanted to do wasn't to clean up and get dressed. Not to lay back down together and savour the moment either, but to *draw me.*

Brow crinkling, I twisted my head to meet his eyes, but when I saw the silent plea, I couldn't help the next word out of my mouth.

"Yes."

There was something about Bash that made me want to say yes to him, not because I had to, but because I wanted to. His passion was contagious. He set me down on my feet and gestured to the bed with one hand.

I perched on the edge, looking up at him to see a frown on his face.

"No, like, lay down, and spread your legs."

What the fuck?

Bash was kinky.

I decided I liked that about him.

I did as he said, laying flat on my back and spreading my legs. With an irresistible grin, he went to grab the cardboard, giving me a perfect view of his ass. I might be beyond sated, but I could still appreciate the taut muscles as he reached for his materials. Placing them on the chair, he went to retrieve his pants when I cleared my throat.

"Um, excuse me, but if I don't get to wear clothes, neither should you."

With a chuckle, he looked back at me, the grey joggers in hand. "Because I'm about to sit on this hard chair and my balls will stick to them. I figure you have a vested interest in that part of me. Unless I'm wrong."

That fucking lopsided grin had me laughing along with him.

"Why didn't you say anything before when we were in the chair together?"

He quirked an eyebrow and smirked. "I was otherwise occupied."

Yes, yes, he was.

I laughed, the sound coming from me in a delightful rising crescendo.

This fucking man.

"Okay, but no pants. Put on some underwear or something."

With an eye roll, he moved to his dresser, retrieving a pair of boxer shorts and stepping into them. I watched, appreciating the hard-won definition in his legs and the way his stomach stayed taut even when he bent. My body reacted to the sight of him, and I swear I could go again. Could come just watching him put on a pair of boxers. This was ridiculous. Good sex was one thing, and I'd had an awful lot of sex since joining Pack Breeders 103C, but none of it had been this all-consuming haze I'd been helpless against.

Controlled.

Purposeful.

Enjoyable, sure, but never this.

Bash settled back in his chair, bringing one leg up to hook his ankle over the other, and made a table out of the cardboard garbage he used for his art. What a shit piece of cardboard he'd found. I was sure I could find him something better, and I would. It couldn't be comfortable to draw on such a flimsy piece of ripped up cardboard. He needed a proper desk.

"Use two fingers to spread yourself." His breath hitched as he waited for me to obey.

With a grunt of approval, I did as he asked, wondering if he could see his seed spilling out of me.

I watched with rapt attention as he drew me, realizing how beautiful he looked. A large man hunched over a slip of paper, his hand gliding across the sheet and his eyes darting up. It should've looked ridiculous. *He* should have looked ridiculous, only he didn't.

He was stunning, and I was drawn into the passion painting his features. I wanted to know what he was drawing, to get a glimpse into his world. But the spell was broken with a series of loud bangs on Bash's door.

Right. There was a whole other world out there beyond Bash and me. I'd been lost to him for however many hours since he confronted me in the shower, but now...

This place. Our purpose. Everyone else in the dorm. It was all still there.

Incredible perception-altering sex couldn't change that.

Not even Bash could.

With a wince, Bash set his supplies carefully back down on the floor and gave me an apologetic smile. Curious, I moved to the end of the bed and leaned forward, so I could see and hear whatever had interrupted us.

"Hey, man, it's time for the daily run." Bash had his hand on the door, his knuckles tense like he was ready to slam it. His broad shoulders eclipsed whoever was speaking, but I didn't think I recognized the voice anyhow.

Maybe it was one of the new guys? Strange they would send someone who just arrived, but then, I listened closely and thought there was something familiar about his voice, something tickling at the back of my mind. Like a voice I used to know but hadn't heard in long enough for it to fade into memory.

Bash argued with the familiar stranger.

"Why can't we stay back?"

"Nope, not allowed. We used to allow it, but no more. New rules ever since—Well, let's just say now everybody comes out for the run."

"Listen, man."

"Jace."

Fuck. Jace. That cocky bastard was back? I hadn't seen him since my first cycle, but there'd been a time when he'd been obsessed with my body, taking me anywhere and everywhere. I'd thought myself so special to have received his attention. Just before he found someone new and did the same to them. I later found out he called us his "puppies".

Fuck, I hated him. If there was one man here I hated more than Carter, it would be that asshole, but at least now it made sense why he was going around banging on doors.

Jace, supreme asshole commander though he may be, was an alpha in his squad, which gave him a certain position within Pack Breeders 103C. A position he'd obviously slid back into with little complaint from Carter or the other top wolves.

When had he arrived? My stomach twisted at the thought of him having been a participant in my breeding party.

"Jace," Bash corrected. "Syl and I are—"

"Wait, Syl?" Jace peered under Bash's arm and grinned, his green eyes lighting up. Pathetic. He gave a friendly wave that stirred nothing in me except a desire to vomit what little food I'd eaten in the past however many hours.

"Hi," I said dryly, wondering why he thought we'd still be friends after he'd used me and left me friendless, making it so I'd had to quickly ingratiate myself with another group or be forgotten.

Jace cleared his throat as if to shake off my chilly reception, and turned his attention back to Bash, falling out of sight.

"So anyway, nobody stays back. Simple as that."

Bash's body stiffened, and I frowned at his tense posture.

"Syl and I are having a bit of fun here, and we're very busy. Can't you make an exception?"

His words ripped at something barely formed inside of me.

A bit of fun. My mouth went dry, and I missed whatever else he had to say. Of course. Fuck, I was dumb. I was turning into Bash's puppy, just like I'd once been Jace's. Just a little idiot following him around, expecting there was anything substantial behind the sex. Maybe because I was the one to take his virginity, he was obsessed with me, with drawing my body, but he clearly knew his purpose.

He was here for the pack, just like everybody else.

Tears burning my eyes, I scanned the room for my clothes, quickly remembering I'd left them on the shower floor.

Fuck, I was so stupid, getting caught up with someone. This wasn't me, wasn't why I was here, and it certainly wasn't why Bash was here.

Bash. He closed the door and turned to stare at me, his jaw tight, eyes searching. His face was pained. He looked worried.

"You okay?"

Fuck him. I stood up, not bothering to look for something to wear anymore. I'd left my clothes like the damned fool I was, and I wouldn't cover myself with something of his. So, where did that leave me?

Naked and alone, as usual.

"Great. Listen, Bash. This was great. Really. But I've got to go get prepared for the run." I moved to sidle past him, unphased by his wide eyes. But it was still hard to pass close to the heat of his body. His warmth called to me, and all I wanted was to press into it. With a shiver, I paused when his hand reached out to grasp my forearm.

"Wait, Syl, I'll go with you. Just give me a minute—"

"No, thanks." I didn't meet his eyes—couldn't. Instead, I pushed the rest of the way through, stepping out into the hallway with him still staining my thighs.

"Hey, Syl, looking good." Gale's lust-filled smile twisted my insides, as did the way his eyes roved over my body freely. Like he had the right. Like he owned me.

But he did. They all did. I was here to be sucked and fucked until I could ensure the next generation came about. That was all I was good for.

And fuck Bash for making me think there could be anything more. I didn't have time to be anyone's puppy. Sex with Bash had been beyond expectation, and I would certainly do it again, but The Party Girl was back.

It was her who smiled back at Gale, a skip in her step as she skirted past him on the way to her room.

Chapter 14

BASH

She left. Everything we'd shared, and she'd just gotten up and left like it meant nothing. It was all I could do to stare at the swirling woodgrain of my bedroom door where Syl had stood. I'd screwed up. Somehow. Something I'd said had set her off, and damn, she was pissed. Not just pissed, furious, and I swear I'd seen tears shimmering in her sky-blue eyes as she'd moved past me.

Those tears had stopped me when she'd shrugged off my hands. To allow her to leave the room. Like we'd just been fucking around—nothing more.

More, yes. I wanted more. A lot more. I wanted to live in Syl's beautiful body, to know her mind well enough that we barely needed words anymore. Frowning, I tried to puzzle through what the fuck had just happened.

Jace. That shaggy-haired motherfucker. Everything had seemed fine before he'd arrived, and I'd tried to get him to leave us alone, so I could spend more time drawing and fucking my girl in equal measure.

With a sigh, I returned to where I'd placed my sketch on the ground.

Syl had thought I'd meant to draw her pussy, and I'd certainly made a few sketches of it, but having her pose for me in such a sultry position was to capture her expression. I wanted to know what she looked like when she was laid bare for me, watching me sketch her most private parts.

Syl's face looked up at me from the paper. Vulnerable, sweet, adoring.

So, what the fuck had gone wrong between us? I wracked my brain for the words said when I'd tried to get rid of the jackass at the door. I'd told him to leave us alone, that we were busy having fun, and—

No, I hadn't said we were busy having fun. I'd said we were busy having a bit of fun. My fists clenched. Right. That was it. With a groan, I dropped my head into my hands. I'd made it sound like we were in here doing kinky shit, and not like I'd just been to heaven with Syl's pussy clenching around my cock.

I couldn't have said that to Jace. Syl must know I had to play their game, to make it seem like we were just fooling around. Anything else was forbidden, and if I crossed any lines someone might go down to Sebastion's squad and have a word with his squad leader about his behaviour. Only they'd find the real Sebastion, and I'd be fucked.

They'd haul me out of here so fast I wouldn't have a chance to say goodbye to Syl, let alone get closer to her. Syl must realize how strict they were here about any relationships forming between couples. She must.

Only she hadn't. I wanted to punch myself in the face for it. And rough up the asshole who had hurt Syl until she could be sensitive to such comments. Only doing so wouldn't solve the problem, and I had a run to prepare for.

Spending time with Syl wasn't my only reason for wanting to get out of the run. I took a deep practice breath, wincing when there was a wheeze at the end. The air fresheners permeating this place had done a number on my lungs, a factor I hadn't considered.

Now I'd be expected to run, to hang with these men who had been running every day of their lives while I'd been told as a child never to attempt it. I could still hear the doctor listening to my chest and shaking his head.

With those lungs, I wouldn't recommend it. A shift and a walk will be suitable to appease his animal side.

Only a shift and a walk wouldn't appease Pack Breeders 103C, and I dug out my blue puffer from where I'd stashed it in my sock drawer.

I could put it in my jean pocket and circle around to my clothes. The puffer would fit in my wolf's mouth if I needed it to. Only the bright colour made it stand the fuck out.

It was dangerous, both because there was a chance of being caught and because I could have an attack without my medicine and die out in the woods today. But I couldn't miss this. The thought of Syl out in those woods, pissed at me and ready to take on any of the other wolves, made my heart pound. Could I even catch her? If I did, would she want me to? Would she turn those furious eyes on me again and push past me on her way to someone else?

It didn't matter if she did. I wasn't going anywhere.

Hand in my jean pocket, I clenched my puffer, hoping the stiff fabric would be enough to hide the shape of it from anyone looking too closely. Unfortunately, there was a girl on my left, with soft brown hair blowing in the light breeze, whose eyes kept drifting down. She wasn't looking for the puffer, but I shifted uncomfortably under her scrutiny. Hopefully Syl would join the line soon, so I could talk to her before we shifted.

She came out just as the others were stripping, and she didn't look my way. Not fucking once. This was no good. I knew she was pissed, but had my thoughtless words really screwed things up this badly? How could they have so easily damaged such an indescribable experience we'd shared?

The connection. The heat between us. It had been gripping. Consuming. And yet here she was, already stripping off the thin white tee she'd worn and stepping between two men at the other end of the line, a teasing smile quirking up her kissable lips.

I was about to go over there, to stand beside her and demand her attention, when Carter stepped in front of the line. Interesting, and here I thought that guy Jace was about to take over our dorm. He'd had a confident way of speaking that set him apart as a leader, a higher-up, and I'd felt it more keenly than the overwhelming distaste churning my guts whenever Carter spoke.

Jace outranked him, or he should.

"I want a nice clean run. Well, okay, it can get a *little* dirty." A chorus of laughs followed his words. "Run until you're tired. Run until shifting back into your human form doesn't seem so bad. We're here to fulfill a need, but let's also have some fun with it." He winked and removed his black shirt, signaling all of us to do the same.

I whipped the cotton shirt over my head in a single movement, quickly enough that I could take extra care, pulling my jeans and boxers down without exposing or dislodging the puffer within. I heard an appreciative moan and looked over to find the woman with her floaty brown hair staring directly at my cock.

This place was definitely strange, but as pretty as the woman beside me was, I still peered around her to see what Syl was doing. I found her naked, pointing out something on her chest to the stocky guy with a buzz cut beside her. Everyone was naked now, and I wanted badly for us to begin, if only because Syl would be forced to shift and run instead of flirting with a naked man whose interest in her was becoming apparent to everyone in line.

Fuck, she was beautiful, and the sight of her lithe body twisting as she flipped her hair at him was making me hard. She could flirt with that douchebag all she wanted, but I would be the one to catch her.

Because I fucking had to be. I sucked in a deep breath, willing the wheeze at the end to dissipate, and turned my attention to the forest ahead. This would be hard. Ill-advised. Foolish. But it was also necessary, and I'd die before letting anyone else catch the Syl-wolf.

It was happening, and I was startled to find the girl with her flowy brown hair beside me, changing into a fierce russet-coloured wolf. Her bones snapped and joints popped as her body twisted and bent, fur springing up.

My eyes sought Syl, eager to see what she looked like in her other form, and she did not disappoint. A gorgeous silver wolf stood where Syl had, and I knew I would be drawing her later, struggling to get the curve of her proud ears right. She'd ignored me ever since coming into line, giving her affectionate attention to those surrounding her. But now, she met my eyes, the golden hue of them piercing me across the distance until it felt like she was standing right in front of me, close enough to touch.

My mouth hung open the longer our gazes connected. She didn't look away, and I knew I couldn't. The spell was only broken by a single word shouted across the field.

"Run!"

Her eyes held mine for an extra moment, and I swear I could hear her voice in my head.

Catch me.

Not a question. A demand, and one I intended to honour.

She took off into the woods with her tail high in the air and one last playful look back at me. Whatever anger and resentment my careless words had caused, she still wanted this. The chase. The hunt. The catch ending with me buried deep inside of her.

Just like that, I wasn't the little boy with asthma being told he couldn't run, that shifting and going for a walk was all the poor little defect could do. No, I was powerful. Unconcerned. Capable. And Syl was waiting.

With a grin, I rolled my shoulders, feeling the powerful muscles of my back and all the strength I'd hammered into my body. For her. All of it for her.

The smile didn't leave my face as I embraced the animal part of myself and fell to the ground, twisting. The sounds of my body changing and snapping into place, killing the shape of a man so I could assume my other form, were sickening. The sensation was a mix of pain and pure pleasure as the beastly part of myself tore through the man, shredding his skin and replacing it with fur. The wolf part of me knew what to do, and he was done with walking. Done with playing it safe. Done being careful.

His mate was waiting in the forest.

It was time to run.

Fucking Bash.

I'd discounted him. He'd hurt me in a way I didn't think anyone would ever be able to again. Him with his deep blue eyes and vulnerability. He'd tricked me, damaged me. Taken the stirrings of my heart and shut them the fuck down, but I still wanted him. Even if it was just for a "bit of fun". I couldn't help it.

From the second I'd stepped outside, I'd picked him out of the line even with his back to me. It wasn't that he stood a head taller than anyone else. If he'd been the same height, I would've known him. Something about his posture, about the way his shoulders were relaxed but his neck tense, was exactly Bash. Luckily, I'd been able to tear my eyes away from him before he noticed, finding a place far enough away in line that I would be safe from his mesmerizing presence.

A presence I knew would consume me again, and soon, if I wasn't careful. I needed to find a way to keep the incredible sex between us to just sex and stop expecting another being to actually give a shit about me. I knew better than anyone that you could only count on yourself.

Elise was proof enough of that.

CHAPTER 15

Running always calmed me. Even wondering how far behind me Bash was, couldn't distract from the feeling of sheer freedom of racing into the forest beyond the field. The soft grass traded places with the wild of rocks and sticks, but I barely felt them through the thick padding of my paws. The forest was home to me as much as the pack, and I eagerly breathed in the scent of pine, reminding myself that out here, I was a wolf. Not a party girl, not even Syl, but an animal eager to fade into its natural habitat and become one with the environment.

My fur on the back of my neck prickled, and I knew he was behind me. I didn't see him. Didn't catch his scent, but I felt his presence, and it filled me with wild excitement. Fueled by elation, I yipped and darted to the right. The thrill of being chased and hunted driving me all the harder. If he wanted to catch me, I'd make him work for it.

Dropping my nose to the ground, I picked up another wolf's scent. Male. I found myself going the other way. Fuck me, but I didn't want another male to smell me and chase me, not when I knew Bash was in pursuit. As much as I was eager to prove to him he wasn't special, my body rebelled at the thought of taking another man when Bash was so close.

And he was close. I could almost taste the hot sex. Hear the heaving of our bodies.

Splashing through a stream, I was momentarily tangled in the brush before bursting through. Well, that would slow me down, but with lust pumping through my veins with every beat of my foolish heart, I didn't mind.

I wanted to be caught, and I feigned a limp, stepping out of the stream to carefully navigate the bank on the other side. Oh no, I'm so helpless with my hurt leg.

I whined, hoping the sound would help him find me.

He was there. I looked up to find him in front of me. A beautiful brown wolf with silver patches on his side. The tufts of hair around his face were tinged grey on the ends as well, highlighted with it. Like he was part one, part another, and I stared at him in awe.

Seeing Bash as a wolf for the first time was otherworldly, and yet completely expected, like I'd seen the stranger wolf before me a hundred times before. Only I hadn't. He dropped his head and growled. The sound reverberated through me, creating a delicious mix of fear and arousal that made me shuffle in place. Unsure whether I wanted to run or move closer to him.

Instead, I stayed rooted to the spot, only my eyes able to move as he took the decision from me. Softly padding closer. Stalking me. A delightful shiver raced up my spine as he came close enough that his hot, sticky breath whispered across my face.

He growled again—the sound low. Vicious. Feral. The closeness of him scrambling my senses, and the sheer hold he had over me was too much. I dropped my head before him, rolling over to expose my belly and place myself in his power to do with as he pleased. He gave a satisfied huff, sniffing my stomach, his teeth near my most vulnerable part.

But I felt safe. Certain. Bash would never hurt me. Never.

He'd die for me.

What the fuck? The thought had come out of nowhere, and with it a surge of affection that had me lifting my head to nuzzle into the thick fur of his neck. He nuzzled me back. The sensation of him pressing deep into the fur of my neck almost too much, but then he pulled away. The beautiful brown wolf before me looked startled and took a step back.

There was a mad panic in his eyes as he backed further away, and I lifted my head to stare at him in shock.

What had happened? There was no answer, no explanation from him, as he turned from me and headed off into the woods, leaving me laying with my belly exposed on the forest floor. Needy for him, wanting him, and sure I had been on the verge of some great revelation, here in the wild with his wolf.

But now he was gone, and I was alone. Always alone.

I'd been a fool to think otherwise.

BASH

No, no, no. Not now.

I hacked.

A wolf coughing. Pathetic. But I didn't have time to feel sorry for myself. There was no air. My lungs tightened with each step, and I was grateful Syl hadn't made me chase her very far into the woods.

I'd left her, and a surge of guilt swelled up within me, even as I all but crawled across the lawn, searching for my pants. Spots danced in my vision by the time I reached the clothing. My airways were squeezing tight, and I shifted back to my human form with a regretful sigh, searching through the pairs of pants at about the place where I'd stood in line. I'd meant to bring the puffer just in case this happened, but when Syl had shot off into the woods, something had taken hold of me, and I hadn't thought to circle back around to bring it with me. I'd been consumed by the chase, by the promise of what waited for me when I caught her, feeling powerful and not able to comprehend I might need medical help.

Well, fuck past me, I guess, because the spots were getting bigger, and I was whooping. I'd avoided an attack like this for years. Never overdoing it. Always keeping my puffer on hand. Even when I'd been breaking my body down to build muscle, I'd had my puffer nearby for any flare-ups. My condition had become an annoyance, nothing truly dangerous.

But then I'd run, compelled to chase Syl through the woods like something bigger than myself was possessing me and driving me towards the beautiful silver wolf skirting along the edges of my vision. The tip of her tail taunting me. The wind blowing the scent of her arousal directly into my flaring nostrils.

Shit.

The sight of my fingers turning blue had me scrambling with the pocket of the jeans I'd finally identified.

I located the puffer, falling to my back and putting it into my mouth in the same movement. I sucked in the medicine, letting it ease some of the burn in my lungs. Some but not all. I was still gasping like the pathetic, defective creature I was.

It was all I could do to stare up at the passing clouds, breathe and take additional puffs of medicine when I felt able until the breaths came easier. The vice across my chest eased, allowing me to take in life-giving air. I wondered what Syl had done after I'd left, if she'd looked for me or if she'd found another wolf. The thought was painful, and I turned my head as though turning physically away could change whatever Syl would do. But I couldn't get past how she'd responded to me, the trust she'd shown baring her belly, and the joy I'd felt when she'd nuzzled into my neck like she didn't find me pathetic or defective.

Like I was a thing worth loving.

Fear clenched my heart as I raced around the woods, searching for Bash. What had caused him to panic? He'd seemed as intent on me as I was on him, but the way he'd looked at me—like he couldn't stand to be near me. I couldn't understand it. His wolfish growl still sang in my bones with the rightness of it, and I couldn't stomach trying to find another male to proposition.

The Party Girl wasn't in the mood to fuck, and it pissed me off, as did Bash's continued absence. I skirted the other wolf scents, trying to find him and failing. I had no idea where he'd gone, but I knew what happened out on these runs when you jacked up a group of breeders on the sheer adrenaline of shifting and racing.

He'd found someone else. Whatever he'd panicked about. Whatever had made him decide not to choose me and to leave—he was probably being comforted by some horny she-wolf right now.

Melanie had been right beside him, and the few side glances I'd stolen while we were in line had revealed her to be fixated on him—much to the chagrin of the stocky blonde on her left. She'd wanted Bash, and maybe that regret I'd noticed had been a panic when he'd realized his mistake in choosing to chase me. What had he seen that had made him run from me? Tears pricked at my eyes.

Maybe it had been the way I'd stormed out of his room, practically in tears at being slighted? I'd let my emotions get the best of me. I'd forgotten we were all here for a bit of fun—a lot of fun, actually. But why did it hurt so fucking much where he was concerned? If all I could ever be to him was a bit of fun, I'd take it.

My desperate, needy soul would soak up every bit of fun he gave me, feasting on it like a dying man discovering some gruel in his cupboard. Resigned to it, but so fucking grateful to have something in his belly.

I shifted, my body settling into its human form so I could sit on the forest floor and hug my knees into my chest. Tears slid their way down my cheeks, and I bit into my fist to stifle a sob, cognizant of the many wolves prowling these woods and not wanting anyone to find me just yet.

This wasn't how I had expected this to go. Yet here I was.

Abandoned.

Cast aside.

Not worthy.

Someone as big and strong as Bash entering Pack Breeders 103C had surely attracted a lot of interest from the other breeding women. He had alpha written all over him, and the way he'd shoved the other breeders out of the way to get to me in the shower had proved it.

I'd just been too blind to see how desirable he would be to others—that he wouldn't want to sleep with just one woman during his time as a breeder. Wrapped up in the idea of him being obsessed with only me, I'd let myself believe I was the one with the power between us. Now I knew how wrong that was. I knew I'd crawl to him on my knees if he would only kiss me again, and let me back in.

A kiss. Was that what I was fantasizing about? Not Bash's light touch coaxing my body into a fiery passion I couldn't—and didn't want to—escape from. Instead, I wanted to be held and kissed, comforted like a child.

Fucking Bash. I swiped angrily at a tear threatening to drip off my nose. I hated what he was doing to me, and that he'd left me in this pathetic state. This creature sitting on the forest floor, surrounded by decaying leaves and broken sticks, wasn't me. She was a weak thing who hadn't had to fight, and I refused to acknowledge her.

Clearing my throat, I stood up, brushing a few leaves from the backs of my thighs. Heart sore and limbs stiff, I made my way back to the building, intending to go straight to my room and work on some of my designs. That always helped to settle my mind, to remind me I was Syl, and not just a party girl.

I wasn't anyone's anything. Not Bash's little puppy, or my mother's rage outlet. I wasn't anyone's anything.

I belonged to myself, and I needed to take care of my shit.

Chapter 16

Puffer in hand, I crawled my way back to the building. Using the walls and furniture to steady myself, I headed to my room. The air fresheners in the dorm had once only been a tickle at the back of my throat, now created an inferno.

Stumbling my way down the hall, I finally reached the relative comfort of my room.

My door closed with a snick, and I collapsed onto the bed, tossing the clothes I'd carted along with me onto the floor. I'd been so stupid to think I could be normal. Staring at the popcorn ceiling, I tried to imagine what Syl had made of my sudden departure. Had she been affected, or was this just another day for her? Cast off by one, off to find another. I squeezed my eyes shut at an assault of images. Syl being railed against a tree. Syl being chased through the woods by another wolf—that asshole plowing her in the shower before I'd stepped in and taken her myself.

Who would want me?

I'd been so sure of my plan to come here and meet Syl. Certain I would know what to do when I found her. But now that I had, and with my own inadequacies so painfully on display, what happened next?

She was a pack breeder, chosen for her genetics and aptitude to bear a new generation of wolves. It was one of the highest honours the pack could bestow.

Then there was me.

Even my family hated me, and the pack? Oh sure, we were all valuable. We all had our place, but those places were far from *equal.* Mine had been the worst of them—forced to watch and monitor the breeders in a position I was told held so much *honour.*

I was helping to ensure the breeding went okay, that everyone was safe. Thus maximizing a chance of pregnancy and contributing to the new generation the only way I could.

But then there had been Syl, the fucking angel I was supposed to watch from afar but never, *never* touch. I'd said fuck you to the system, but Syl? I couldn't dismiss her as easily.

My presence here—my name, my file—was a lie meant to fool the higher-ups, but I was also lying to Syl. Making her believe I was something I wasn't. The crushing sensation in my chest from the weight of my faulty lungs inflating was a reminder of why I'd never be anything but her watcher.

Sleep wrapped my mind in comforting fuzz, and I pulled myself more fully onto the bed before darkness creeped into the edges of my vision. My exhausted body needed rest to recover, but my heart needed a lot more than that.

SYL

Where the fuck was Bash?

I'd meandered around on my way back, avoiding crossing paths with any of the other wolves, and when I'd come back to the starting line, I'd gotten dressed and sat against the red brick of our building, waiting for the others to return.

One by one, they emerged from the woods. Some still in their wolf form and others as humans. No one came to speak to me. I'd become the loner.

My eyes caught on Melanie with her arms wrapped around the waist of someone I couldn't see. Scarcely willing to breathe, I watched until I could ascertain the man wasn't Bash. She was smiling up at him. Her soft brown hair flowed across her shoulders in waves. Looked to me like they were pretty cozy, which hopefully meant Bash hadn't left me to go fuck her.

Jace wandered in, entirely human and obviously alone. I almost felt sorry for him as he walked across the field, his arms swinging at his sides and brow furrowed. Carter emerged next, an arm around a tall blonde who exceeded his height by a couple of inches. He grinned at her, and she smiled back shyly. I wondered if he'd used the spikes on her yet.

I waited, but still no one acknowledged me. Of all the guys there who'd fucked me in various holes and used me like a fuckdoll, Jace was the one to saunter over. Now fully clothed in a grey tracksuit, he leaned up against the wall next to me. I guess it made sense. There was something new about him. It was in the way he carried himself–his shoulders slumped forward–and it set him apart as surely as it did me. We were loners together.

At first, he lounged beside me, content to let the comfortable silence between us speak for itself.

"You okay?"

Fuck. Even Jace could tell something was wrong with me. I pressed my cool hands to my cheeks nervously, trying to clear any lingering flush from crying earlier.

"Fine."

He chuckled, giving me a conspiratorial wink. "Sure, sure."

"What do you care?" I sneered, regretting my tone almost instantly. At least Jace had thought to ask, to approach me when everyone else was chatting with each other, and acting like I didn't exist. Clearing my throat, I tempered my tone. "I'm okay. Just something in the woods."

"Something with that Bash guy?"

My eyes shot to his. How the fuck did he know about Bash? Right. He'd walked in and found me there in his room.

"Yes." My words came out in a whisper, and I dropped my head back to the brick behind me.

"You know that shit's dangerous, Syl."

Dangerous. Jace the Player was going to lecture me about guarding my feelings? Then again, who better than the man who had first showed me the trouble they could cause if misplaced? There was no denying the truth to his words, but I didn't know how to answer. I lapsed into silence, watching a hawk soar across the field, hunting for prey in the grass not tall enough to conceal it.

Jace didn't say another word, but I was oddly grateful for his presence. The sight of him didn't offend me nearly as much when Carter announced we could return, and I stood to go inside. He felt almost like a friend, despite our past, and I couldn't help smiling when he opened the door with one hand and gestured me inside.

"You know I'm not going to fuck you ever again, right? No matter how many doors you open?"

Jace grinned, bowing his head and making a flourish with his free hand.

"Message received, my lady."

With a snort, I headed inside, eager for the quiet of my room and my designs. To lose myself in the work and dream of one day having the fabrics I needed to make a ballgown.

I was sure Bash had chosen to stay in the woods longer, my mind whispering that he was otherwise preoccupied and not yet ready to return. There must've been another she-wolf missing who I hadn't remembered joining us. But he still didn't appear as I made a quick salad in the kitchen or when I lingered to play foosball with Jace, who kindly stuck by my side to warn other men off with his presence.

No, there was no Bash to be found. I retired to my room, sick with worry that his beautiful obsession with me and my body had easily transferred to a new target, and I wouldn't see him again. I wandered past my door to pause at his, hand raised in the air.

Did I dare knock? I didn't think he could've slipped past me, but if there was a chance he had, then maybe I'd have a chance to read his face and know where we stood.

Firming up my resolve, I knocked twice but heard no reply. Even with an ear pressed to the thick wood, the sounds inside were too muffled. I didn't hear a thing.

Sighing, I returned to my room, pulling out my magazines and the extra paper I kept in the bottom drawer. Who would I dress today? Melanie came to mind with that gorgeous hair of hers, so light it framed her heart-shaped face like a halo. She'd need something to draw the eye to her exquisite waist and away from the broadness of her shoulders. I sketched out a poor excuse for her figure and set to dressing it.

I'd give her long sleeves with flowing cuffs extending almost to her fingertips to highlight her petite hands. The cut of her dress would go low, exposing the tanned skin of her chest down to her waist where I would secure it with a rhinestone belt, like the one on page fifty-three of *Chamel*.

She looked pretty, but not perfect, and I hated the way I couldn't draw out the vision in my head. My hand was an alien thing, moving in every direction but the one I wanted, leading to jagged lines and uneven shapes. Unable to match the perfection I tried to recreate. Thoughts of drawing carried me back to Bash, and I slammed the pencil down on my nightstand.

He could draw. But would he teach me? Could I be taught? My mind was swimming just thinking about being able to do my designs justice. I found myself on my feet, about to go to him, when I remembered I had no idea where he was or who he was with. He could be in his room, yes, or he could be behind one of the other silent doors with a different breeding female. With a huff of frustration, I sat back down on my bed, deciding to flip through my magazines again for inspiration instead of trying to draw another sketch.

Oh well. Melanie would've looked gorgeous in my dress, and I retrieved the sketch and pencil, intending to add a lace brocade to her sleeve cuffs. The tight bodice and flare would complement her perfectly. She'd be stunning. Too bad I would never make it, and she'd never wear it. Just another bit of disappointment to sour my day. I drew X's over her eyes and scribbled out my terrible rendition of her face. She was clearly attached to the guy she'd walked out of the woods with. So, why did I feel a burst of jealousy whenever I thought of the sweet brunette?

No reason. Just Bash playing with my mind again.

This was ludicrous. I barely knew him. Sighing, I pulled out a fresh piece of paper and sketched him out. Tall and lean with muscular arms and broad shoulders. His waist cutting down sharply in a V. He'd look spectacular in a suit, I decided. One left open intentionally with a cummerbund in dark blue to match his eyes. With a bit of playfulness, I gave him a grin, imagining him loving the three-piece suit I'd prepared for him.

Mm-hmm.

Bash, where'd you disappear to? I asked the figure, half expecting a response.

He really had done a number on my head.

BASH

I didn't know how long I'd slept, but I woke up stiff as hell, my joints creaking as I sat up at the edge of the bed and took a proper deep breath. The lingering effects of the attack had dissipated, leaving me with a manageable wheeze I could easily avoid by taking shallower breaths. What I needed was to avoid going for runs, but with them required every damned day, I couldn't see how that would be an option.

One thing was for sure, I wouldn't be chasing down Syl anytime soon.

"Fuck!" I shouted into the room, slamming my fist down into the covers. First my mess up with Jace, then I abandoned her after hunting her down. So full of lust I had barely noticed the attack creeping up until I was too far gone to stop it, and now I'd have to disappoint her again, to somehow skirt the rules of the run and sit it out.

But sitting it out when Syl was somewhere in the woods, hunted by a pack of horny wolves, was not something I could tolerate. With a growl, I took a handful of coverlet and twisted, wanting to break something, anything.

My eyes drifted to the battered doorknob I'd first noticed when I'd arrived. I imagined the previous occupant consumed with the same frustration I was, compelled to act out on something in this torture chamber, to leave a mark on this place that had left a mark on him.

But I didn't need to be in here any longer. My lungs were better, if not yet fully healed, and Syl was waiting. I stood up and the blood rushed to my head, leaving me dizzy. I sat down hard. *Fuck.* Guess I was staying put for a while longer. I eased myself back down, counting the seconds until I could go out into the common room again and find my girl.

I just hoped she'd wait for me.

Sleep claimed me, and I must've been out for a long time because I woke up starving. My energy had returned, and I tested sitting and then standing, pleased when neither made me dizzy. I slipped on the first clothes I found in my drawer, a pair of black sweats and a grey cotton t-shirt, and took a few tentative steps.

Good. I could go back out to the common area and find Syl, make sure everything was okay between us after I'd left her dripping with arousal in the woods.

It must've been pretty late because the common room was empty. Even the kitchen was sleeping, the normally obnoxiously loud slamming of cabinets and oil sizzling absent. Instead, the TV was on low volume, and there she was.

Fuck, she was beautiful. The TV cast an ethereal light across her delicate bone structure, emphasizing the angles and making her seem more mature. She looked exhausted, but her eyes were open and fixed on the screen like a doll propped up and made to stare at a blank wall. The long pants and loose tank top looked like pajamas, and I wondered if she'd been unable to sleep. Even her features were devoid of emotion. I stepped out into the open, and her gaze shifted to mine, locking on it in an instant.

"Hey."

"Hey yourself." Anger coated her words with a sharp edge I hadn't heard from Syl, and I paused to study her. I guess we were doing this. Jaw tightly set and brows puckered, Syl stared accusingly at me. I had no idea what to say. "Well, what do you have to say for yourself?"

Shit. You'd think I would've come up with a clever excuse for leaving her in the woods, but my first thought each time I'd awakened had been seeing her. I sighed, leaning back against the wall and studying an air freshener on the ceiling. At least the lights were low, and I didn't have to dodge the cameras.

"Sorry." Maybe not the best apology, but there was no way for me to elaborate without outing myself.

Sorry Syl, I'm really a defective watcher who snuck into the breeding program, and I really wanted to fuck you in the woods, but I'm not supposed to run, and I almost died from an asthma attack.

Yeah, fucking right.

The air was thick with silence, and I hazarded a glance at Syl. She stared at me, her beautiful eyes wide with confusion and outrage.

"Sorry? Bash, where the fuck have you been? It's been *a full day* since the run. Did you have someone else in your room, is that it?" Her voice squeaked, and it was my turn to stare at her in astonishment.

With an outstretched hand, I approached her.

"Syl, I—"

But she stood in a flurry, turning away from me and moving around the other side of the couch, her hair blocking her face as she shook her head furiously.

"You know what? I don't even want to hear it. It's good to see you. Goodnight, Bash."

She stormed off, skirting around me like she couldn't stand the idea of accidentally touching my arm.

I'd fucked it up, and I let myself feel the misery of my situation as I flopped down on the couch Syl had vacated, hoping the feeling of warmth she'd left behind would somehow soothe the ache I felt for her.

No sooner had I turned my attention to the television program Syl was watching than she stormed her way back into the room, stopping to stand in front of me with her finger leveled at my face.

"You will never disappear on me again," she demanded, and I gave a shaky nod. "Never," she reiterated, leaning in, her finger inches from my nose.

"N-never," I stuttered, knowing I might if I had another attack but eager to put the run behind us.

She studied my face, and what she found there must've been satisfying because she dropped the finger and a little shudder ran through her body, shaking her shoulders. The movement reminded me of the beautiful way she came for me, and I looked on helplessly, feeling myself hardening as the images swirled to life in my head. Syl naked before me. Syl pressed up against the shower door. Syl clawing at me as she found release.

"Good." She said the word almost to herself, and then she was climbing onto my lap, nuzzling into my neck. I groaned, slipping into the rightness of touching her, my hands coming up to run the length of her smooth back.

"Syl, I don't under—"

She cut off my complaint with her mouth on mine, the wet heat of her tongue making me lose track of whatever the fuck I'd been about to say.

"Sh, I don't want to talk." She was so close. Her lips brushed mine with each word until they were almost incomprehensible to my frazzled brain.

Straddling me, she rose to her knees, pressing my face into her neck. I groaned at the taste of her, peppering kisses along her collarbone. She rubbed herself up and down my hardening length. The friction of her through the thin pants I wore sent a shiver up my spine. My breath came out in pants, my hands moving awkwardly against her back as I encouraged her, feeling like a helpless participant in her able hands.

She sat back down hard, and I grunted, cursing the fabric between us. When I moved to pull down my pants, she grabbed my hands. Obediently, I returned them to her back, holding her at the waist and rubbing circles through her ribbed tank top. I became aware of her staring at me, and I met her gaze, seeing the same lust swirling within her eyes that was surely in mine.

"You want me?"

What the fuck kind of question was that? I gripped her hips and rolled my own, pressing myself against her so she could feel just how badly I wanted her.

"Good."

Good?

I watched in amazement as she climbed off my lap, straightening her shirt—the peaks of her nipples showing through. She cleared her throat before grinning down at me.

"Now you know how it feels."

What? Horrified, I could only stare when she turned with a spring in her step towards the hallway, a hand raised over her head, flicking her fingers.

"I'm going to get some sleep. We'll talk later. Bye."

Then she was gone, disappearing around the bend and leaving me feeling deeply fucked up. I heard a door close and then nothing but silence.

After sitting there for a few minutes with nothing but some stupid animated mouse to keep me company, I found myself laughing out loud. Deep snorting, body shaking laughs that didn't sound quite stable.

Well, shit. She'd shown me, taken her revenge for leaving her out in the woods. No matter how wound up I was, I'd done the same, if not worse, when I'd left her on the forest floor without an explanation.

She'd made her point, and all I could do was salute her for it.

SYL

I leaned against the door to my room, breathing hard. Had I just done that? It hadn't been my intention to mess with Bash and leave him like that. I'd barely been able to stop, but something vindictive in me had risen up when he started getting into it. I'd remembered how I'd been at his feet in the woods, begging for him to take me when he decided to run off and disappear on me.

He'd left me in the woods and then in a state of agitation, not knowing if he was hiding out in his room or what had happened to him. I'd had nightmares of him secretly in his room or someone else's. I couldn't help but think that holding up in Bash's room for a few days was exactly what I'd intended to do before Jace had shown up and forced us out.

At least Jace had stuck with me, and as many misgivings as I had about the man, I was grateful for his presence. Whether it was Bash's challenge or Jace's presence, Carter had been watching me from a distance, his dark eyes hugging my figure every chance he got, but he stayed away.

Bash unaccounted for, I'd found it increasingly difficult to sleep. Like a tiny machine inside my body had refused to stop whirring so I could rest. Which was how I'd found myself out in the common room when he came out, his bedhead sexy as hell. Clearly ready to get back to us.

I hadn't wanted to waste time. Hadn't wanted to miss this chance to feel something in this place before I went back to the family compound, but the anger had risen up in me, like it was a living thing I had no control over.

Taking another calming breath, I pressed my back into the cool wood, feeling it keenly through my thin tank top, and hoping it would cool the heat of my body.

It wouldn't. Nothing would except the man I'd left grousing in the other room, but something in me demanded more from him than sex after he'd been such an asshole.

Maybe it was silly for me to taunt him, to demand he beg for forgiveness. He could decide at any moment I wasn't worth the effort, that maybe he'd take one of the other girls to ease the pain in his aching cock, but I wanted him to prove himself to me, to show me he cared.

Maybe it was foolish and selfish. I had only this cycle and the next to get pregnant, and here I was moping over Bash. What was worse, I was now passing over an opportunity for sex when The Party Girl was always supposed to be up for anything so long as it got her laid. But I couldn't shake the feeling that Bash was going to be the one to get me pregnant, and I wanted him to work for it.

Yeah, like banging another breeder in the breeding program should be work. No, we were here to party, to drink, and listen to loud music until the inhibitions of even the shiest of us were lowered. That's what a good pack mother would do, and it was what I aimed to be.

No more messing around. I'd lost myself with Bash, and the traitorous organ in my chest agreed. So long as he still wanted me in the morning, I would make myself his.

But when I woke and went straight to the common room to find him sitting in the same damn spot on the couch, grinning and patting a spot beside him, I felt rage burning in my chest. I walked stiff-limbed past him to go get a bowl of cereal.

I wasn't even hungry, and the sugary flakes swam miserably in overpowered milk before I went to perch on the cushion beside him, grateful no one else seemed around save for Jace and Sid playing a game of foosball in the corner. They'd be well out of earshot.

Clearing my throat, I kept my attention on the food, or the illusion of my attention. In truth, I was hyperaware of where Bash sat next to me, the little hairs on my body zeroing in on his presence and threatening to send a jolt of arousal strong enough to make me shiver and spill cold milk on my bare legs.

"We've got a couple of hours before the run."

I turned his words over in my head. Was he asking if I wanted to sleep with him?

"Yes, we do," I replied tightly, the warmth of his arm sliding along the couch behind me.

"So, you designed clothes for fun before coming here. You must've been popular."

I gave him a smile I knew dripped with sadness. Yes, the other girls had wanted me to design them beautiful clothes, and I'd been obsessed with their different figures and looks, crafting outfit after outfit. But they'd taken advantage, demanding more and more from me until my fingers were red from working the needle, and my back ached from poring over fabrics.

Sure, designing clothes had made me popular, but it hadn't made me any friends. If anything, it had set me apart from the others and driven the thought of friendship from their minds. Paired with the strange standoffishness my mother had instilled in me with her torment and I'd grown up lonely.

Sensing my mood, Bash's arm dropped to rest gently across my slumped shoulders.

"Well, I think it's amazing, and I'd love to see some of your work."

I hadn't shown anyone here my work, hadn't wanted to play dress up with a new group of wannabe friends, but Bash? He was watching me with such genuine interest that I couldn't help but smile back. Okay, maybe I would show him.

Just him.

"And I'd like to learn how to draw like you do. I have to draw figures you see and gowns before I can start cutting and sewing. It helps to get those images out of my head and onto a page, but—"

He watched me intently, his eyes drifting down to my mouth occasionally. It was distracting, and then my eyes dropped to his mouth and I was pulled towards it. Imagining the taste of him. How good it would feel to run my tongue along his bottom lip. Even knowing how the fire would consume me when I kissed him, I was helpless.

"But?" he questioned. My eyes shot to his, noting the way he watched me intently.

Shaking my head to dispel the effect he had on me, I tried to remember what we'd been talking about. Right clothes. Drawing. Art.

"But I can't get the figures to look right, and I thought since you know how to draw, maybe you could show me?" I fussed with the spoon, dragging flakes around until they clumped on the side of the bowl in a soggy mesh that didn't look appetizing in the slightest.

"I'd love to help."

I smiled at the cereal, bouncing up from the couch. "All right, I'll go dump this out and let's get started."

"Is it okay if I eat in your room?"

I stared down at him in surprise, and he looked away with a nervous smile.

"Kinda hungry."

"Sure. Grab whatever and come to my room. I'll get us some paper and pens out."

"Pencil."

"Excuse me?"

"We'll start with pencils. Easier to erase our extra line work that way," he said with a wink. Unfolding his long legs, he stood in front of me, his presence nearly overpowering my thought. Taking my shoulders, he dropped a kiss on my forehead. "Be right there."

Navigating around the kitchen while avoiding the camera was tough. I turned my head like I was talking to someone and pulled open the refrigerator door, quickly blocking my face with the door.

I knew Cam was one of the watchers assigned to Pack Breeders 103C, but he wasn't the primary. Who that would be, I didn't know, and that was the point. Getting Jerry reassigned had ensured the new primary wouldn't be someone I was as familiar with.

Unless they picked Cam. It was a worry I couldn't dwell on. The odds of them selecting Cam out of the ten watchers who switched off with Jerry were slim, but it was possible. The more I thought about that possibility, the deeper I buried my face in the fridge, avoiding any accidental captures by the camera embedded in the cabinet hinges. Cooking would show the side of my face unless I was very careful. Luckily, the guys had cooked up a whole turkey at some point, and I snagged a meaty drumstick.

Not bothering with a plate, I turned my head again as I closed the fridge door and hurried down the hall to Syl's room, tilting my face the other way as I passed the camera pointed at the common space.

Inside her room, I found Syl sitting on her bed with a paper and pencil on the nightstand beside her and another on her lap. That fucking skirt she wore was so short, the paper covered more of her legs than it did. A growl rumbled through my chest, and I coughed to disguise it, looking away when her cornflower blue eyes shot up to mine.

I wasn't here to ravage her. I was here to help her with her drawing.

To support her passion.

Except I was painfully hard as I sat down beside her. My cock twitching as the bed dipped from my weight and her breasts jiggled at the movement. That little tinkling laugh did all kinds of things to me, and I avoided her eyes. Not wanting her to think I'd come here to ignore her request and ravage her body the way I wanted to.

And I did. I wanted to suck, lick, bite every bit of exposed flesh and then remove the flimsy spaghetti strapped tank top hanging low on her chest, to get at the bits she dared to cover from me. But instead, I fought for control of myself and took a bite of turkey, chewing the stringy meat so I wouldn't have to say something about Syl's clothes and occupying my hands so I wouldn't rip off her skirt.

"Is that supposed to be lunch?"

Offended, I looked down at the drumstick in my hand. It was a perfectly good lunch. What was she talking about?

"Yes?"

She chuckled. "Don't you ever eat, oh, I don't know—anything other than meat?"

Did I eat a lot of meat? I thought about it. Ever since I'd started training, I'd made protein a philosophy, and it'd done my body and my muscles good.

"I don't see the point."

She giggled, the sound tugging at something in me, and gave my arm a shove. She almost fell back from the force, but I was unmoved.

"The point is, it's good to have some vegetables in your diet. Maybe the occasional carb. You know?"

I didn't know or care. Protein, protein, protein. That was my mantra, and the one that had seen me through the dangerous training regime I'd set for myself.

"Sure, next time you make a bowl of air, I mean salad, you can make me one too."

She laughed, and I looked up to find her wavy hair dancing with the force of it. "I'll hold you to that."

Fucking perfection. I wanted to tangle my fist in the silky strands. Shaking my head to disperse the vision of Syl mad with lust as I twisted my fingers tighter into those ash-blonde strands, I smiled back, hoping my dirty thoughts weren't etched onto my face.

Syl leaned over and began rummaging through her nightstand drawer, putting my willpower to the test as she waved her round ass in my face. My hand clenched so hard on the drumstick, it was a wonder the thing didn't shatter into splinters in my hand. But then she was done, moving to resume her position beside me with a stack of papers in her hands.

"These are some of what I've done. I can't get them to look right or to move right. My designs and fabrics need motion and life." She spoke quickly, and my heart clenched when I noticed her eyes glistening.

The drawings were definitely the work of a beginner, and I swallowed down a lump of half chewed turkey. Wiping a hand on my pants before reaching out and taking the top paper to inspect it. This was important to Syl, and it was something I could help her with.

Unsteady lines completely masked what she was trying to do. The motion she was trying to capture in this drawing was that of a woman walking, but without a good basis for a figure and with such unsteady line work, it was easy to see why Syl was frustrated with what she was producing.

I studied the drawing carefully, trying to think where we should start, and it kept coming back to her lines. When I thought about how I'd learned as a child, it'd been the result of endless practice and determination, of trying and failing over and over until, at last, my lines were straight. The objects and people I was drawing started to emerge from the paper. Each success had fueled me for a hundred more failures, but Syl wasn't like that. She had a purpose. A mission. Reproduce a single image in her head so she could bring it to actual life through cloth and thread. So, what to do with her? How to help?

What she needed was hundreds of small failures, mixed in with some success.

Step one.

"Okay, we're going to start by just practicing your line work until you can draw a steady line without thinking. I'll make the parameters and check your work." I looked down at the paper balanced on her lap. As much as I wanted to stay in Syl's bedroom, this bed wasn't going to work. It'd be better if we had something hard to put behind the paper. Even better if we could use the dining room table. I tried to think of a time I'd seen the large table unused, and I couldn't. Even when I'd been observing Pack 103C through the monitor, it seemed to always be occupied.

"What about late at night?"

I looked up at her in surprise. "At night?"

A small smile rose to her lips, and she looked away. "Yeah, I know the parties go a bit late, but eventually everyone goes to bed."

Yes, they did, and that table was fucking perfect. Smooth across the top and at a great height. Plus, it'd mean extra alone time with Syl until she started letting me back into her bed. I started imagining what else we could use the table for, but I cleared my throat before my fantasy could play out and demand I act on it.

Help. I was here to help her.

"Yes, we could do that. I'm used to staying up late."

After three years of fucked up breeding party schedules, I could sleep whenever and be awake as needed. Late night didn't bother me. Hell, it was so dark in those fucking tiny observation rooms I couldn't tell if it was night or day half the time, anyway.

Giving a nervous cough, I handed her back the paper. She took it with a shy smile, ducking her head as she placed it back in the drawer instead of in the pile with her others.

Had the one I'd chosen been special to her?

Shit. I'd been too busy thinking about her short skirt and unsteady lines. I hadn't spared much thought for the design. She turned back to me with a bit of ash-blonde hair curling over her eye, and I couldn't help it. It was right in front of me. I reached out to tuck it behind her ear, nearly losing it when she shuddered as my fingers grazed the shell.

We both froze, my hand still holding the silky strand. She leaned into me, her eyes hazy and soft with lust. My hand dropped to her jaw, and I brushed a thumb across her plump bottom lip. The things I wanted to do with that lip. Fuck, she was beautiful. She leaned in closer, the sweetness of her warmth so close I could taste it, taste her, and the memory of what it'd been like when our bodies had merged.

But she stood abruptly, leaving me staring at an empty space, my hand dropping uselessly to the coverlet.

"Okay, thanks, Bash. I think it's almost time for the daily run, and you should probably finish eating that." She nodded to the turkey leg still clenched in my other fist, completely forgotten when my body had been consumed with other needs.

She was right, though. It was almost time for our run, and I'd need to figure out a way to keep myself safe through it. Swallowing hard, I nodded, my mind already churning away, coming up with ideas for how I would trick the others into thinking I'd gone for a run with them.

I stood, saluting Syl with the turkey leg.

"See you at the run?" I watched her expression, to gauge how pissed she still was about last time, half expecting her to freeze up at the mention of the upcoming run.

Instead, she smiled shyly, and I loved it. She was so seemingly open with everyone else, but I was starting to see the real Syl. Maybe her sending me away instead of fucking my brains out was a good thing. She hadn't seemed willing to turn anyone down, even when Carter had been hurting her, but here she was smiling and gesturing to the door.

Maybe it was fucked up to take it as a good sign when she was actively kicking me out of her room, but I didn't think things were so simple with Syl.

And if she wanted to wait to take me to her bed again, I'd make sure I was ready for her.

Chapter 17

Syl was lined up with the others when I came out, and she didn't seem upset when I squeezed my way in between her and a muscle-bound guy with a buzz cut. Instead, she gave me a flirty grin, her eyes twinkling before they fixed on the tree line. She was already naked, her back straight as she looked out dreamily at the forest.

Beautiful. I ached to draw her expression, but that wasn't why I was here. So, I committed the light in her eyes to memory and busied my hands, pulling off the joggers and hoodie I'd thrown on. When I pulled it over my head, I emerged to find her eyes glued to my body, roving over my muscles with a hunger I was eager to sate.

Too bad I had to be an asshole today.

I cleared my throat, and her eyes shot guiltily to mine. Fuck. She could stare at me all day if she wanted to. I welcomed her attention. Every muscle, every ridge of definition had been put there for her. A costume that allowed me admittance to her exclusive club.

It was all for her, and it was all hers.

I scrubbed a hand through my hair.

But I couldn't say that.

"I hope you're not going to take off on me again." There was a warning growl in her voice, but I caught the underlying lust and frustration. If I chased her, would she submit to me? Allow me to take her as I'd been about to last time? I could imagine it, how healing it would be. I'd stay, unlike last time, and finish what we'd started.

Only, that might kill me. I drew a deep, steadying breath and looked down at her. My angel, my muse.

"Sorry, Syl, but I like to be alone on my runs. It's weird, I know, but I'm a bit of a lone wolf that way," I said the last with an awkward laugh, hoping to soften the blow I saw already falling and crushing the excitement in her eyes.

She looked away, her brow puckered and bottom lip protruding. Her slim shoulders filled with a tension my palms longed to ease.

Fuck.

I wished I could chase her down like she wanted. Every part of me screamed to do so, to hunt her through the forest and hold her down, but I couldn't. There was no way to explain why without outing myself.

We were out here for a scheduled run. To maintain our bodies in peak physical condition. To let the animal part of ourselves soak up the glory of the pines and the crunch of leaves as we raced through them.

But it wasn't meant for me, and I never felt more like an outsider than in that moment with Syl's eyes glistening as she fixed them on an empty space across the field. No longer looking to the tree line but at something that didn't exist.

I'd never wanted to disappoint her, and I'd never hated myself more than in that moment. All my mother's and my sister's words about my defective nature couldn't compare to the disappointment in Syl's eyes. A disappointment I'd put there myself.

A disappointment in me.

Always a watcher, never a breeder. Never anything more than the little defective boy held back from runs, from participating in anything even remotely straining, and then locked in a room to watch more able-bodied men once I was old enough. Better men.

Fuck, I wanted to scream out my frustrations, but Carter stood in front of the line, giving some shit speech about nurturing our other forms.

I didn't know if he was really giving a bad speech or if my hate for him was strong enough to downgrade even the most eloquent of words, but the thought of that slimy jerk out there with Syl, able to chase her through the woods when I couldn't...It filled my mind with rage until whatever words he continued to spout were lost to the thundering in my ears.

There was cheering around me as everyone began to shift, but I stood there in my human form watching as Syl took off across the field and into the woods, easily winding a path between the pines. Beautiful. I could watch her run all day. Just plant myself out here and watch Syl-wolf do all manner of mundane thing.

I longed to be out there with her, to hunt her like an animal and take my reward when I caught up, but that wasn't me.

So, I shifted, taking my wolf form and falling to my paws as my bones cracked into their new position and hair sprouted across my body. Even with my heightened senses, I could feel the crushing pain and anger at having to stay back. I loped my way into the woods, ensuring an easy pace that wouldn't irritate my lungs.

I hid in the woods like a coward, pawing through the decaying leaves and falling branches to make enough space for my oversized body so I could lie in the dirt, cursing my pathetic existence.

If wolves could cry the way humans did, a stream of my tears would have caught in the wind and trailed behind me as I raced through the woods, trying to outrun the pain and disappointment. I'd been so sure when I came out here today that we'd pick up where we left off, that the hurt caused by Bash abandoning me on the forest floor would be healed tenfold. Instead, he'd muttered some stupid bullshit about wanting to be alone.

Alone and not with me. Was I really so undesirable? But I knew I wasn't, at least not to Bash. The way he'd been watching me when I'd invited him into my room had been dirtier than most of the sexual acts I'd fulfilled since coming to the dorm. He hadn't just undressed me with his eyes. He'd fucked me with them, and I'd ordered him out, wanting him to take me out here the way he'd failed to do before.

Only he wouldn't. Tragic yips escaped my throat, and I ran harder, pushing my legs until they burned, leaping over a fallen tree and barely slowing my pace. I'd left a moment behind the rest, but I knew I was ahead of them now, and I wanted to put even more distance between myself and any other wolf.

If Bash wanted to be alone, then I'd be alone too. Maybe that way I could feel close to him again.

But the understanding wouldn't come. He wanted me, and he'd wanted me during our run last time. Why give me a shitty excuse so he could go off on his own? It didn't make sense, and I couldn't stop the images of him chasing down a different she-wolf from forming in my mind. She'd be a beauty with long legs to match Bash's height and a mane of silky-smooth dark hair. Never mind that no one in Pack Breeders 103C fit that description. Bash's girlfriend took shape in my mind until she became a real person, and I fucking hated her.

I knew how stupid I was being. If he chose to take another woman, it was none of my business. We were here to conceive. Nothing more. And multiple partners weren't only encouraged, they were practically demanded. Everyone knew they'd be going home after they were involved in a pregnancy as a man or made pregnant as a woman.

Back to their real lives away from this place of fiction, and relationships deeper than the physical were discouraged. Bash should take another lover, and I should too. It was what we were meant to do, but winding through the trees and tearing through the brush didn't change how badly I wanted Bash, or the feeling that he'd be the one to finally get me pregnant.

And that was the goal—a pregnancy. Then they could all leave me the fuck alone. I'd hand the red-faced infant, or infants, off to a gaggle of eager aunties and make my dresses in peace. Safe from the poison fields and able to live my life.

I'd lost sight of the goal—distracted by Bash and our connection—but he didn't care enough to chase me. Even knowing the way most runs ended with wolves tangled up with one another—sometimes shifting, sometimes not—with the adrenaline of racing through the woods and feral needs of our animal sides brought to the surface, had me concluding that he didn't care.

Maybe he was happy to be rid of me, to lose me out here and let another wolf hunt me down the way he'd started to do before turning away.

I had to face the facts.

He didn't want me.

Sex with Bash was dangerous. Sex with anyone else was just sex, but with Bash—it was something more. Something that went beyond the physical.

All of it amounted to one thing. The Party Girl was back. I'd still draw with Bash, soaking up his presence and artistic skills, so I could return to 14F better able to draw out the fashions in my head, but I'd stay away from him physically and avoid his touch at all costs. I knew where it led now, and nothing good could come of it.

It could get me cut from the breeding program and sent directly to the fields. Icy fear gripped my heart, and I stumbled, coming to a stop.

I'd give up on him. The next time I saw him, I wouldn't allow myself to be drawn in. He didn't want me, and I was done letting heartache and longing interfere with what I was doing here.

But I couldn't stop the mournful howl from leaving my throat. It echoed up into the branches, flushing out a group of birds with inky black wings previously unseen within their depths. Why had I dared to hope for more from this place, from him? Stupid. Stupid. Stupid girl.

I'd miss Syl, but she didn't have a place here.

Not anymore.

Chapter 18

By the time Syl returned from the run, she wouldn't even look at me, and I didn't blame her. I could barely stand myself. My mind went through different possibilities, things I could tell her, excuses I could make for avoiding her on the run, but none of them felt real enough to work. The thought of directly lying to Syl when my whole identity here was already a lie made me sick.

So, I followed along behind her when she returned, not surprised at all when she made no move to put her clothes back on. I was close enough to touch, and I raised a hand without thinking, wanting to feel the smooth skin of her back to remind myself that she was really here, that I was really here and not back in that shitty room watching her through a monitor.

But things with Syl felt grainy and soundless, like I was watching her through a screen again. I hated the distance between us, and I was too worked up to think about much else when we returned to the common room.

"Did you have a pleasant run?" Stupid. Even though I spoke to her back, I could tell she heard me by the stutter in her step. A new tension settled into her shoulders, but she didn't reply.

She still didn't put on clothes even when we were back in the common room, going to the kitchen to pour herself a tall glass of ice water. It was all I could do to stand across the counter from her and stare.

"Syl, I—"

Her eyes shot to mine, and the words died on my lips.

"Yes? Did you have something you wanted to share?"

I couldn't. My mouth worked, but no words came out. Anything that did would be a lie, and fuck, I didn't want to do that.

"Then here's how it's going to work." She leaned forward on the counter, pressing her breasts together and eyeing me up and down, sizing me up. "You're going to stop scaring off the other guys since you don't have the balls to take me yourself, and you're going to teach me to draw at night like we'd planned."

My mouth hung open.

This unspoken thing between us was fire and passion. It was everything, but here she was talking about taking other men like it was no big deal, and I couldn't say a fucking thing about it.

Nobody here was supposed to be exclusive, and she was right. I'd rejected her out on the field. Let her believe I'd wanted to be alone when all I'd wanted was to hold her and cry into her shoulder, to let her soak up my pain until I could breathe without it squeezing my chest.

She stared me down, waiting for me to say something, to demand she not take other lovers—but I couldn't. The words wouldn't come. Not when my very presence here was a lie, and I couldn't explain what I'd done without outing myself.

The truth was, I could offer her nothing, and why I'd ever thought otherwise was beyond me.

I was her watcher, not her breeder. Meant to stay on the sidelines and observe. Keep her safe. Make sure rules were followed.

Never interacting.

Never touching.

Never thinking about the us that couldn't be.

Accepting my silence, she nodded and looked down at her water, swirling the liquid while she spoke.

"Tonight, I'm thinking we meet out here at three AM. Everyone's usually cleared out by then."

Straight to the point. Emotionless. Almost dead. Her tone was cutting. I shut my mouth and nodded.

She gave one quick, decisive bob of her head, like she'd played out this scene and it had gone exactly as expected, and there was nothing I could say otherwise. The silence stretched between us—a gaping chasm I had no way to bridge.

"You should get some sleep." I hated the short biting tone she used and the way her luscious lips pressed together.

I shouldn't get to sleep. It was six PM at best, and the last thing I felt I could do with Syl so obviously pissed was go rest, but I could hear the dismissal in her tone and the way she avoided my eyes.

That and maybe some alone time in my new box of a room was just what I needed. What I deserved.

I nodded sadly, and that's when I noticed it.

Fuck. I was standing in full view of the kitchen camera, and I turned quickly, heart pounding.

This shit with Syl had completely wiped caution from my mind. She was everything and having her so obviously upset with me had made me stupid. The camera had been right in my face for anyone on the other end to see.

"Goodnight," I called over my shoulder, not daring to turn my head.

SYL

With his eyes off me, I watched Bash walk away, noting the slump of his broad shoulders—a ridiculous posture on such a tall man. Maybe I shouldn't be meeting with him tonight to work on my drawing skills, but I badly wanted to learn, and Bash seemed willing to still teach me.

He'd been contrite, but I refused to let it touch my heart. Not when he offered no words of explanation. Other breeders filtered back into the dorms, loud and excited from a successful run. I wanted to join in that excitement, to be as carefree as they were. So, I grabbed a beer from the fridge and took out a few other cold ones to set on the counter. Kevin was the first to walk up and grab a beer from the counter, pulling a bottle opener from the drawer and snapping the top off with a satisfying crack and fizz.

"Hey, Syl, where's your shadow?"

My shadow. What a great fucking way to describe Bash.

"Gone back to his room. I guess the run made him too tired." I pouted, knowing my lips always attracted attention.

"Oh, yeah?" Kevin's eyes widened, and his cheek dimpled with a smile. I wouldn't let Bash scare anyone off anymore. Fuck him. He'd rejected me, and as much as I was drawn to him, he didn't own me.

No one did.

"Yeah," I purred, leaning forward on the counter and stretching out a hand to lie across his long-sleeved shirt. It was a tightly woven cotton. None of my favourite fabrics on men. The material was so pliant and easy to work with. I toyed with a frayed bit on the cuff, looking up at him through my lashes.

"Hey, Syl, you got a beer for me, babe?" Carter sauntered up to the counter, all swag. His face was still flushed from the run and the way it had undoubtedly ended with his cock inside of an eager she-wolf.

He grabbed a bottle, popping the top while looking over my nakedness with eager eyes. "Get lost, Kevin."

Fuck. Kevin I could deal with. He was a nice enough guy, but Carter staking a claim? Shit. The sight of his windblown hair and smug smile made my skin crawl.

"Where's the new guy?" His eyes roved over my body while he spoke, and I made no move to cover my exposed breasts.

"He's-he's gone to sleep. I must've worn him out during the run." It was stupid to lie, but Carter wasn't someone I wanted to deal with, and as the most dominant wolf here, no one could challenge him. If he decided to continue things with me, he'd demand I be only with him unless he chose to share me.

Carter nodded, then gave a dark chuckle.

"His loss. My gain." Carter's white teeth glinted in the waning light, white and predatory.

BASH

I passed the time drawing endless sketches. No way I could sleep knowing how things stood with Syl, that she was out there offering herself to whoever would take her.

Of everything I drew, Syl was the easiest and the hardest. I didn't have to think to conjure images of her face, her breasts, her silky soft hair and how it reminded me of moonlight, almost white with a hint of gold. But I was also never satisfied with the result.

Fuck, why did this have to be so complicated? I drew until my hand cramped up and my stomach reminded me I hadn't grabbed any food before retreating to my room. By the time I looked up to check the time, it was nearly three.

My heart leapt, and I stood up in a hurry, scattering papers on the ground. What an idiot. I quickly collected them and shoved them haphazardly into a drawer, not caring about the way they spilled out. Normally I would place them into my portfolio carefully, each sketch of her a treasure, but with the real thing waiting for me out in the common room, I didn't much care what happened to my drawings.

I brought some of my 3B pencils. No need to confuse her with different thickness of lead, and avoided the ones I'd worn down nearly to the nub.

With a handful of pencils clenched in one hand and a few sheets of paper in the other, I emerged into the hallway and followed the light into the common area to find Syl already seated at the table, her back to me. She wore a white shirt, and I could pick the edge of her bra out of the thin material. Had she worn it for me? Maybe she'd already been wearing it for someone else and hadn't cared what I saw her in.

The thought was a miserable one, and I grumpily approached her, coming around her front to find she had paper and pencils already set out. She looked up at me almost absentmindedly, and inwardly I groaned. There was an air of disinterest and stiffness in her posture that was difficult to process. But then she sighed and gave me a weak smile.

"You're late."

Was I? I spun around to look for a clock, and realized I was under a light and in full fucking view of that damned kitchen camera again, and the one near the foosball table. Clearing my throat, I moved to the other side of the table, putting my back to both while Syl watched me curiously.

"Sorry." No explanation again, and I caught the look in her eye that told me she'd noticed. But I couldn't exactly tell her I'd been drawing pictures of her, trying to understand her better so I could find a way through this. Find a way back to the us that was barely beginning but felt so damned good.

I rolled my shoulders, mindful of the cameras at my back. I wouldn't even be her watcher anymore if I was discovered. I couldn't afford to let down my guard.

I cleared my throat and dropped my materials on the table, taking a sheet of paper and drawing two horizontal lines. I handed it over to her, and she stared down in surprise.

"You're going to draw perfectly straight lines between those bars until you can draw an unbroken line with no mistakes. Only then will we move on to, you guessed it, longer lines. This is all we're going to do tonight. It'll be hard, annoying work, but this is the best way to get your line work improving in as short a time as possible." I didn't want to think about our limited time, but I'd only booked off family time for two months, and my absence would be missed. If she got pregnant this cycle, we'd only have a few more weeks. No matter which way I turned it over in my mind, there wasn't much time to teach her, and I was determined to make every lesson count.

"Like this?" She drew a line, but it had a curve to it as I expected.

"Perfectly straight, Syl. Like this." I took the paper, wincing when I brushed her hand, and she pulled back as if I'd bitten her. A reaction I chose to ignore, instead showing her an example line to use. The bars I'd drawn were only two inches apart and the further I made them, the harder keeping the line straight would be. Once she mastered lines, I'd move her on to circles and we'd start putting things together.

Syl cursed, and I chuckled. The words that came out of this woman's mouth were remarkably crude, and though she could have been left to complete her task independently, there was no way I would pass up a minute in Syl's company. Dreamily, I thought of the painting I was working on in my room, the one that occupied my hours when I couldn't sleep for thoughts of her.

How precious those paints were. In trade, the schoolteacher had me draw out entire books filled with foreign animals restored from ratty old pictures—great grey beasts with trunks, and oversized cats with stripes—before she would give me the meager supplies I had requested. All of my correspondence with the auntie teacher had been through a runner, the boy's cheeks always flushed and a twinkle of excitement in his eye from the exertion, but I'd gotten the colours I'd wanted, and it had been worth the cramps in my hand.

Of course, I'd never known I would use them for something as magnificent as what I'd carefully slid under my bed.

But with no chance of working on it tonight, I took up a sheet of paper and began sketching. It felt inappropriate to sketch Syl while she sat beside me and with everything going on between us. Instead, I focused on some of the nature I'd seen while outdoors.

Nothing that would bring Syl's mind back to the run and how I'd rejected her, but on simple things. A broken cloud lazily crossing the sky. Blades of grass stretching to bask in the sun's light. The wind giving them a dancer's sway.

"That's beautiful."

I glanced up to find Syl studying my page. On it was a sea of grass stretching across a field with the sun opposite, every blade tilting towards it even as the wind pushed them away.

"Thank you."

With a sigh of frustration, she put her pencil down. "And how do I get from these shitty lines to that?" she huffed, gesturing at my paper, and I laughed.

"Years of practice, Syl. A lot of years. The lines are the best place for you to start, trust me."

With an annoyed glance my way, she picked up the pencil and began the next row. "Fucking, shit-balled, son of a bitch, ass-twat-fucker-sandwich," she muttered under her breath, the uncouth words so at odds with the casual elegance she always seemed to exude. Her breath disturbed the hair falling softly to the sides of her face, framing her beautifully, and I allowed myself a drawing of one errant wave.

No, we weren't fucking.

No, we weren't together.

But this felt somehow worth every bit of pain I'd suffered to get here. Every torn muscle. Every strain I'd pushed into instead of backing off from. Hanging out with Syl, teaching me so many new swear words, as I quietly sketched out the beauty of the world.

This felt right.

Which is why my heart broke when Syl started yawning, looking up at me with tired, droopy eyes.

"I think I'm going to have to head to bed, sorry."

Was I so obviously disappointed? Sighing, I took in her slumped shoulders and the weak way she held her pencil. She'd tried to stay awake, for me, and the thought warmed my heart. Maybe she'd given up on us for the moment, but I'd find a way to convince her to give us another try.

"Of course. Goodnight, Syl." I dropped a kiss on the top of her ash-blonde head, gathering up my papers in a quick scoop and giving her one last parting smile before heading to my room.

With a sigh, I opened the door, miserable at not bringing Syl back with me, at having to spend another night alone in a boxy room, when I noticed it.

Right in front of my main floor window was a folded up piece of paper, the edges curling. Brow furrowed, I retrieved it.

They'd left it by the window, not the door, and a chill crept up my spine at the realization of what this meant. If any of my fellow breeders wanted to leave me a note, they could've slipped it under my door. It wouldn't make sense for them to go outside, find my window and slip it in there, which meant whoever sent it was no breeder.

My hand shook as I unfolded the note.

What the fuck are you doing?

Meet me at the tree line, tomorrow, one am.

They'd left off their name, but whoever had written this note knew who I was, which meant they had the power to end everything. No more getting to know Syl. No more teaching her how to draw. No more hoping I could continue trying to understand the connection between us. It'd all end, and what was worse, Syl would know.

She'd know I was a defect, unworthy of the title of breeder. Just some asshole who had conned his way in to fuck and party. Only that had never been my goal, and if I was taken away, I'd never have the chance to tell Syl why I'd really come here. How a grainy, crying version of her had ensnared my heart and given me a purpose I'd thought long gone.

Guess I'd find out tomorrow. Whether the note writer was aware of my nightly appointment with Syl at three, I didn't know, but a one AM meeting would, thankfully, allow me to do both.

If I wasn't hauled out and thrown in front of a red-faced Administrator Sampson.

Fuck.

Fear left me numb, and I barely managed a few hours of sleep before joining the others for lunch and having to watch Syl get fucked in the ass against the foosball table by that slimy asshole Carter. She was drunk already, her head bobbing, and her eyes glazed as she grabbed the foosball handles, causing the little plastic men to clatter as she took him soundlessly.

She didn't seem happy about it, at least, and she shot me a death glare if I came anywhere near her, but it still hurt. I got the impression Carter was fucking with me by taking her in the common room where everyone could see.

We'd know soon if she was pregnant, and whether I'd have another turn with her in the breeding room, but not even the thought of sinking into Syl's wet heat could properly distract me from my meeting with whoever had sent me that note. I watched Syl from the corner, almost unaffected by what I was seeing.

The run passed with a flicker of pain, unable to penetrate the gloom as Syl took off for the woods with Carter's wolf right behind, and I moved to the sidelines, stepping aside so she could be with a breeder, as she should.

But if I was outed, I wouldn't even have my nights with Syl anymore. Wouldn't see her in the flesh ever again, and the worry kept my stomach in knots the rest of the afternoon until a drunken Syl wandered up and broke briefly through the haze.

"Hey, Bash. What's up? What are you working on there?"

I looked from my sketch pad to her, surprised she was speaking to me outside of our drawing sessions. I'd been so lost that I hadn't even heard her come up.

Knowing where Syl was at all times was my obsession. I frowned at the sketch I'd been doing of her face, this time focusing on the gap beside her incisor and how I wanted to dip my tongue into it. I pulled the paper to my chest along with its cardboard backing.

"Just—Nothing really."

Her eyes twinkled playfully, and I knew just how drunk she had to be to look at me like that.

"Nothing? Really? Come on, Bash. Let me see."

She made a grab for the paper, but I quickly pulled it away and stood up from where I leaned against the wall to hold it out of her reach. But I'd underestimated her, and she jumped, snatching it at the same time the cardboard fell.

I watched as her eyes widened and she held the paper up, looking at a mirror image of herself.

Beauty, meet beauty.

I sighed, knowing this couldn't lead anywhere good, but she looked up at me in surprise, a question in the crease of her brow.

"I can never get the eyes right." It was true. I'd been trying ever since I'd seen her on the monitor, and I knew it was part of the reason I'd made so many sketches focusing on her face. To get the expression just perfect, I felt I needed to understand Syl better, to know her soul so I could represent it correctly.

Or maybe I was just way too stressed and tired.

"Cool. Well, keep trying, I guess." She gave me a watery smile, and I blinked in surprise.

Keep trying, I guess. It sounded like more than the drawing, like I should keep trying with her. Keep pushing, keep trying to make the dream of us a reality. I grinned back at her, taking the offered paper.

"Count on it."

Syl returned to the foosball table, thankfully to actually play foosball this time, and I felt a renewed sense of certainty. She was pissed at me and playing the role of a breeder—fucking anything that moved like she was supposed to, but she'd also said to keep trying, and that gave me hope.

The hope clung to me like a second skin as the afternoon wore on until Carter took Syl back to his room, and I retreated back to mine. I tried to sleep, but it was fitful, and I woke up in a sweat bad enough that I needed to change my shirt.

Time to meet my mystery letter writer.

I slipped out of my window at quarter to one, not wanting to be seen leaving on the dorm cameras, and headed into the pines. The cool night air was the kind of damp before a storm, and the tension in my body mirrored the weather.

This meeting could break me and everything I was trying to do.

Which was what? I still didn't know. I'd thought meeting Syl was the answer. I'd meet her and know why I'd gone through the trouble of remaking myself and becoming Bash, but I hadn't. Not then, and not now. I felt no closer to understanding my fascination with her.

But one thing I did know was that I couldn't leave. I felt on the verge of knowing Syl and having her know me, of some greatly important discovery. The letter writer had the power to take it all away, to send me back to the role of watcher or worse.

What would be the punishment if I was caught? I'd long been deemed too weak for the fields, but if word got out of what I'd done, how I'd infiltrated the breeding program—well, it would set a precedent for the other watchers. Prove their system wasn't infallible—that it could be done.

"Hey," a voice hissed in the dark, and I followed it, nearly fainting in relief when I caught a flash of red hair and found Cam standing next to a large rock.

"Fuck, man." I gasped in relief, stepping closer.

Cam studied me for an anxious heartbeat, his eyes searching my face before pulling me into a tight hug. The shorter man only came up to my chest, and I awkwardly patted him on the back.

"What the hell do you think you're doing?" He pulled away, glaring up at me. "Breaking into a dorm, posing as a *breeder*. Are you crazy?"

All I could do was wince at his sharp tone and nod apologetically. I'd clearly worried Cam, and I felt truly bad.

"So, this is why you took family leave?"

I nodded, eyes focusing on the rough bark of an unruly pine behind Cam's head.

"I couldn't believe it when I saw your face on my monitor."

My eyes shot to his. "Did you take over for Jerry as the primary?"

"Yes," he answered slowly, not giving anything away.

I nodded, swallowing hard. "That's good. You're a great choice, and an excellent watcher."

Cam balked at me, his mouth hanging open. "Yeah, except I'm a terrible fucking watcher, thanks to you."

He hadn't reported me, not yet. The tension holding me rigid eased, and I slumped forward, not realizing I'd been waiting for him to confirm he hadn't reported me before I could relax.

"Yeah."

He glared at me, and I winced. "Fucking yeah. So, you've had your fun, and it's time to come back. I can doctor the reports, tell them Sebastian the breeder was needed by his squad and had to drop o—"

"No." Icy dread gripped me, and I grabbed Cam's shoulder. "You can't. I can't leave."

Cam shook his head, ginger curls dancing across his eyes.

"Why? Is it the sex, the booze? I thought you were better than that."

It was safer to let him believe I was only here for a good time. But I couldn't stand the look of disgust in Cam's eyes.

"It's nothing like that. Cam, it's about Sylvia." I used her full name, hoping he might've seen her file.

His blank stare met mine. "A woman?"

"Yes, I—well, I was her watcher, you see. For her breeding party, and, well…" My mouth opened and closed ineffectively as I tried to think how to explain that I'd been drawn to her from the moment she'd appeared on my monitor. How her tears had gripped my heart, and her body had pulled me into her heat like a helpless, unthinking pawn.

"Do you love her?" Steely eyes met mine, demanding an answer.

Fuck. Did I love Syl? There was a fine line between obsession and love. I'd been obsessed before with a flower or an animal, sketching it out over and over again, trying to recreate its perfection, but Syl? She was more. She was everything. Her laugh, her smile, the secret drawer full of dreams she tried to keep hidden from everyone else. The way she swore like it was a second fucking language. Her gossamer-soft hair.

"Yes." The word came out strong, firm, and I saw something fall in Cam's eyes just before he turned his face away.

"And how long do you intend to keep this up?"

"Until she knows it." There, that was my next step, somehow finding a way back to being with Syl, and confessing the feelings swirling in my gut. In my heart. In my bones. I didn't think it would go anywhere, and maybe it would mean nothing to her, but I couldn't leave the dorm and resume my role as a watcher without her at least knowing.

"Right." With a sniff, Cam reached down for a black canvas bag hidden in the shadow of the rock. He pulled something out and pushed hard into my chest.

Surprised, I took it from him. It was hard, and when I unfolded it, I understood.

A baseball cap.

"At least cover your fucking face. I'm not your watcher all the time." He hugged me again, a long lingering hug. Then, just as I was about to say something, he pulled away and left me to lean against the tree for support as I tried to process the relief spreading through my limbs.

Just telling someone about Syl was freeing like a weight had been lifted from my chest. I could breathe again. I had someone on my side, someone who cared.

Now if I could just get through to Syl.

CHAPTER 19

The next few days passed in a drunken haze. Sometimes Carter passed me around, but mostly, he kept me to himself, taking me to his room so he could ply my body with a variety of pain-inducing toys.

Daily runs became the most dreaded part of my day. I always felt a twinge of hurt when Bash's wolf set out with me before careening off into the sidelines. The reminder drove the wedge in my chest deeper—he didn't want me. Wouldn't give chase. Couldn't care less.

But Bash at night was a different creature. More patient than I'd expected for someone of his impressive skill. He didn't say a word when my hangover interfered with the perfect circles I'd been able to produce the previous night. By the third night, I was so sick of circles and lines I could scream, but Bash just sat there, completely oblivious, his eyes glued to the page as he drew a squirrel with fur so real I wanted to brush my hand across it to see if it was as soft as it looked.

There was no conversation between us, just quiet words of instruction when I showed him my work. Until one night, he reviewed my page and gave a curt nod.

"Okay, we're ready to move on."

Fuck yeah. I squealed, wiggling in the chair cushion, making all kinds of embarrassing sounds on the fake leather. He watched me, drinking in my excitement without reacting. The same way he'd been watching me get fucked on the couch in front of him this week.

It pissed me off.

Just more of the fucking same.

He cleared his throat and took a clean sheet of paper. I expected him to draw some guidelines on it. Maybe some more curved lines to practice drawing between or a tortuous slope within which I was to draw more circles, but he held it in his hand before sliding the blank paper in front of me.

"Draw one of your figures."

Incredulously, I looked from the paper to Bash, studying his face to see if he was serious.

Draw one of my figures? I'd drawn nothing but random shapes and lines since his instruction had started, and now he wanted me to draw figures?

"What?"

He smirked, and I hated how sexy it looked on him. "I want you to try drawing a figure, just as you've been drawing them before we started."

I stared at him, wide eyed. He was supposed to be teaching me how to draw figures, not giving me blank papers and telling me to do it.

"I can't. They're shit. I showed you what they were like. Aren't you supposed to teach me how to draw?"

His smirk spread into a grin, and fuck him for looking even cuter. He slammed his stained hands down on the table. "That's the point! You've been practicing the technical skills you need to draw figures, Syl. I want you to see how much progress you've made. Basics are boring, but they're important." His smile was contagious, and I felt a matching one creep onto my face.

"So, I'm doing good?"

He slammed the table again. Loud enough I glanced behind me at the hallway of doors, sure Carter was about to wake up and come snatch me away.

"You're doing fucking fantastic. Don't believe me?" He waggled his eyebrows. "Draw a figure. Just like you used to. Don't try to do anything differently. Let's just see how it comes out."

The challenge issued, I turned my attention to the blank page, picking up a pencil and blowing out a breath. I could feel Bash's eager eyes on me, and I glanced up to find him leaning my way, peering over my arm to get a better view.

"Do you mind not watching?" It was stupid and sheepish, but the way he studied my paper made me nervous.

"Right, right. Of course. Sorry." He turned back to his own page, adding more details to the squirrel's whiskers, as if the woodland animal didn't already look ready to jump off the page and go hunting for nuts. He still glanced up at me occasionally, and he grinned when I caught him, a twinkle of pride in his eye that warmed my heart.

"Sorry, I can't help it. I'll be good." He fixed his eyes on the page, and I could almost feel the effort it took him not to watch me as I put pencil to paper and began trying to sketch the human shape I wanted to dress.

No way. The figure still didn't look right, its arms and legs disproportionate in my failed attempt at tilting her sideways, but my goddess.

Fucking Bash.

She took shape.

The body was wrong, and I could see the errors, but I could also see how much smoother and easier it was to translate my vision to the page. Her head was a bit oversized, but it was perfectly round—the circles. The lines of her body didn't bounce around. They were perfectly straight—the lines he'd had me draw.

Amazed, I sat back, staring at my hand and the pencil I held.

"Can I look yet?" Bash's voice was strained. I looked up at him in surprise, almost forgetting another person was at the table with me, and that was saying a lot. I was usually painfully aware when Bash was present or not.

I'd done this. Drawing the figures had been hard before, every line a challenge, but now those movements were second nature, and my vision on the page was faulty but clear.

"Y-yes."

Bash practically threw his pencil away and grabbed my paper, holding it in front of his face and grinning.

"This is what I'm talking about, Syl. We started with the line work because of this. You did this."

Embarrassed by just how far outside his scope of skill my pathetic excuse for artwork was, I moved to take it back, but he held the paper away. "No, this calls for a celebration. I could fucking frame this thing."

Frame it? The thought made my stomach churn. Nothing about my drawing deserved framing, but Bash stared at it like it was a fine piece. Like it was worthy. Like I was worth something other than fucking and making babies. I teared up, not sure why, and turning my face so he wouldn't see.

"Syl? Are you okay?"

I nodded, not willing to turn towards him and show him just how not okay I was.

"Yeah, fine. Just emotional. I've been trying so hard to get these right, and I've never been able to. I'm going to—Excuse me." Keeping my head turned, I gathered my papers and pencil and retreated to the quiet of my room.

But the joy springing to life in my chest was squashed when I used the washroom before bed and found a smear of blood on the toilet paper. I dropped my face into my hands and let the tears flow, a seemingly unending stream mirroring the pain inside. I gasped in a breath, my body remembering I needed it to survive. Cleaning up only took a few minutes, but mentally retrieving a sanitary product from the shelf, knowing I would need to tell everyone my period had come, lasted an eternity.

This cycle was a bust. I'd failed. Which meant I had just one cycle remaining in my extension. One last chance to prove my value to the pack as a mother before they would deem me infertile and find another use for me. One that did not require me to keep my fingernails.

The hall was silent, and I was grateful for it. I didn't think I could stand seeing another person right now. The soft padding between my legs haunted me, a reminder of my failure. All my efforts, everything I'd done, and it hadn't mattered.

I wanted to scream. To punch a wall and break through the plaster until I splintered the wood beyond, damaging the very stability of this place. But doing so would bring people out of their rooms, and then I'd have to explain to them—to tell them I'd failed yet again.

Walking in a haze out of the dorms to face the forest, I tilted my face up to bask in the light of the crescent moon, imagining it was a better mother than the one I had and would dry my tears. The moon couldn't do that, but the light and imagining was a comfort in a harsh reality. Not in the mood to shift, I ran down the path to the left, heading back to the houses and hoping I wouldn't run into any guards.

The wind blew across my face with a chill to it that froze the tears to my cheeks. The sensation only made me run harder, faster, until my muscles screamed at me to stop, and my chest burned. My useless limbs gave up, forcing me to halt and double over, panting as I tried to catch my breath.

The world seemed against me, and I let a few more tears leak out before making my way silently down the tree-lined path and back to the dorms. I settled on not telling anyone, but answering if I was asked, unable to stomach the idea of announcing my failure to the others.

But it wasn't all bad, and as I opened the heavy front door with dread weighing me down, my eyes fell on the dining table and a smile tugged at my lips.

Another month to spend with Bash.

CHAPTER 20

When I'd gone to bed, it'd been with the image of Syl's grin in my mind—the sheer joy on her face at realizing her progress had been a wonder to behold—and I'd drifted off easily, imagining how her happiness would grow now that we could move on to proportions and perspective.

But when I woke up and headed into the common area, I found a very different Syl sitting at the dining table in the same spot. Her hair was pinned back, and she wore a black turtleneck that covered more of her skin than I was used to. She looked like a completely different person, nursing a steaming cup of coffee, with her hands curled around the earthenware like she was warming them by the fire on a chilly night. Her rosy cheeks were pale, her face drawn, and she stared at nothing.

Shocked, I took a seat beside her, settling into my usual spot without thinking and placing my hand on her arm to get her attention.

"Hey."

Startled blue eyes met mine, and I squeezed her arm comfortingly, my fingers digging into the thick knit of her sweater.

"Are you all right?" Would she even tell me if she was? I knew Carter was doing shit to her when he took her back to her room, but she'd been so resistant to me that I hadn't known how to intervene.

"Yes, fine."

But she didn't look fine, and the tight-lipped smile she gave me was anything but. I shook her arm gently, careful not to jostle her enough to jeopardize her grip on her coffee.

"You can tell me." *You can trust me.* The words were unspoken, but I hoped she understood that I'd do anything to help her.

Her gaze met mine and softened. I smiled encouragingly, but just as she opened her mouth to speak, Carter came into the room with one of his buddies. He laughed at something the other man had said, startling us. I jerked my hand back without thinking, uncertain if it was for Syl's sake or for mine.

"Hi yah, another beautiful day. Hey, babe." His arm rested on Syl's shoulder protectively, and I didn't miss her tense or the brief look of disgust flitting across her features. "Sup, man?"

I was surprised to find Carter addressing me. After Syl had gone back to him, I'd avoided any form of contact with the asshole. I gave a noncommittal grunt in reply, hoping he'd leave so I could keep talking to Syl. He didn't, instead pulling a chair around so he could sit next to Syl.

Obviously out of sorts, she tensed when he settled an arm across her shoulders, and I felt a deep growl rumbling into my chest. I quickly masked it with a cough when Syl shot me a glare.

I brought my hands under the table, pressing my white-knuckled fists into my thighs to keep my rising temper hidden for Syl's sake.

"Hey." There was nothing encouraging about her greeting to Carter, but he pulled her stiff body towards him and whispered something in her ear while watching me.

She cleared her throat and gave him a watery smile. "No, sorry, I'm on my period, so..." Her voice trailed off into a whisper, but I wouldn't have heard it if she'd continued at her normal volume.

Her period. Elated, I tried and failed to keep a smile from flitting across my face, pulling the brim of Cam's baseball cap forward to hide my expression. She'd be here for my second month of leave. I'd felt she would be, but part of me had worried she'd get pregnant this cycle and return home. I had just one more of her cycles before I would be forced to return as a watcher.

She didn't sound elated, though, and I studied the way she clung to her mug all the tighter. Her shoulders hunched forward to make herself small.

Carter had gone rigid beside her, his casual demeanor disturbed by her words.

"Okay, cool. Let me know when you're ready to get back in the saddle." He chuckled at his own joke, gesturing to his crotch as if we wouldn't understand he was the saddle, before standing up. I wanted to punch him in the dick. Now that Syl was on her period and not interested in sex, he headed off with his friend to the kitchen, abandoning her, and not caring for the way her eyes stayed downcast.

I bristled, glad he was gone, but annoyed I could still hear his aggravating voice and that of his friend in the kitchen. But I had Syl to think about.

"Can we go back to your room? Please?" My only thought was to get her out of here, somewhere quiet where she could unburden herself, and I could find a way to dispel the dark cloud she'd fallen under.

Syl's eyes shot to mine, and she nodded.

Just like that, I was back in. I followed close behind as Syl opened the door to her room and ushered me inside. She took a seat on the bed, her legs pressed together nervously. I sat beside her, leaving some space between us and trying not to rock the bed. But I needn't have worried about her spilling her drink. She still clutched it tightly in her hands like it was a lifeline.

"So, are you all right?" I repeated my question from before we were interrupted.

"Yeah, it's just. My period started last night, and—" She didn't elaborate, tilting her head up to the ceiling and breathing as though she had a weight pressing down on her chest.

"And?"

Tears streamed down her face, falling backwards to trace the contours of her face. Beautiful. An angel crying.

But I was no angel, and I wanted so badly to find out what exactly was bothering her so I could fix it.

"And I'm not pregnant, Bash. I-I—" Her words dissolved into tears, and she abandoned her mug to clutch me instead, falling into my chest. My arms wrapped around her shuddering body to offer her the comfort of my presence.

"You want that so badly to be a mother?"

She shook her head against me, crying all the harder, and I shut my stupid mouth, stroking the soft gossamer of her hair.

The love I had for the woman in my arms was endless, and I felt her pain as if it were my own, thankful she couldn't see the tears welling in my eyes and threatening to spill over to wet her head. I couldn't help her with what she wanted, and the pain of knowing just how fucking useless and defective I was cut deep. I tucked her into my chest, pulling her onto my lap so we pressed together, every inch of me wanting to comfort her, all the while knowing I couldn't be what she needed.

She wanted to be a mother, but I was no breeder. Just a watcher, an ineffective piece of equipment meant to ensure she moved along on her journey to motherhood. But at least I could do this. My useless body could be warmth and tenderness. I stroked her back, reveling in the way her soft body curled into mine, settling into me like it was perfectly natural. Like she felt safe with me.

Lost in thought, I didn't notice she'd fallen asleep until a soft sigh caught my attention. Her hair had come undone from its clip, the wildness of her waves unwilling to be contained, and I gently brushed a few ash-blonde tendrils aside, trying not to disturb her.

Now I knew why the crying girl cried, and why it could never be me who made her happy.

Chapter 21

I woke up alone, tucked into bed with the covers pulled up above my shoulders. Shaking my head, I cleared the fogginess of sleep, and the sting of embarrassment at losing it so completely in front of Bash. I was glad he'd left, that I didn't have to face him after weeping like a child and drenching his shirt with my tears.

Pain blossomed in my chest at the thought of his face twisting in distaste, and I closed my eyes tight to clear the image. That wasn't Bash. It was just my imagination and anxiety. No, he probably had a perfectly normal reason for deciding to leave, and at least I didn't have to explain myself further now that I was more clearheaded.

I couldn't afford to be such a victim. With only one cycle remaining, I needed to try even harder to be everyone's best friend. That is, until I could leave this place forever and banish everyone here from memory.

With a jaw-cracking yawn, I quickly dressed in some jean cutoffs and a white tank, throwing a shirt on top before I could stop myself. After my emotional outburst with

Bash, I was still feeling vulnerable. Weakened—like a piece of cracked glass held together with glue. The glue was busy hardening, and it would—I would—be okay. But all it would take was one more hit, and I'd have to start collecting the pieces and fitting them back together all over again.

So, I stayed in my room, flipping through my magazines as if they would magically yield new designs and not the same ones I'd pored over a thousand times before, until my mind settled. Focusing on the design work and fabrics instead of the challenges the next month would present. At last, I was bored and hungry, forcing me out into the hallway and down to the common room.

Bash leaned against the wall opposite the kitchen, his long legs crossed at the ankles in front of him. He wore a baseball cap tucked low over his face, so all I could see was the outline of his jaw and the press of his lips while he concentrated on the cardboard-backed paper he worked on. If I snatched the paper away and looked at what he was working on, would I find my face staring back at me?

I couldn't deal with Bash right now—didn't want to dredge up the emotional turmoil that had drawn me to seek comfort in his sturdy arms.

Jace fried something on the stove, and I walked over to the kitchen, intending to get myself something to eat.

"What's up, Syl?" His eyes barely flickered to me, too fixated on frying what appeared to be brown sausages with rapidly crisping edges, drowning in a sea of sizzling and popping fat.

The smell penetrated the disgusting air freshener florals and made my mouth water.

"Can I have some of that?"

Jace looked up and frowned, giving his food a protective shake in the pan. "Yeah, I could spare a half piece."

"Thanks."

"Here for another round, huh?"

He must've heard I was on my period. I supposed it was good the news was spreading so quickly through the dorm. This way, I wouldn't have to explain myself to anyone. I mulled his words over, getting lost in my head.

"Come on, Syl. Another round here isn't so bad."

I gave a careful nod, wishing I'd gone over to Bash or had some way to excuse myself from this conversation, but I was stuck waiting here while the meat bubbled and popped.

What he wanted from me, I didn't know, and I looked back towards the hallway to find Bash watching me. He quickly looked away, his cap shielding his face again as he continued his sketch.

"Naw, it's not so bad here." But I wasn't thinking about the dorms. I was thinking about the man still leaning against the wall, his concentration focused on his drawing. I wondered if the chairs were uncomfortable for someone of his height and if maybe that was the reason he chose to stand.

Jace cleared his throat, and I looked back at him guiltily.

"Yeah, not so bad at all." He studied my face, and I tried to bring The Party Girl to the forefront.

What would she say? Probably something about how great this place was. The music. The food. The drinks. The men. But the men had narrowed down to one man in terms of my interest, and I could never tell him *that*.

Never be exclusive.

You're here to party.

Get laid.

Get pregnant and get out.

That's what they told us, and it'd been my motto. Maybe it would be different if this was my second cycle, if everything in the dorm felt shiny and new. Back then, I hadn't been worried about getting pregnant, and it had been fun to cut loose and drink. But now? I just wanted to be done. My interest in Bash was the only thing with even a slight hold on me about this place.

"You know, it's-it's okay to feel things here."

My gaze shot to his, but I saw only concern in his eyes. Not judgment. This from Jace, who had taken my feelings and shoved them into a blender. The man who had made me one of his puppies.

"I know why I'm here. I don't need the reminder." My tone was harsher than I'd meant it, and I instantly regretted the reprimand. Jace had been nothing but kindness and friendship since he'd returned to the breeding program, and he'd saved me several times, providing male attention that had warded off the others without demanding anything in return. "Sorry Jace, it's just been a bad couple of days."

He nodded. "Food's ready." He grabbed two plates out from the drawer in front of him and dropped a greasy sausage onto one of them. Rolling, it left a smear of brown across its path. I licked my lips, my stomach rumbling at the thought of the greasy meat.

He'd given me a whole one after promising only a half, and I looked up to find him, smiling.

"I know all about bad days, Syl. Keep your head up, okay?" He patted me on the arm and moved to prepare his plate, emptying the pan of meat into a bowl.

I took my plate over to where Bash stood. It was better to get this over with than to have it worrying me when there were so many other things I should be thinking about.

"Hey, Bash."

He grunted in greeting, and I playfully went on my toes, trying to see what he was working on. But he just hugged his makeshift table closer to his chest, looking up at me with a coldness I'd never expected to see in his deep blue eyes.

"What is it?" His icy reception was so unexpected that I fumbled for words.

"I just—Well, I wanted to apologize for earlier. I wasn't myself and—"

He cut me off before he could continue. "It's fine. Don't worry about it." His words were clipped, his tone tight, and I studied him more carefully. He appeared relaxed, but he didn't look up. Like he couldn't be bothered.

My mouth hung open. He'd never cut me off mid speech like that, and he was already returning to his sketch in obvious dismissal.

"Hey, Bash." I put my hand on his forearm, trying to ignore how the physical connection with him always made me feel. I didn't need the split focus right now. "Everything okay?"

"Yeah, I'm fine. Great, in fact. I finally got some time alone with Rebecca on our run today."

On the run I'd slept through. I guess they'd let me skip it when they'd realized I was in my room alone. Always alone. Tears threatened, and I pulled my hand away from his arm. Thankful his eyes were fixed on his paper, and he didn't notice the way his casual mention of fucking someone else killed something inside.

But that something wasn't entirely dead, and it demanded to know more, to understand the change in Bash.

"That's good. So, you're happy then?"

It was stupid. We hadn't been together, hadn't even slept together since he'd left me begging for him on the forest floor. I had no claim on him, and he had none on me. He'd stood in the corner watching me get fucked without batting an eye. No one here was exclusive. I should be happy he'd spent some time with another woman. Maybe she'd draw some of his attention, and I could stop peering over my shoulder to find him watching me, always wishing it was him taking me and not whoever I was with.

Only, I wanted every bit of his attention on me.

Anything less was unacceptable.

"Yeah, sure." Still not looking up, Bash nodded, his lips pressed together, and his brow furrowed as if he were lost in deep concentration. A concentration I was clearly disturbing.

"Well, all right then. I guess I'll, um, see you later?"

"Yep."

And just like that, I felt more alone than I ever had in this place. More than when I'd been brand new and Jace had left me. More than when I'd returned from my house with my sister's state and my mother's abuse fresh in my mind. Bash had become a permanent fixture in this place, a touchstone that I'd depended on as my time slowly dwindled and the fear of failure became more difficult to deal with.

"I'll see you tonight?" Maybe it was the tremor in my voice at the possibility of even that time with him being lost, but Bash looked up to meet my eyes, and I saw a hint of sadness swirling in their depths.

"Of course." His tone brooked no argument, no consideration of stopping, and I gave a weak laugh, hoping the tears wouldn't fall and embarrass myself further. Imagining I had some stake in a man who was here to fuck whoever he could, whenever he could, and party as much as he wanted.

He was a breeder, as was I. Even if I wished things were different, there could only be one purpose in this place, and with my last cycle starting, I needed to remember that.

Now more than ever.

The tears shimmering in Syl's eyes almost compromised my resolve. Then I remembered the pain from earlier, and how it had been so great she'd cried herself into exhaustion, passing out against my chest. I had to protect her, to make sure she had everything she wanted and needed, and I couldn't be the one to do that.

She was better off without me.

Uncomfortable with the way she studied me and the plea I saw in her eyes, I shifted my weight onto my feet. If I asked her to, would she take me into her bed again? Could we resume where we'd left things when my asthma had flared up and forced me to abandon her in the woods? Something in her expression told me we could, but doing so would be selfish and cruel. I'd be dominating her time—me, a watcher—better spent on the one thing that would make her happy. Motherhood.

Smiling at my muse, my angel, I returned my attention to drawing, letting it remind me why I would deny myself her company.

"See you later?" There was a question in her voice that I hated.

Of course, she would see me later. She'd see me all day, watching her from the shadows, as I should. And she'd see me in the night, giving her drawing lessons. If I could superimpose myself onto her eyelids so she saw me every time she blinked, I'd do that too.

Sighing, I added a few more strokes, satisfied my sketch was near completion. I had a new crying picture to replace the ones I'd drawn of a smaller, grainier version of her on the monitor. This one was in a terrible amount of crushing detail. Syl's beautiful face, so alive and real and fucking sad that I wanted to wipe the tear running down her cheek away and do whatever I could to make things better. Only staying the fuck away from her was how I did that.

Fuck.

At least the baseball cap from Cam was proving helpful, and I tugged it down, ever aware of the cameras in the room.

Syl mostly kept to herself, and with my resolve firmly set, I did my best to stay out of her way. Knowing I would at least have her one last time at her breeding party was my only comfort. I'd leave right now if I wasn't a selfish bastard who wanted her badly enough to stay these last two weeks. But then I had it planned out. I'd claim food poisoning from some bad chicken wings and head back to wait out the final two weeks of my family leave at the cabin in the woods.

I'd leave Syl in peace, to have what she wanted and be who she wanted—things only achievable with my defective self out of the picture.

I'd known it was coming, but Family Day still crept up on me, and I didn't miss how miserable Syl seemed about going for her visitation. Pale-faced, she startled when her name and house were called, not sparing me a backward glance as she headed out the door. I took that as a good sign. My goal now was to be forgettable, to enjoy her presence while making my own as small as possible.

But then they called me, or rather, the man I was impersonating, and I was led down the path to a house I'd never seen in my life. With a smile and a nod, I dismissed the ruddy faced coordinator who had first brought me to Syl's breeding party.

The cabin was a walk from the house, and I took it slowly, letting the cool breeze soothe the burn of air freshener lingering in my lungs. The longer I stayed indoors, the worse the stuff affected me, and I knew they'd be replacing the air fresheners during the monthly deep clean. Which meant the shit would be new and more irritating to my tight chest when I returned.

A light drizzle started, and I stopped to tip my face back and feel the cooling droplets on my skin. The pine scent and birdsong of the outdoors had always soothed me, and I let it remind me that once I left the breeding program, left Syl, I would still have this.

Only, for my three years as a watcher, I'd barely stepped a foot outside. Would I go back to the way I was then, once Syl was out of my life? Or worse, would I return to my box of a room to find her on my monitor going through her heat with a new set of breeders?

A vise gripped my heart at the thought of once again being her watcher, but that's the role I was working to accept. I watched her now, not participating. Sure she wasn't a grainy image, and her laugh came through in surround sound, but it would be much the same on my soundless monitor.

Always an observer.

A defective like me could be nothing more.

My cabin came into view, and I gratefully climbed the two planks of wood serving as front steps to seek shelter within. I'd left a few articles of clothing inside and changed out of my wet gear before sitting heavily on the bed. The mirror I'd used to cut my hair to become Bash still stood on the counter and the food I'd brought but never used had gone moldy from being left out.

That was a travesty, and I looked away guiltily. Humans starved just outside our borders. I could've at least thrown it outside, but I'd been too consumed with the idea of meeting Syl to think it through. Not when my angel was so close to being within my reach.

Only, now I'd had her. While sinking into her body and hearing her laugh had truly been a taste of heaven, I knew just how far apart I was from her, and how stupid I'd been to think I could be worthy of her attention. I screwed my eyes shut at the pain of losing her, wondering if it would ever ease or if the dark place that had consumed my years as a watcher would rise up and welcome me home.

I could feel it threatening to claim me already. Every plan I made that brought me further from Syl also took me away from the spark of interest she'd pulled from me. An interest in a life that hadn't felt worth living before she'd cried on my monitor and her pain had made me feel something again.

With a sigh, I stood up and cleaned the cabin, taking the moldy food out into the woods and leaving it there, hoping some animal might find it palatable enough to eat before packing my scattered clothing and mirror. I left the cabin tidy and ready for me to return to once I'd said farewell to Syl.

SYL

Elise looked worse than she had when last I'd seen her. The hair on her head that peeked out through a colourful bandana, no doubt set to hide its thinning, was brittle and lifeless. Her arms, too, were thin, and the smile she gave me was skeletal.

"You could leave, Elise, run away. You don't have to stay in the fields."

But Elise just shook her head, a strange fire coming to life in her eyes—the most alive thing about her.

"No, Syl, what I'm doing is important. It's right. This is the only way I can serve the pack, and while it might be uncomfortable sometimes—"

"Uncomfortable? You call this uncomfortable? Elise, it's *killing* you." I'd wanted her to shout and scream when I laid out her fate so clearly, but Elise only smiled wide enough to show me a gap in her front teeth.

"Yes, but this is my choice now, Syl. I might die, but the pack will live on, and the pack is everything. Besides, I'm about to start my rest cycle. I'll heal up and get back to the fields soon." Elise's eyes took on a dreamy quality, but I didn't think she'd be able to rest up from this.

She was a living skeleton where once had stood my sister. What's worse, she sounded so sure of herself, and I hated it. I wanted to grab her arm, to shake her and scream until the fiery woman who had put on lipstick and danced naked under the full moon would rear her head, but I couldn't. Not when her arm was pathetically frail, and I worried what shaking her would do to her depleted body.

"I don't want this for you. Maybe you could ask them to release you."

"What? And accept banishment?" Elise shook her head firmly, her eyes clear. It wasn't much of a choice and I knew that. She could take her chances in the world—packless, friendless, likely hunted by starving humans for her meat—or she could face the certain death the poisoned fields were rapidly leading her towards.

What would I pick if faced with the choice? I had no idea what was out there, but now, seeing Elise, maybe a chance was worth the certainty of the horrific death she faced. Would I make that choice? I didn't know, but with one cycle remaining to conceive, the choice might be mine to face one day, and I turned it over in my mind. The pack was all I'd ever known, and while I'd met a human raider once who had tried to spear me as a child, the fear of them was foggy and old compared to the horrors ravaging Elise's body.

Her rainbow bandana came loose, exposing a patch of flakey skin on the side of her head where hair should've been growing—thick and luscious brown.

"I want my life to mean something more. I won't leave my pack, Syl. It's not who I am."

My mouth dropped, and I struggled to find the right words, the ones that would change her mind. But there weren't any, and I could only nod thoughtfully at her words.

Tears sprang to her eyes, and she pulled out a deck of cards from her pockets. "Now, do you want to play rummy?"

I fucking hated the game, but I knew this could be one of the last times I saw my sister alive. Nodding, I reached for the offered cards, shocked when I had a three king meld right off the bat. I was devising a strategy around my other cards, my focus on Elise and the glimmer of life I saw in her eyes when I heard the sound of someone approaching.

But I hadn't been to visit my mother, and she entered the room with an indignant huff.

"Not even coming to see me, Syl? This is family day, isn't it? Am I not family anymore?"

I'd seen the look on her face a thousand times before, and I didn't miss the way Elise hunched her shoulders forward to make her tiny body that much more invisible.

"Yes, and Elise is my family, too, Mother. So, I'm visiting with her."

My mother's face went red and blotchy with rage, and she reached down to roughly grab my upper arm and drag me to my feet. I twisted out of her grasp.

This place, this world, had left me pissed off and itching for a fight, and I wasn't going to take her punishment anymore.

"Don't fucking touch me. You've never been my family, Mother. You've been my bully. Now, you get the fuck back to your compartment, or I'll go to the administrator of 14F. Maybe no one would listen to a child, but they'd listen to a future pack mother, wouldn't they?" I grinned, relishing the way my mother's face went pale with fear.

"You wouldn't dare."

Laughter bubbled up in my throat, spilling out in a mad cackle. The situation was ridiculous. My sister, her *daughter*, sat beside me half dead, and my mother was worried about a reprimand from the higher-ups?

"I'd do that, and more." I took a step forward, getting into her face and staring her down. "If you lay a finger on me again, I swear to the goddess, I'll bite it right the fuck off. Now get out. I'm visiting with my sister."

Swallowing hard, my mother cast a bewildered look at where Elise sat on the couch, as if just realizing she was there, before turning and stumbling out the door.

I'd done it. Years of suffering her pinches and jabs, of allowing her to push me around, I'd broken free.

Sitting back down on the kids' couch, I turned to my sister. Elise held the cards she'd brought in trembling hands. I should've felt triumphant at having at least risen to my mother's challenge and bested her, but Elise's gaunt figure brought me back to my new sad reality. Her decision to stay meant I would lose her soon, and if I failed to become pregnant this cycle, I might be joining her. With a sigh, I settled back into the patchwork cushions.

"Come on, Elise, let's play."

Still emotionally reeling from standing up to my mother, Elise's state, and my own failure to conceive, I eyed the mattresses being spread across the floor with distaste.

Movie night. Of course.

Heading to the kitchen, I fished out a beer from the fridge. I needed the numbness that alcohol brought, and I chugged it back when Jace approached.

"Hey, you gonna be okay tonight?"

I eyed him, noting the concern in his eyes and fucking hating it.

"I'm fine, and I don't need you blocking the other guys anymore."

Jace cocked an eyebrow at me, reaching past to grab a bottle of his own.

"No? You sure? Because you're not looking so hot."

I wasn't, and I knew it. Seeing my sister and saying what I felt sure was a goodbye to her had taken its toll, especially because it was starting to become clear that I was looking into my own future. Every bit of iron willed resolve I had going into this cycle was starting to give way to despair. Six cycles and not a single conception, even with all the bed hopping I'd been doing. It seemed unlikely this would be the one to take, but I had to try.

With my emotions and my need to play The Party Girl so at odds with each other, the numbing haze of alcohol was my way forward, and I nodded at Jace.

"I'm sure, Jace. You don't need to worry about me anymore. Your job is done. Go, be free or whatever. Fuck around. Do your thing."

But this Jace was different from the one I'd known, and he lingered a moment before taking his beer and going to help with the movie night set up.

I didn't see Bash anywhere. His spot at the wall was sadly empty. I fucking hated how I still looked for him, as if I expected his recent coldness to have abated, and I'd find him smiling at me and welcoming me into his arms.

Into his arms. What a joke I was. With tears threatening, I reached into the fridge and pulled out another beer. Cracking the twist, I took a swig of the cool, frothy liquid, savouring the way it tingled on my tongue and the release of tension it would provide.

I needed this to drink until Elise and Bash faded from memory, and I could just sink into oblivion. Get myself to the place where I could successfully play The Party Girl for my remaining time.

One last cycle. One last try—and fuck everything if I wasn't going to give it my all.

Bash

When I returned to the dorm, Syl was getting plastered in the kitchen and the couch had been pushed back from the TV with mattresses getting spread out across the floor.

"Hey guys, what's going on here?"

Kevin dropped the mattress he was positioning with a thud and looked up with a grin.

"Movie night, man."

Brows furrowed, I tried to make sense of the room's rapid readjustment from couch space to one enormous bed.

"This is...for a movie?"

Annoyed, Kevin adjusted the mattress on the floor to align with the surrounding ones until all the mattresses were flush with one another.

"Yeah, man. Somebody found this old fucked-up horror movie behind their dresser. Something about a weird shadow hunting down and flaying a group of students. Should be good."

"I see, and won't people be missing their beds?" I gestured to the setup.

Kevin looked up at me, his eyes twinkling and the whites of his teeth shining.

"Oh, there are quite a few of us already planning to double and triple up. 'Sides, we can always sleep out here, right?" He laughed, grabbing a pillow from the couch and fluffing it before he threw it onto the middle of the mattress he'd just placed.

Right. This place was so strange sometimes. Just when I was getting used to the bone-rattling music they played every night, now we were hanging out and watching a movie like a group of kids. With a shrug, I kept my back to the camera in the painting on the far wall and sidled around the setup, making my way to the kitchen to grab a bite of food.

But when I opened the fridge, it was filled with fresh beers already chilling, and I grabbed one by its icy neck. I'd had alcohol from time to time, but worried I wouldn't be able to keep my wits under its effects. I hadn't had all that much since coming to the dorm. With thoughts of saying goodbye to Syl still tormenting me, I decided I'd indulge. Just this once.

At the very least, it might make this crappy sounding movie a bit more interesting.

But just as I was about to claim a spot on the couch, the same shaggy-haired blonde guy who had interrupted Syl and me in my room stepped in my path.

"Hey, man. It's Bash, right?"

I eyed him up and down, noting the way he fidgeted with his hands and shifted on his feet.

"Yeah, who wants to know?" I checked my hat, pulling it forward to shield my face, though I knew I'd put the camera to my back.

"Jace. We met a while back. Anyway, that's not important. Can I talk to you for a sec? Alone?"

Palms growing sweaty as I pondered what reason he'd have for wanting a private audience, I said, "Sure."

I followed Jace down the hallway. He was a relative stranger in this place, so what could he have to say? Did he find some kind of clue that I didn't belong here? I felt for the puffer in my jogging pants, feeling the comforting shape of hard plastic through the cotton.

With a nervous cough, Jace led me into his room and gestured for me to have a seat on his unmade bed. Unwilling to see just how popular Jace was with the ladies, I declined his offer to sit with a shake of my head and looked at him expectantly.

"It's about Syl."

Surprised, I stood a little straighter, my whole being activated by that one word. "Okay."

"Well, she's..." Jace licked his lips nervously, rolling his shoulders like he was buying time to think. "She's off somehow. Behaving weird, and I'm worried about her."

Behaving weird. That wasn't much to go on, and I wracked my brain for the last time I'd seen my angel. She'd been clearly nervous about going to visit with her family, but otherwise her normal self.

But Jace, a legit member of Pack Breeders 103C, couldn't know just how interested I was in her. I shrugged my shoulders, leaning back against his wall and doing my best to be nonchalant.

"Okay, so?"

Jace's mouth fell open and his eyes widened comically, surprise so evident on his face that I knew he'd never had to be discreet. Never had to hide anything from anyone. Never had to play a role in order to survive.

I hated him for it. This legitimate breeder who had been given everything in life that I hadn't.

"So, I've seen you watching her, man. I figured maybe you'd care."

I stood away from the wall. "Guess you figured wrong."

Jace's mouth worked. "Well, she cares about you, and she's a good person, so maybe you could show some decency and listen for a minute."

That stopped me in my tracks. How the fuck did this guy know Syl cared about me? The thought of her caring for me, of pining for me even a little bit, stayed my hand on the knob.

"All right, I'm listening." Turning half my body towards him, I waited for Jace to say more, but I kept my hand on the knob so he'd know I wasn't planning to stay long.

"She's acting erratic. Off. I don't know what she'll do, but just help me keep an eye on her?"

My heart clenched at the look of concern on his face. "And what's she to you? Why are you so invested?"

Jace looked away guiltily. "Because I owe her."

He kept his eyes averted, and I realized that was as much as I was going to get from him.

"I'll watch her." I turned the knob, and as I left, I heard him mutter a thanks before the door clicked shut.

The common room was filling up, and I took my beer over to secure the last spot on the couch. Syl was perched on the arm at the other end, beer in her hand, and laughing and touching the guy beside her.

Was she okay? She looked pretty damned good to me. Her loose ash-blonde waves framed a flushed face. Nothing seemed amiss, but I thought of Jace's words and looked for any signs of strangeness, noticing how she seemed to be too into the guy beside her. Handsy even.

Speakers blared to life, and whoops from excited movie watchers echoed around me. Somebody had set up a surround sound for movie night, and of course I'd sat right the fuck next to one. Probably why nobody wanted this spot.

Syl moved onto the guy's lap, and I had to look away, fixing my eyes on the TV to see a man being brutally murdered. His attacker followed him to the ground and stabbed him repeatedly in a spray of brownish red that didn't quite look like blood. I laughed, really laughed, at the sight. Fucking cheap effects. The beer was doing its work, and my muscles loosened as it worked its way into my system.

The man's shadow came to life just as somebody handed me another beer. Fuck yeah. Shadow motherfucker took revenge on the murderer, somehow peeling off his skin with shadow power? I didn't get it, but the peeled face of the murderer was very satisfying. Only the shadow didn't stop there, drifting out through a window like a puff of smoke.

A soft moan that haunted my dreams caught my attention, and I looked over to see Syl with her pants off, riding the cock of the guy on the other end of the couch.

Fuck. She faced the screen, her mouth parted as the guy pulled up her shirt to play with her breasts. The guy in the middle had stopped watching the film and started playing with Syl's other breast. She moaned beautifully under his touch.

Perfection. That's what she was. An angel that I could only covet from my position on the ground. My cock strained as the man she was riding helped lift her up and down on his length, and the guy in the middle pulled down his pants to give his cock a pull.

The movie forgotten, I watched Syl in profile, drinking in the way she placed her hands on his thighs to lift herself and drive him back into her body. A body I wanted so badly to taste. My cock was rock hard by the time she came with the sweetest little coo, and the guy pulled her to him, squeezing her breast mercilessly as he worked through his own release.

Shit. This was too much. I had to pick the fucking couch. Syl turned around with a drunken awkwardness and settled on the lap of the guy next to me. Her thigh settling next to mine made me jump, and it was all I could do to stare as she positioned him at her entrance.

He was a smaller guy with curly brown hair, and he pressed his head back into the cushions, groaning as Syl took him into her body. She gave a chuckle, grabbing the beer from his hand and chugging it before lifting herself up and sliding back down along his length.

I should leave. I should really fucking leave, but I couldn't. My body simply wouldn't obey my commands. Too intrigued at the possibility of having her again, right here, right like this in front of everybody, even if they weren't really watching us. Hell, just having her again after pushing her away and planning to leave.

Aroused beyond imagining, I drank the rest of the beer and reached down to set it on the floor beside me.

It was going to be a long fucking wait for my turn.

Lost in sensation, the world felt far away and yet impossibly close. I swayed back to find the man in front of me swirling as the dizziness set in. I laughed, sitting more forward and working his cock as I pressed his permanently confused face into my breasts.

It was like he'd never done this before, and I squinted at him, trying to bring his name to memory. But fuck it, whether he was new or had been here all along, he was just another cock for The Party Girl to impale herself on. I reached down to play with my swollen clit, still tingling from my last orgasm.

Yeah, he was close already. Definitely not someone who had been fucking around all that much in the dorm, and I picked up the pace, feeling myself getting closer to cresting. Fuck boy came before I got there, shooting himself into me with panting breaths and an "ah, ah, ah", his legs shaking as he spilled his load.

Maybe this would be the one who got me pregnant, this boyish man who didn't know what he was doing. I'd have his children and be safe. A tear threatened, and I laughed through it, burying myself in his neck.

But the man was spent, and there was another waiting beside me. I turned to face the screen, not surprised when I found he had already pulled his pants down in readiness. He was large, and his hands matched his body, taking hold of my hips as he speared me on his eager cock.

The stretch of him burned before melting into a feeling of fullness that made me gasp. His hands moved up my body, cupping a breast gently, before pinching a nipple. Fuck, that was hot. The mix of rough and gentle was exactly what I'd been craving, and I let the drunken haze take over, settling into the sensation as I bounced up and down on his large cock.

Only, it felt too fucking good. Like, really good. The kind of fuck I'd been craving, and I wanted more than his hands on me. I wanted every bit of his flesh to touch mine.

I pulled away briefly to turn and face him. Burying my face in his neck, I settled back on his cock with a relieved gasp as the fullness of him returned. Then he tilted my chin up and brought his mouth to mine, his hands moving up and down my back. The alcohol made everything blur, but the sensation between us stood out, refusing to be numbed.

Fucking heaven. I stayed completely still as my body adjusted to him, not able to comprehend increasing the friction between us. I wanted to soak in this moment, but the man was eager, cupping my ass and lifting me to thrust upwards. It was all I could do to cling to him, pulling his head to my chest, knowing my long fingernails were scraping into his scalp but not caring.

He lifted me higher. More friction. More tension. Swirling and rising within me. It would break me. This feeling was too much. There was a familiarity to it, and a strange sense of relief, like I'd been gone too long and had finally come home. I pulled back to taste his lips, and my drunken mind recognized who it was.

Bash. The dark blue of his eyes, filled with feral need, stared back at me. Emotions swelled up to the surface, and I stroked his cheek, seeing him more and more clearly. Bash, on the couch, his lips swollen from my kisses, his cock moving in and out of me in a maddeningly steady rhythm that I knew would be lost once he gave in.

The alcohol was supposed to numb this, to take away all feelings, but now I felt them more keenly. I leaned forward to kiss Bash, rubbing my thumb across his cheek.

If he wouldn't set the rhythm, I would. Faster, I worked him, my hands moving up and across his chest. My fingertips knowing the shape of him from a memory that had been rapidly fading.

Not anymore. I gasped into his mouth as his thumb found my swollen clit and circled it. Faster. Harder. I barreled towards it, the fire in me rising up to meet him. He wrapped me tight, looping his muscular arms under mine and gripping my shoulders. He lifted me and pulled me down hard enough to fill the air with the slapping of flesh.

The Party Girl had been fucking around endlessly since I'd been with Bash, but now it felt like I hadn't had sex in months. My body was achingly desperate for each stroke of his, and then he was slamming me down and groaning into my neck. The release took me, my walls clenching on him even as he throbbed inside of me.

But I wasn't done with him. Would never be done with him. I pulled back to kiss him, stroking his face, his body like I had to convince myself he was real. He was doing the same—kissing me back with a heart-wrenching tenderness as he explored my body with trembling hands.

"Bash." His name felt so good on my lips, in my mouth, and he trailed kisses along my jaw and across my neck, worshiping every inch of my skin. I'd missed him, and the ache in my chest was soothed by his presence. "Where have you been?"

Goddess, I sounded so stupid, like he hadn't been right here in the dorm this whole time, watching me get fucked by other men but not trying to take me himself. Not trying to chase me during a run—just not there.

He didn't answer me, and I yelped when he nibbled along my neck, the sharp edge of his teeth on the sensitive skin awakening something in me. I arched my neck towards him, and he licked along the nip, soothing it with his tongue.

Could he taste my blood? I wanted him to, wanted his teeth in me.

"Syl, I—"

The husky edge of his voice sent a shiver through me. I pulled back to study his face.

"What?" He'd been about to say something, and I wanted that, wanted some kind of explanation for his behaviour, but he just stared at me. His eyes drifted from mine and down to my lips until he leaned forward to kiss me.

Only opening a conversation with him had swept back the curtain, revealing the depths of hurt he'd left me with when he'd grown cold after I'd cried myself to sleep in his arms.

"No, you tell me what. I cry myself to sleep in your arms, show you I'm a person, and suddenly you don't want me anymore?" The painful reminder of that moment before he'd changed so completely had ruined the fragile peace between us. Tears flowed, rolling down my cheeks, and I sobbed, hoping he'd explain himself, wanting him to talk to me, but he didn't. His lips pressed together. He studied me while I waited.

Too fucking long. I'd waited too fucking long, and I'd done exactly what I'd promised myself I wouldn't do. Had sex with Bash again.

Tears still streaming from my cheeks to dribble pathetically from my quivering chin, I stood up with a sob. Everything in me rebelled at the loss of comfort and contact. But I had a shred of dignity left, and Bash could offer no explanation for his cruelty. Stumbling back towards my room, I sobbed my way down the hallway, crawling into the softness of my bed and curling into a tight ball.

Sex was supposed to be just that, sex. A bodily need being fulfilled by another. Sex, I could do. Sex, I was used to. The problem was, with Bash, it didn't feel like sex.

It felt like love.

CHAPTER 22

Still raw from the night before, I woke up sore and with blood on my arm from an unknown cut that had apparently stopped bleeding. Stumbling down the hall, I went straight to the little coffee maker, scooping myself some beans and grumbling a hello at anyone who passed.

Not that I didn't drink coffee every day, but after a night of drinking and then what had happened with Bash, I needed it desperately. Once I had a cup in hand and doctored it to my tastes, I slid onto a barstool with my back to the hall. Fuck, I hoped Bash didn't show up, that he was still sleeping or just choosing to stay in his room. My eyes craved the sight of him, my ears the sound of his voice, but his lack of explanation the night before had made me more certain than ever of how dangerous he was for me.

My weary heart couldn't take the sight of him. Not right now. So, when a hand settled on my shoulder, and Carter slid onto the barstool next to me, I stiffened beneath his touch.

"Hey, babe. I missed you at movie night. I thought we'd said you were to come to my room when it was done."

Yeah, I suppose I should feel lucky he'd let me fuck around, but just then, the possessive way he leaned his weight across my shoulders pissed me off.

He growled and pulled me closer, his hot breath hitting my ear. "I have the perfect punishment in mind for your disobedience."

Pulling away, I straightened, curling my hands around the porcelain mug in my hands and savouring the last bits of warmth it possessed.

"No thanks. I'm not in the mood."

He laughed. A full-on, head thrown back laugh, his brown hair bouncing with the motion, and I stared at him in surprise. He looked crazy and hot, but I couldn't care. He sat forward, his arm on my shoulder once more.

"Your mood doesn't matter. You'll get your ass into my room in five minutes."

Fuck this.

Why had I ever tolerated this asshole of a man?

Furiously, my heart threatening to pound its way out of my chest, I flung his arm off my shoulder and snarled in his face. "You don't fucking touch me, you donkey-fucking, cunt-sickening asshole." My finger jabbed into his shocked face, and I was on my feet without knowing how I'd gotten there. "Keep your punishment and shove it up your ass. Maybe use the spiked one." I cupped a hand as if I was sharing a secret. "I've heard you like that one best." I turned to leave, a chorus of laughter following me all the way back to my room.

It wasn't until I was in my room, sitting on my bed with clenched fists twisting at the fabric of my thin pajama shorts, that I realized what I'd done.

I'd lost him, lost Carter, and with him went the status I relied on to get laid as often as possible. Well, fuck it. My heart didn't just pound anymore, it throbbed—the pain of Bash's repeated rejection cut deep, and Carter had come at me on the wrong day at the wrong time.

I was still The Party Girl, but I wouldn't put up with his shit anymore.

Not now.

Not ever.

Fuck it, fuck them, and *fuck* Bash. My eyes burned with the need for tears, but I ignored them, pulling out my magazines. By the end of this month, I'd be done with this place once and for all. I'd either have conceived or bound for the fields, but at least I wouldn't have to deal with this bullshit anymore.

But the bullshit was never ending, and I knew I'd have to face Bash at some point.

He was already outside for the daily run when I showed up, his tight ass easily standing out to me in the lineup. I took up a place on the far end, trying not to look over at him. I swear I could feel his eyes on me, but I also noticed something strange. The two guys beside me weren't hitting on me or talking to me, but to each other. I recognized Jessie, and he smirked, saying something to his friends and meeting my eyes briefly. I felt left out of the joke and I sauntered up to them, expecting to be let in on it.

But they huddled up without a word, and I was met with Jessie's broad back, still shaking with laughter.

Luckily, I didn't have long to dwell on the asshole epidemic sweeping the line before Carter stood before us and announced the run's start.

Gleefully, I shifted, falling with a sigh onto my four paws, and relishing the pain and pleasure of my spine twisting and reforming. A glance back as I hit the tree line showed Bash's brown wolf veering to the right. I refused to let the pain of his choice hurt me the way it had, and I took off at a steady lope, hoping to lose myself in the trees and avoid the others.

The strain of my overworked muscles was just what I needed, and I felt much more clear-headed by the time I returned to the great brown building. Bash could do what he wanted. I'd made a mistake sleeping with him again, letting him get in my head, but no more. Already, signs of my heat were starting—my nipples darkening and sweat staining my sheets at night. At most, it would be a week before they would induce us in a group again to keep us all on the same point of our cycle.

I could do this. Just keep sleeping with whoever was willing for a few more weeks, and hopefully—

Fear clenched my chest, and I shifted back to my human form to distract myself, rolling my shoulders as the joints resettled into their new position. I wouldn't think about the consequences of failing.

This was it. The cycle I would become pregnant. I'd leave this place with a child, or children, in my belly and be done with it forever. Done with Carter, Kevin, Jessie, and all the rest. Finished with booze and back to an environment that made sense, where I would use my newfound drawing skills to make my designs bigger, better. More detailed and easier to work off of.

We'd just gotten into figure drawing, and while I now needed to end things with Bash if I was to push him out of my mind, I was much better than I'd been. I was capable. I was strong. I didn't need him anymore, not when I was a few weeks away from being free.

I had to think that way. A few weeks, that was all, and I would be pregnant. Somehow, some way, I would make it happen. Ensure my success. I wouldn't end up like Elise. I refused.

This time, I would cut Bash out completely. Rid myself of him like a snake shedding its skin. I didn't need him or the vulnerability he so effortlessly pulled from me. I could sacrifice a few weeks' worth of lessons and just pretend he didn't exist. I could, and I would, but I caught myself looking at the flattened grass where he'd lined up to see if he'd come back to retrieve his clothes, and felt a sting when I found he'd already retrieved them.

Fuck it. With an irritated shake of my head, hard enough to jolt my neck, I threw on the tank top and the slinky thigh-revealing skirt I'd worn out and headed back inside, hurrying to catch up with Kevin who was just about through the door.

He didn't give it the extra push to keep the door from slamming, and I found that strange. It was such a basic gesture of courtesy, but then, maybe he hadn't noticed me run up.

Inside, everyone gathered around the counter with beers in hand. Carter sat casually on a stool with one of the other breeding females on his lap—a petite blonde with a pointed nose and unusually long eyelashes, wearing a wrap dress I knew could easily be undone.

No one looked up when I approached, and when I went to reach into the center to grab a beer, I was met with a wall as the guys closed the gap and continued their conversation.

What the fuck?

More people filed in behind me, the remaining few who had lingered in the outdoors, no doubt lost in the midst of passion or enjoying the fresh air for a few extra moments. I ignored them, trying to find a new gap in the group, but when the guys there moved together to block me, as well, I knew something was wrong.

Panicked, I went up to the last remaining gap. Of course, it would be next to Carter.

"Hey, can I get a beer? Good run, right? So, now it's time to party?" I tried to sound enthusiastic, but my voice wobbled, and my palms were sweaty as I moved towards the opening by Carter.

"Party? With you?" Carter laughed, merriment twinkling in the emerald green eyes I'd once found so fetching.

"Yeah, I mean, why not? We always party, right? We have a good time."

Carter's smirk curled around the mouth of his beer as he took a swig. "No one wants to party with you, Syl. Fucking defective, infertile. If we fuck around with you, we'll never get out of here, right, guys?" A chorus of laughter echoed Carter's sentiment, and a few of the guys glanced back at me, the same disdain reflected in their eyes.

"What? No, I'm not defective. I'm here to—"

"You're here to what? Breed? You've been here for how many cycles, Syl? It's ridiculous really. Here I was taking pity on you and fucking you when nobody else would, but to be honest, babe, it's pathetic, and I want to get back to my squad, you know?"

My eyes burned. Pain in my chest flared to life. Infertile. Defective. Not worth their time, and the guys were going along with it. Smiling and nodding their agreement, and clinking beers like I hadn't shared my body with them, given myself over to them in trust.

Apparently, none of that mattered to them. I spun just before the first tear fell, and tore off for my room with sobs already choking my throat. Their laughter followed me down the hall, and I swear I could still hear it when I slammed the door. Those fucking assholes.

Alone in my room, I let the tears flow freely, taking great heaving, gasping breaths as I fought to breathe through the pain of their words and their rejection. Defective. Infertile. Their hateful words echoed in my mind, each repeat causing more damage to the delicate structures within.

How dare they? I'd tried everything I could to succeed in this place, to please them, to be the breeder I'd been chosen as, and now they abandoned me.

The Party Girl had died with their rejection. No one was going to party with her now, to stuff her full of their cum until she could take no more, which meant my chances of getting pregnant this cycle just plummeted.

Shaking and cold, I wrapped my arms around myself in a hug I sorely needed. This place, these people, I hated them. Violently.

With total clarity of my hopeless situation, I stood and yanked open the top drawer of my dresser. Pushing my underwear aside and all those slinky pieces I'd chosen to entice the guys until I found the vial I'd stolen from the coordinator during my last breeding party.

If I took this, if I induced a heat, they'd have no choice. I could do it. Induce a heat twice and double my chances.

The glass vial slid between my shaking fingers, but I managed to hold it firm and pull the cork stopper. I'd show them. If they wouldn't have me willingly, I'd force them.

The door banged open, and I startled as I turned to find Bash, his face a mask of fury and pain.

Those fucking pieces of shit. Overhearing Carter's damning words to Syl had frozen me to the spot with rage. Then she'd taken off, tears streaming down her cheek and their laughter seeing her out. I hadn't been in a place to chase her.

No, fuck them. I'd walked right up to Carter, shoved the girl off his lap and punched him in his stupid mouth. I shouldn't have done it. They might look into me if I needed to be called for discipline, but the sight of him toppling off the bar stool to land sprawled out on the floor had been worth it.

Piece of trash didn't deserve to be in the same universe as Syl.

No one had said anything or challenged me, and Carter stayed down cupping his rapidly swelling nose, so I turned my attention to Syl. Rushing into her room, I found her standing at the dresser fisting something in her hand. With a concerned look out in the hall to ensure I hadn't been followed by anyone seeking revenge, I shut the door behind me and gave Syl my full attention.

"Syl? Are you okay, baby?" The term of endearment sprang to my lips before I could stop it, and I ground my teeth in annoyance with myself. Syl barely responded. She'd glanced up at me when I'd banged open her door, but now her eyes were fixed on whatever she held in her hand.

"This is the only way, Bash."

Frowning, I took a cautious step forward, getting my first glimpse of the vial she held and the purple flower within.

"Syl, no. That's—where did you get that? Those aren't supposed to be used outside of the breeding rooms after prep, and with supervision. You can't take tha—"

"I can and I will." She looked up at me, her eyes red rimmed and burning with rage. "I'm sick of people telling me what I can and can't do. They don't want to fuck me? I'll fucking make them." She brought the vial to her nose, and though I reached out intending to stop her, she managed a deep breath before I could wrestle it from her hands.

"No, please. Syl, this isn't the way. Those guys are complete assholes. Syl?"

Her eyes had gone hazy, and she pushed her way past me to the door. "Hey, door's open, and I'm in heat if anyone wants to fuck me." She was already yelling between bouts of sobs before the door was open, and I threw myself at it, pinning it closed. She glared at me, tugging on the knob as if she could shift my weight and pull it open. Why she wanted to prostrate herself before the sea of filth in the other room, I couldn't fathom, but I wouldn't let her debase herself so completely. She was worth so much more than that.

"You're not doing this." My words came out in a growl, but I was instantly disarmed when she dropped to the floor and buried her face in her hands, the shaking of her shoulders causing her ash-blonde waves to move around wildly.

"Why not? What good am I if I can't even fucking conceive? Who the fuck would want me now?" Her face crumpled, and I found myself on the floor with her, pulling her into my lap and wrapping my arms around her heaving body.

"I want you, Syl. I've always wanted you, and I couldn't give a shit about anything else."

She cried harder, turning to me and pressing herself into my neck. I was barely aware of it when her sobs turned into ragged pants, and her skin burned straight through the thin material of her tank top.

Gasping at the bolt of arousal she triggered in me, I rubbed her back soothingly, my cock straining for her. I adjusted her in my arms, fighting through the rapidly growing arousal she was pulling from me. Safe. She had to be safe, and the bed, she could fall off. Fuck. This was a terrible idea. The floor was best. When had she drank water last? Food? Before being induced, breeders were required to eat and drink at preplanned intervals, so their body could weather the lengthy heat process. I should know, it'd been my job to make sure they made it through the heat safely.

With a growl, I gathered her in my arms and stood. Thank fuck she'd had a couple of water bottles in the corner of her room. Syl arched in my arms, and I groaned right along with her as I stumbled my way across the room, unable to let her down and break our connection even for a moment. I had to do this while she was still lucid enough to accept it.

One-handed, I pulled her comforter onto the floor to use as padding, and laid her down onto it, grabbing the two water bottles as I dropped to my knees.

"Drink this." My voice wasn't my own—the deep gravelly tone was unrecognizable, but I'd gotten the words out. Syl looked at me in confusion, the heat madness taking hold. "Drink this," I repeated, cracking open the bottle and pulling her into my arms. Cradling her and tilting her head back, I slowly trickled water into her waiting mouth. At least her mouth was open, but her eyes were still frantic, darting around, and the occasional arching and tensing of her muscles meant we spilled about half the bottle. But I'd gotten some water into her.

Syl sobbed with frustration, my cock hard against her back.

"One more and I'll fuck you," I promised. Cracking the next bottle and trying to keep my hand and her head steady as I worked to get my water into her system.

By the time we'd managed the next bottle, I was feral for her. I threw it aside, not caring where it landed, barely processing the smack of plastic on hardwood somewhere at my back. Pushing Syl on her back, I fumbled with her pants and mine. Needing to feel her, to sink into the wet heat that called me home. I groaned when I managed to pull both my pants and her skirt low enough that they were around our ankles. I kicked them off, settling back against her.

I kissed the skin of her neck, and tasted the salt of sweat already beading on her skin before sinking into her and losing myself to the heat.

CHAPTER 23

SYL

Need. Want. Desire.

Every thought was consumed by it and being held down while Bash poured water down my throat was torture. I could feel how hard he was for me. How easy it would be for him to fill me and slake the terrible emptiness quickly turning painful the more my heat took hold.

Then the bottle was gone, and I felt his hands at my waist. Words escaped me, forgotten, unable to be formed, and I whimpered for him to hurry. It was all I could manage, and I hoped he understood. Then he was inside of me, and the emptiness faded. The stretch of him satisfying the monster clawing at my insides.

Friction. I needed it. But he stayed seated, licking at my neck and panting. His hot breath danced across my feverish skin. I couldn't scream. Screams, just like words, were lost to me, and it was all I could do to wiggle beneath him in a silent plea.

Then he was moving in and out of me. Never all the way out, pushing in deep to fill me and withdrawing just enough that he rubbed against me in the most fulfilling way. An orgasm crested, and I held him as it shuddered through my body, knowing it wouldn't be the first. He'd slammed the door. No one else was coming. I had only Bash, only this one time, and then I would have to wait for him to recover.

The thought of being empty and at the mercy of his stamina made me weep, but then he pressed in again with a grunt, and I saw stars. It was all I could do to cling to his back and feel his movements as he pounded into me, chasing his own release.

He found it, and the throb of him within me sent me higher. I gasped as I lost myself in the sea of sensation. Prepared to cry out when he pulled away—only he didn't.

Instead, he nuzzled into my neck, kissing it and nipping in an equal measure that sent firecrackers chasing along my nerves.

The ache for more friction was painful, and I arced my back, settling into the familiar sensation of burning alive and shooting towards heaven that the heat provided. Bash rose up with me, becoming hard again, and it felt so good I could cry. May have been crying. I didn't know. Couldn't tell. I was barreling towards heaven again, squeezing my eyes shut and crying out as the tension within me unraveled, and I shattered.

He pulled out, but he didn't go far, like he was stuck in place. Never leaving me empty as he rolled his hips against mine.

It never ended. All animal instinct, our bodies moved with one purpose. The heat consumed us both, but the continued contact with him never left me empty and waiting for the next man to come. It made the heat bearable. Enjoyable even. Each time the heat consumed me, he came with me, his body satisfying my needs just as they started. I clung to him, not sure where we were or what existed beyond us. Beyond sensation. Our hearts beat in sync. Two bodies, now one. Combined. Interwoven like a piece of knitting with no loose strings. Something kept us together, held us with a force beyond either of our understanding.

He slammed into me, moaning, and I clung to his shoulders as an orgasm tore through me. His mouth on mine, pure fire in his kiss and awakening a need in me that couldn't have been from the heat. It was as if he, too, was going through a heat and bringing me into it surely as I brought him into our own.

Hours passed. Or maybe days. I didn't know. Every moment was pleasure and pain, need and satisfaction, bliss and famine—until, at last, I lay boneless on his chest, his warmth a soothing comfort as sleep claimed me.

When I awoke, he slept soundly beneath me, and I looked up to study his face. Bash had given me himself, completely and wholly. Something nobody else had done. What would have happened if I'd managed to follow through with my plan to leave the door open and hope those assholes in the common room lined up to take turns?

What if they hadn't? They might have left me in here, suffering in agony through my heat. Alone and afraid.

Bash hadn't let that happen. He'd been there for me, and for the first time, I understood what a heat was meant to be. A bonding between mates, a time of togetherness and peace. I wondered if it would be less intense without an induction. Smiling, I rested my chin on my hands, trying not to move and disturb Bash while he slept.

He really was beautiful, and I wanted to look at him a while longer. My man. Mine. The thought was a truth my body and soul had whispered to me from the moment I'd met him as The Stag, but it hadn't been something I'd been willing to acknowledge until this moment. I'd been right. He would be the man to get me pregnant. He had to be.

Because he was my breeder, and he'd bred me. Fucked me so deep and so well that the heat had passed without its usual terror. Once I was pregnant, I'd be released from this place, but Bash would still be mine. Even if we weren't together, because something inside of us had joined during the heat. The thought put a smile on my face.

Bash's hair was mussed with one long strand hanging almost to his eye, and I gently brushed it aside. He moved towards my hand like he'd sensed it, a small moan rumbling through his chest. He stayed asleep, but his sound had affected me, a shiver of arousal running through me almost reflexively.

I wasn't surprised to find him half hard, and I slid down, my arms on either side of him as I tried not to wake him. I wanted him to wake with his cock in my mouth. A thank you for the way that he'd come to my rescue even when I'd lashed out at him for it. I eyed his cock hungrily, tracing the curves with a light touch. He was long and deliciously thick. My tongue traced along a vein, and he groaned again.

With a chuckle, I admired my prize, trying to decide which part of him to put my mouth on next—when I saw it. Shocked, I peered closer, not able to believe the truth of what I was seeing.

It couldn't be.

There was no way.

But there it was. Scars. A crisscross pattern of scars just underneath Bash's cock, the kind that meant—

No. Not this.

I looked up to find Bash blinking blearily at me. He caught my wrist and sat up in one motion, pulling me along with him until we were both sitting opposite one another.

My mind worked as I tried to think of any other explanation for what I'd seen. Bash studied me, his grip uncomfortably tight on my arm, his shoulders stiff with tension.

"Bash, why would you—why would you have scars there?" Scars. It was hard for lycans to form scars, so hard in fact that there was a special herb used for one kind of delicate surgery they didn't want us healing from.

The kind they gave to defectives to ensure their genes wouldn't accidentally make it into the next generation.

Bash's jaw stood out as he tensed, his eyes falling to catch on where he gripped my wrist. Loosening his hold, he looked up at me with shining eyes.

"Syl, listen, I'm—"

But I lunged forward before he could tell me what I knew he was about to, pressing a finger to his lips.

Shaking my head miserably, the tears threatening once more, I stared at him and let the shock wash over me.

"How? Why? What are you doing here?" Slowly, I removed my finger so he could speak, hating the way the wetness of his mouth had tingled up my arm.

"I'm—I was a watcher. Your watcher, Syl. I-I came here to meet you."

A watcher. The lowest of low amongst the defectives, those who were too weak for the fields, but Bash wasn't weak. He was a big guy. He was strong. I didn't understand. But the reality of what this meant sank in, and I sat back hard on my heels.

"You were my watcher." I was in a haze, my vision unfocused as my sight turned internal.

"Yes, I was your watcher, and when I saw you on my monitor, I knew I had to come here to meet you. Syl, everything was for you, to be here with you, to know you."

My eyes shot to his. "To fuck me."

He grasped both my upper arms hard enough that I winced. "No, Syl, that's not why I came here. I needed to just speak to you, to understand you better."

Tears sprang loose, and I swiped them away. "I thought I knew you, Bash. I thought you were going to be the one."

The one. The one to get me pregnant, to buy me my freedom with a child or two I could take back as a prize to the family compound.

But that had never been possible with him, not once had it been possible to conceive because he'd been prevented from siring a child. It was too much, and I covered my face with my cool hands, letting them soothe the feverish skin as I sobbed.

How could he have done this to me? On my last two cycles, I'd wasted so much time sleeping with a man who couldn't get me pregnant, no matter how much he wanted to or how hard he tried.

"You're-you're an imposter!" I let the accusation fly, parting my hands to see the words hit home in a bloom of pain.

"Yes. I am."

Realization coursed through my veins, and I tried to stumble to my feet, but my leg gave way. Bash tried to catch me.

"Don't help me," I shouted. "I don't want *your* help." Eventually, I made it onto my legs, still shaky from the intensity of my heat, and pulled open my nightstand drawer. I whipped out the magazine I'd found in my room, the one someone had taken and filled in the other half of the dress.

The paper wrinkled in my fist as I held it out to him, but I couldn't give a shit. Bash's guilt was apparent in the way his eyes shifted from mine, his lips pressing together in a tight line.

"Was this you?" I still remembered how surprised I'd been to see this. How it had felt like someone had made it just for me.

My tone would not accept a lack of response, and he nodded slowly.

"Fuck, Bash. I trusted you."

A look of fear flitted across his features, and I felt my heart clench at the sight. "What are you going to do about it?"

Fuck. He was right. I could turn him in. They might even banish him for this. A watcher infiltrating the breeding program was unheard of. He had his place in the pack the same as anyone else. To think he would find a way to compromise the system was something they'd want to squash down as quickly as possible.

Could I turn him in? His betrayal was cutting. I'd come here for one purpose—to secure my future by becoming a pack mother, and he'd doomed me by occupying my time. I'd still had other men, but every occasion we'd slept together could have been another opportunity with someone here who was fertile enough to give me a child.

He'd hidden this from me, taken my choice away, let me believe he could give me something that he absolutely could not. Furious, I stood, cursing the way my legs still shook. My mouth was parched. Fucking heat.

"No, I'm not going to fucking *out* you, Bash, but you need to leave right now." I pointed to the door, my arm stiff and unyielding as he stood and searched the ground for his clothes. Eventually he located the shorts and shirt, and I thought back to when he'd first shown up at my door like a hero set to save me.

Fucking save me, yeah right. He'd occupied me for a heat, albeit pleasurably, but it wouldn't get me pregnant, which meant everything was riding on the breeding party and the next few weeks. I thought he cared, that he was helping me, and he'd really been here for his own selfish reasons.

Bash paused at the door with his hand on the knob, his head bowed. "Syl, I'm sorry. I never meant to hurt you. I just…" He sighed heavily, rattling the handle. "I wanted this time with you."

He left, and the door closed with a definitive snick behind him.

She knew. Syl knew who I was, what I was, and she'd reacted with the same kind of revulsion I'd come to expect from the people in my life, ousting me from her room like trash. As much as it hurt, I couldn't blame her. I'd come here as a man with a secret, and of course, she'd be the one to find out.

I hadn't wanted that, had planned to slip away from this place without her ever knowing where I'd come from or how I'd been so taken by her. At least she wouldn't out me.

After sharing her heat, it was physically painful to be so far apart, and I tried to fill the emptiness with a pile of fried chicken in the fridge and a few bottles of water. I took my meal back to my room, not wanting to see anyone.

There was still a chance she'd come around, but the look in her eyes, the betrayal I'd seen in their depths filled me with a guilt and shame that had carried me out of her room and away from her.

I was a watcher. I couldn't get Syl pregnant, and I'd known how badly she'd wanted to be a mother. How she'd cried when she'd failed to conceive, and I'd still put my worthless self in her path, refusing to let her go through her induced heat with anyone else. I could've called someone else in. A better man, maybe Jace, someone who was fertile and could give her what she needed.

Shit, I hadn't deserved to go through a heat with her, but I also knew I would never forget it. The closeness we'd shared had gone beyond sex or love. It had been the one time in my life I hadn't felt so alone in this cold, cruel world. She'd been there right with me. A comfort—a joy—easing each need as it rose to meet hers and driving us both towards ecstasy. It'd been what I'd been missing when she'd pulled me into her heat before we'd met, and I'd ridden it out watching her on the monitor. My hand cramping up. The room covered in my cum. Alone.

But here I was, alone again, and hating myself for it because it was my own fucking fault.

Furious with my behaviour, I pulled out the black duffel from under the bed and began packing my things. I'd planned to stay until her breeding party, to have her one more time, but would it even work when she'd induced it early the way she had? I didn't know and couldn't face her.

I had to leave.

Each article of clothing I threw haphazardly into my bag felt unbearably heavy—like a dumbbell my achy muscles couldn't bear to lift. My heart wasn't in this, but it had to be. I packed everything I'd brought. Slowly but steadily, forcing myself through the motions, knowing they would take me away from Syl.

My angel. My muse.

SYL

Still pissed at Bash for lying, I struggled to process my new knowledge of him. He'd come here under false pretenses, but why? Bash was perfect in every possible way. Taller and hulkier than any of the other guys here, and so fucking hot it made my panties wet just thinking about him. His mind was keen. It was in the way he spoke carefully and reacted quickly. Then there was his art. Beautiful would be too weak a word to describe his creations.

So why had they chosen to exclude him as a breeder? I thought about it until my head began to ache, and I had to go retrieve a water bottle. Pushing my way through the crowd in the kitchen, I kept my head down the whole time.

Dizziness nearly overwhelmed me, and I caught myself on the fridge handle. Damn, I was dehydrated and hungry. Finding food and water for myself hadn't been my priority when I'd woken up in Bash's arms, completely blissed-out. After I'd found his scars, it had been the furthest thing from his mind.

But my body hadn't forgotten, and I swayed on my feet, pulling open the fridge and grabbing a handful of water bottles and making my way back to my room. I chugged the first eagerly and reached for the second, nearly choking on the cool liquid when my stomach turned and bile rose in my throat. I needed to go slow. The world spun, and I became aware of just how dangerously dehydrated I was. Bash had forced me to drink water just as my heat was starting.

My heart clenched, and my eyes pricked with tears. *Bash.*

He'd saved my life. Without a doubt, with how messed up I'd been and the lack of preparations I'd made before inducing myself, I might have died.

Bash had saved me. He'd saved me in more ways than that. Comforting me when my period had started, making me feel something other than the fear that drove me forward.

But those feelings of betrayal and anger mixed up with all the other emotions I had towards him. If he'd just come to me and told me who he was and why he was here. But he hadn't. Instead, he'd lied to me and consumed my attention when I'd never been able to get pregnant by him.

What the fuck was I supposed to do now?

Pass him in the hall like the heat had never happened? Like I didn't know he was here under false pretenses?

Feeling stronger, I returned to the kitchen. Keeping my back to the guys at the counter, I grabbed some lettuce, cucumber, and radishes and snagged a knife from the drawer to make myself a quick salad to take back to my room. I thought I heard my name at one point, but I ignored it. Whatever those douchebags had to say to me, I didn't want to hear it.

After eating, I was thinking more clearly. I needed to talk more to Bash. To understand what he'd done and why. He'd said it had all been for me, but what did that mean? What else had he done in his pursuit of this position?

Setting the bowl on the nightstand, I went to knock on his door when Jace tapped on my shoulder and stopped me.

"Hey, Syl, this is the last call. Run's starting."

The run. Right. Whatever had allowed them to excuse Bash and I during the previous day's run while I was working through my heat, I didn't know, but the softness in Jace's eyes made me wonder if he'd been the reason for our reprieve.

"Be right out." I smiled and nodded at him, realizing that Jace had been a good friend to me, despite his previous status as Head Asshole of the Asshole Club.

Knowing I wanted to be alone with Bash for this, I waited until Jace rounded the corner and exited the hallway before knocking. I couldn't have Jace overhearing, not when I was still puzzling out what to say. What if I accidentally mentioned his status as a watcher? The importance of keeping his secret was staggering.

They'd banish him. The angry human who still haunted my dreams, his spear raised over his head just before he'd been knocked aside by a guard, came to mind. Bash didn't belong out there. He belonged in here, where it was safe.

Swallowing the lump in my throat, I knocked three times, growing more nervous with each bang before the door opened to permit me.

Hair still mussed from the heat, Bash's eyes widened when he saw me, and he stepped wordlessly back to permit my entry.

"Okay, so you're a watcher, huh?"

"Yes."

Fuck, his voice sounded depleted, like he'd given up on anything good ever happening to him.

"And you watched me."

"Yes."

I moved farther into the room, and he followed. A shadow at my back.

My shadow.

"For how many cycles?"

He hesitated, and I wasn't sure I wanted to hear the answer, even if I needed it.

"Two."

Two cycles he'd watched me getting railed by masked men. I hadn't known there were cameras in the room, much less someone keeping tabs on us, but it made sense. The breeding parties came with a lot of rules about touching and talking, and the watchers must be there to make sure the rules were followed. Otherwise, how else would they know?

I looked around Bash's room absentmindedly while I worked through the idea of him seeing me through a camera.

His dresser drawers were ajar. Strange. Frowning, I pushed one in, noticing as I did so that it was empty. Shocked, I found a black duffel on the floor by his nightstand filled with clothes.

"What the fuck is this, Bash? You're *leaving?*" I toed the black duffel, staring at him aghast, and hoping there was another explanation. There wasn't. It was written on his face.

He. Was. Leaving. Emotion choked me as I stared around incredulously. Anything but this. I couldn't take it. Let us have it out, clear the air, fucking fight, but to leave? Now? With so much unsettled between us? It was unthinkable.

"Oh, I get it. You've fucked me now. Had your fill, so off you go back to being a watcher. Job done. I bet you can't wait to brag about this to your friends." Tears pricked at the back of my eyes, and my face went hot.

I'd meant nothing to him if he could leave so easily. All thoughts of talking things through, hearing the details of his infiltration, slipped from my mind, and I pushed past him, taking off down the hall at a run.

Out the door, I found a line of clothes where the others had shifted for their run. I ripped off my tank top as I went, stepping out of my skirt and shifting before the fabric had hit the ground. I felt Bash at my back, and it brought a fresh wave of piercing pain to my damaged heart.

Joints popped and bones shifted position, halting my progress for a moment, but not long enough for Bash to stop me. I took off at a dead run towards the tree line and into the pines.

My world was in shambles. He'd leave me, now? When we had, at most, a few weeks left before my final cycle ended? He'd leave me to the wolves who had shown their black hearts?

Animal whimpers escaped my throat as I pounded into the dead leaves littering the forest floor. Bash was close behind, almost keeping pace with me, but I was always the fastest wolf. Always. Nobody had ever beaten me in a race, and I pushed myself to the limit, feeling a triumphant surge when I glanced back and saw him falling back, unable to keep up.

Only he was falling farther behind. I hadn't realized how badly I'd wanted him to catch me, to explain himself, but now—I stopped. Something was wrong. A chill went up my spine, and my ears turned directions as I searched for a threat. The brown shape of Bash's wolf was just visible, but it wasn't catching up, and I startled when he shifted back to his human form.

Not understanding what was going on, or why he would shift back to his human form, I raced back, tripping clumsily over a log in my haste. It stung, but I carried on, not willing to spare the injury a moment when Bash was behaving so strangely.

He was lying on the ground with his back against a thick pine. My heart broke, and I shifted, sure my human hands were needed. Eyes bugging out, Bash clutched at his chest and stared up at me helplessly. Seeing him this way–fuck. Panic took hold of me, and I moved without thinking, dropping to his side, scanning him for injuries and running my hands across his chest.

"Bash, Bash. What happened? What's wrong?"

Each of his breaths seemed to come with great effort and an accompanying rattle. *Oh, please.* Tears pricked my eyes. He shook his head, mouth open as he gasped. I looked around frantically, not knowing what to do.

"Help! Help! Someone help, please! He can't breathe." My voice echoed in the forest, and I could only hope someone would hear it. Bash's lips drained of colour, his face pale.

"Puffer. Pants." The words came at significant cost and weren't above a whisper, but I heard him.

A puffer. Pants. I thought I understood, but I needed to make sure. Tears welled up in my eyes. I couldn't lose him. Whatever foolish conflict we'd been having, I may as well have been the one on the ground dying. Not this, anything but this.

"You have a puffer and that will help you. It's in your pants? The ones you took off to shift?"

He gave a single nod, and that was enough for me.

But I couldn't help dropping a quick kiss on his head, not when I could see how much distress he was in. I only hoped my speed was enough to save him.

Shifting even as I dropped, I ignored the sensations of the change, already running as my bones were settling into place. I stumbled, but didn't fall, and once I was in my wolf form, I raced back to the dorm, not bothering to change back to my human form.

Now which fucking pants had he been wearing? Grey. I thought they might have been grey, but a quick check of the two pairs in the right spot revealed no puffer. Fuck. Bash needed this. Where was it?

If it was medicine, it would smell strange. I closed my eyes and let my nose guide me. Yes, a bit of a sting in my nostrils. This was it. It had to be because not finding it wasn't an option. The black sweats were closer to the tree line than the others because he hadn't lined up with them. He'd been chasing after me. My own clothes were strewn across the manicured lawn further up.

Oh, Bash. Please hold on.

I hurried over, using my snout to dig into the pocket, and finding a plastic cylinder. I searched the rest of the pants to be thorough, but found nothing else. This must be the puffer, and a quick sniff confirmed it was where the stinging smell had been coming from.

Carefully, I took it between my teeth and set off to find Bash.

When he came within sight, I stumbled over my feet and almost fell face first into a fallen branch, only catching myself at the last moment. I'd very nearly dropped the medicine. Fear squeezed my heart in a vise, and I knew its icy grip would only let up once I saw Bash well.

His chest heaved, the skin around his ribs pulling with each breath, and I raced up to him. Shifting and hating the extra few seconds I had to wait before having human hands to help him.

"Here's your puffer, Bash. Tell me what to do."

His mouth hung open and his lips were chapped, but he took the puffer and brought it to his lips, fighting with the top part of it.

When I realized he was trying to press it, I helped, pushing the top part in and watching as he took a deep breath of the medicine. I helped him press it again, watching with bated breath as he used the puffer, slowly improving and moving away from the grim embrace of death with each moment of proper inhale.

Tears of relief sprang to my eyes, and I sat down hard on the forest floor, snapping a twig in the process. Now that Bash could breathe, I found I could breathe, too, and I reached out a hand to take his hand in mine. He looked gratefully back, and I smiled reassuringly. He was getting better. He'd be okay. I couldn't remember the conflict between us, hated that it had existed. Nothing mattered so long as he was all right.

I swiped a tear away, putting my head between bent knees.

"I'm okay." His voice was rough and distorted, but clear. "Syl? I'm okay."

It was only then I realized I was sobbing, my back heaving as the fear worked its way out of me in fits and starts. I looked up and found his deep blue eyes fixed on mine.

He squeezed my hand. "It's alright. It's over."

Seeing him well enough to speak, how he didn't need to fight just to breathe, calmed me.

"This was why you didn't chase me? Why you disappeared after that first time?"

A sad smile curled his lips. "Yes. I wanted to chase you, Syl. I wanted so badly to chase you, but I couldn't. I'm defective, you see." He looked away at the last, and it was my turn to squeeze his hand.

My heart broke for him. To think how I'd gone off on him. How angry I'd been thinking he was rejecting me when he refused to give chase. But he hadn't refused. He'd been physically incapable of chasing me. Staring at his pale face, I understood.

He'd given me everything of himself. Had always wanted me. He'd done everything in his power to be as close to me as possible, and I'd rewarded him with my ire. Made him feel less than. Guilt clawed at my insides. I'd lashed out at him for something he couldn't control, punished him relentlessly. The look of panic I'd seen in his eyes before he ran off made sense now. I'd been so sure it'd meant he didn't want to be with me, that he'd left me to chase someone else, but now I understood how all his actions had been for me. My eyes pricked, and a new protectiveness towards Bash surged within me. I vowed right then and there to never let anyone make him feel less than.

A growl rose up in my throat, and I was just about to tell him how foolish the idea of him being anything less than perfect was, when a foot came flying into Bash's temple, knocking him to the ground.

"Well, look what we have here."

A familiar, hated voice chilled my blood, and I was on my feet in an instant, standing between Carter and Bash.

"How the fuck did someone like you con your way into the breeding program, huh?" Carter smiled cruelly, revealing a swollen eye. With one hand, he shoved me aside roughly, and I fell sideways. "You piece of shit. You really thought you could be one of us? You're nothing but pack *garbage*." Carter kicked Bash, spitting on him, before I could struggle to my feet.

Rage consumed every thought. Everything else was gone but the need to defend Bash. Bash, who had almost died. Who was recovering and being beaten like a dog for fucking existing.

I flew at Carter, wrapping my arms and legs around him, and clawing at him with my fingernails. I scraped them across his face, growling.

"You piece of shit, buttmonkey-fucking, cunt-shitting, motherfucking asshole, fucktwat!" I screamed as I attacked, venting everything on Carter—the asshole who dared treat Bash this way.

But then I was pulled off by too many hands to fend off. Pulled off and restrained by a group of breeders who had heard the commotion and come to aid me. To stop Carter? I didn't know, but I'd fucking kill Carter if he touched Bash again, and something in my face must've tipped him off because he swallowed. Wet, hot blood dripped down his cheek from scratches I hoped would be deep enough to scar his face.

Jace stepped between us, his arms raised.

"Okay there, let's all calm down. What's going on here?"

Carter gave him a petulant look, but he didn't touch Bash again.

"This fucker is a defective." He spit on the ground in front of him, wisely away from Bash, whose back faced me. I couldn't gauge how injured he was. "He was out here with his filthy illness and his medicine. No way they would include someone who couldn't breathe without medicine in the breeding program."

Jace nodded thoughtfully, and I wanted to kick him next, to take a bite out of his flesh for not instantly defending Bash.

"And you saw this?" Jace smirked.

"Yeah man, he was breathing funny when I ran up, and he had that filthy medicine they have to use. It's over there."

Jace nodded, giving me an apologetical look before turning his back to me as he faced Carter.

"Then we take him into custody, but you are not to strike a man wounded on the ground. Do you understand me? That is not our way."

Take him into custody.

Bash—in custody, punished.

"No, please, Jace, please," I cried out, but he didn't turn, didn't acknowledge me.

"Her too. Bitch fucking attacked me."

I saw the back of Jace's head nod slowly.

"Her too."

Two burly guys with identical buzz cuts hauled Bash to his feet, and the rough hands holding me by the arms turned me about, marching me back towards the dorms, or maybe to prison.

I didn't know, but at least—at fucking least—I'd be there with Bash.

CHAPTER 24

Carter's kick had knocked Bash out, and it was all I could do to watch him worriedly between the bars of the twin cages they'd put us in.

Each of us had a thin mattress on a metal frame folded down from the wall, but they'd dumped Bash on the floor. So that was where I'd chosen to sit cross-legged, watching him for any signs of consciousness. At least the room was well lit, with a pathway and chairs set in front of each cage, presumably for visitors. Although I couldn't think of anyone I wanted to see.

I passed the time thinking about Bash. If that was even his real name. He'd been put into the role of watcher as surely as I'd been put into the role of breeder. Neither of us had an alternative, a different way to live our lives than the ones they'd selected for us. I watched his brow furrow in sleep, wishing he was close enough for me to wipe the sweat off his forehead.

His breathing was even with only a small wheeze at the end of each breath. A stain of dried blood darkened his hair from a wound long healed, and I hated the sight of it. I wanted to wash it clean, to talk to him and for him to talk to me, but on he slept. And the more I stared at his handsome face, the more I understood.

He'd been on the outside looking in, and he'd wanted more for himself. Wanted it badly enough to take it. How could I fault him for that when it was what I'd always dreamed of doing?

It felt like hours had passed by the time he groaned and opened his eyes, a hand shooting to his forehead. He sat up to cradle his head with both hands, rubbing his palms into his eyes.

"I'm glad you're awake."

He jolted at my voice, his face contorting in pain, before he blinked at me in surprise. Wincing, I resolved to lower my voice.

"Syl? What are you doing here?" His words were laced with concern, and I went on my knees at the bars between us.

"You don't remember?" Perhaps he'd been unconscious when I'd leapt on Carter, a thought which hadn't crossed my mind. He looked up at me, his cheeks blotchy with redness.

"No, sorry. What happened?"

I grinned, knowing the whites of my teeth were showing—and just how savage it looked.

"I kicked Carter's ass."

Bash gave a barking laugh, quickly started to cough, and raised a hand to his head. I reached out for him through the bars, wanting to touch him, to convince myself he was okay.

"Are you okay? Do you need more of your medicine?"

He snorted, looking up at me. "Syl, I'm sorry. I've been such a fool, sneaking my way into Pack Breeders 103C, lying to you, letting you believe I'm something I'm not. This is what I am." He gestured down at himself. "Weak. Pathetic. Unsuitable as a breeder and too sickly for the fields." He gave a self-deprecating smile. "I can't even give you the baby you want so badly. Fucking worthless." He drove a fist into his thigh.

I was incredulous. A baby?

"Bash, where did you get the idea I wanted a baby?"

He looked up and met my eyes with a frown.

"When you didn't get pregnant, and you cried. I know why you cry, Syl. I know how badly you want to be a mother. It's why I backed off. I can't"—he choked up and paused to swallow before continuing—"I can't give you what you need."

It was my turn to laugh. The sound echoed around the room—the merriment at odds with the grief etched in Bash's face. "A baby? Bash, I've never wanted children. Never."

He stared in shock at me.

"But your period, you were so upset."

He didn't get it. Couldn't get it. He'd been assigned the role of watcher. The fields had never been a threat looming over his head.

"Because I have to get pregnant, Bash, not because I wanted to." Tears sprang to my eyes, and I looked down to hide them. I wanted to be vulnerable with him, I did. But this burden had been something I'd shouldered alone for so long. "You don't know what it's like to be a woman in this pack. We aren't allowed in the guard, and if you aren't selected to be an administrator or a coordinator, well, you can either breed or be sent to the fields." I choked in a shaky breath. "My sister failed as a breeder, and every fucking month I have to watch as she falls apart. Do you know what that's like? To watch someone you love die for the glory of the pack?"

A tear slipped loose, the pain too much. I startled when a warm hand cupped my cheek. Looking up, I found Bash watching me with a steady gaze. He'd pulled the confession from me, just as he always had. My hand crept up to hold his in place.

"There is no choice for me, Bash. It's breed or burn."

He should've been disgusted at how anti-pack my sentiments were, how unwilling I was to work the fields for future generations, but I saw only understanding in his clear blue eyes.

"I'm sorry, Syl. I had no idea."

Sucking in a shuddering breath, I licked my lips. "And what you were assigned, Bash, it-it's unfair. You never had a choice either."

It was his turn to look away, and I felt his pain as if it were my own.

"No, I didn't. Once they assigned me the role of watcher, I was shoved into a room to watch better men, chosen men, father children. I was worthless to the pack, unwanted, shoved to the side." I clung to his hand, wanting it pressed tighter to me, wanting to give him some comfort. "And I almost died in there, Syl. I was close to giving up, letting myself just waste away into nothing, and then I saw you on my monitor." He looked up at me, his gaze piercing. "I saw you cry, and I wanted something I shouldn't have. Something I had no right to. I wanted to know why."

And cry I did, blubbering and kissing his palm, wishing the bars weren't between us so he could take me into his arms. He didn't say anything, just stroked my cheek with his thumb and waited until I regained my composure enough to speak.

"You're not worthless to me. I don't care if sometimes you can't run or need medicine. You're amazing. You're perfect, and you're not unwanted, because I want you and anyone who doesn't is a fool." I laughed, and he gave a small chuckle, his hand darting up to his forehead as a flash of pain crossed his features. I leaned forward to clutch the bars and waited for him to look at me. "I love you."

Bash's eyes cleared, and he moved on his knees in front of me, covering my hands with his own.

"Syl. I'm nothing next to you. You're special, beautiful. I'm a lowly watcher. I can't give you—"

I cut his words off with a kiss, pressing my lips against his and darting out my tongue to taste him.

"Shh. I don't care about any of that. I love you. Even if I don't know your real name." I looked down, and we both smiled at the absurdity of the situation. After everything we'd shared, the love I bore for this man in front of me, how badly I wanted to be his and for him to be mine, yet I didn't know his true name.

"It's Ashton, but I chose Bash for you, Syl. Please call me Bash. Ashton is"—Bash licked his lip, fixing his gaze at something over my shoulder—"not who I want to be anymore. I left that life and that name when I chose you."

I nodded, looking down thoughtfully.

"They'll banish me for this, Syl. I know it. They can't allow a watcher to get away with this, and I've been deemed unfit for the fields."

I nodded my agreement. It was the only punishment available for one such as him.

"Yes, they will, and I'm going with you."

Bash stared at me, his eyebrows raised and eyes wide. His mouth worked.

"No, Syl. There's no way I'll allow you to make that sacrifice."

I laughed, reaching out to lay my hand across his cheek and feel the prick of his stubble.

"You can't stop me. If you leave without me, I'll just follow you."

His face fell, and I felt a stab of guilt at the sight.

"Syl—"

"Bash, there's nothing for me here. This was my last cycle to conceive, and I've already had an extension. Seeing as how you can't get me pregnant, I don't think it likely I've conceived, and I won't"—fire entered my words—"I won't go to the poisoned fields to work them, for a pack that wouldn't give me that choice. That would do this to you. I won't sacrifice myself for them. As to leaving, I don't care what's out there. I'm not afraid of going into the unknown with you, Bash. The only thing that scares me is a life without you in it."

"Syl." He spoke my name in a whisper, leaning forward to touch his lips to mine tenderly. "I love you. I'll always be your watcher, your shadow, your protector. I'll do whatever I can to take care of you. I swear it." His voice took on a different tone. One I could feel in my bones. One that sang in my heart. "I'll be your teacher, your lover—whatever you need me to be."

I stared at him in shock. My body was alight with his words, and I sensed it was my turn.

"They called you defective, but I will never call you that—could never call you that. You're perfect, and you're mine. Mine alone, every word, every touch is for me, and in turn, I give you everything I am."

He hummed his agreement, and the thing in my chest flared to life again, edging me closer to something.

"From the moment I saw you, you awoke something in me. You don't burn for them, Syl, you *burn for me*," he said the last with a growl that echoed through my chest and sent a shiver of arousal straight to my core. Heat rose to my cheeks, and I realized he was right. I did burn for him. It was the right word to describe this insatiable, living thing between us.

My trembling lips collided with his, my hand seeking his nakedness even as he sought mine, both of us fighting with the bars and the bit of distance they put between us. I'd put on a white cotton shirt and shorts, but they hadn't been willing to dress Bash and had left his clothing on the concrete floor.

Something wild rose within me, and I felt the need to sink my teeth into Bash. To mark him, claim him, make him mine. I wanted his neck, but I couldn't fit my face through the bars, and all I could do was whimper at the strange need going unmet. He pulled away to look at me, the same feral need etched into the snarl on his face.

"Your wrist, Syl, give me your wrist."

I thrust my shaky hand through the bars, my eyes rolling back when his head dropped to it and his tongue darted out to trace a vein.

"Bash," I pleaded, but for what, I didn't know. I only knew that he wasn't doing it, was holding back. Then his teeth pierced the flesh, and the arousal I'd been feeling increased tenfold until it was almost at the height of heat madness. A bolt of need coursed through my veins, all emanating from the teeth embedded in my wrist. It should have hurt, and in some corner of my mind, I felt the sting of his teeth, but the pleasure it brought was so extreme that the pain was an afterthought.

The need to sink my teeth into his flesh consumed me.

"Give me yours." My voice was low, almost unrecognizable.

Bash watched me, his pupils dilated. His breath had gone raspy, and while I worried for him, I knew I couldn't stop this. I paused a moment to lay a hand on his heaving chest.

"Easy." I waited until his lust heavy gaze met mine and his breathing slowed before I pulled his arm through the bars.

I'd always loved his hands. They were an artist's hands, roughened in a strange place on the side of his finger where no worker was likely to hold a large tool. His fingertips were soft, and I brought his hand to my cheek, turning to trail kisses across his palm and down to his wrist.

"I claim you. I mark you. I mate you," I whispered, not knowing where the strange words came from, but feeling the rightness of them a moment before I could resist no longer, and my teeth sank deep into the flesh of Bash's wrist.

He cried out, and I recognized it from my own experience—arousal and pleasure so intense it was nearly orgasmic, and that feeling of connectedness, only now it was nearly complete.

Blood pounded in my head as I lifted my eyes to meet Bash, and a moment of understanding passed between us.

"I need to feel you."

He nodded in understanding, and we both stood. Bash on shaky legs worrying enough to dull the moment, but then he was standing before me, his cock straining as he positioned himself between the bars.

He was taller than me, and he lifted me into his arms, holding me high enough to kiss my lips before lowering me slowly onto his length. The bars prevented him from sinking fully, and I moaned against him, wanting all of him as he'd promised. Wanting to give him all of me as I'd promised. But his lips were on me, his hands soothing across my back, and I knew we'd get a chance to properly consummate our union.

This would have to do for now.

He lifted me up and down on the part of him that could reach through the bars, a few precious inches that made me desperate for more. I climbed the bars like an animal, and he helped hoist me up until I could hook my legs on his forearms, but the moment he took my full weight, he wheezed. And no wonder after his breathing episode in the forest and then that asshole Carter. The noise stabbed at me, but I knew we needed this, so I gripped the bars above his head, using my upper body to relieve some of my body weight. He gave me a thankful look just before he squeezed my ass, panting into my neck. He groaned, his breath hot on my neck as his palms massaged my cheeks.

How it must've hurt him to not take me fully. I reached through the bars, stroking along his length to soothe the distance between us. He moaned and the sound went right to my core.

Faster. Harder. Damn, I wanted it harder, but his hands massaging my ass and the few precious inches I could get were all to be found. The cold metal bars clanged as I pumped him, squeezing his cock mercilessly as he thrust into me, one hand snaking around my front to find the delicate bundle of nerves crying out for his attention. I threw my head back, panting and wriggling against his hand. His touch was everything, but I wanted more, wanted every inch of my skin to be touching his, until we were as one. More. More. More.

Stroke. Thrust. We found a rhythm. A way through the restrictions, until he throbbed beneath my fingers. I arched back, almost falling if Bash hadn't caught me at the last second. Every fiber of my being burst apart, shattering as release tore through me, different from any I'd experienced. This one was doing something to me, changing something in me, and I emerged from it to stare at Bash with perfect clarity.

Bash.

Ashton.

My shadow.

My watcher.

My mate.

CHAPTER 25

Syl eschewed the bed in favour of the floor where we could sit nearer to each other, and I couldn't refuse her the contact I also craved. She fell asleep, holding my hand to her face. How badly I wished I could sketch her, sleeping peacefully, her breath puffing against my wrist where her mark remained.

Scars had formed where we'd bitten each other, though the wounds had healed quickly enough that no mark should have been left. It was almost like the sheer force of our will to be marked and claimed by each other had forced the scars to form, to leave an impression on our bodies as we made an impression on our souls.

How long would they keep us here, and would they truly let Syl leave with me? I'd had no idea her time in the breeding program had been extended, and I'd foolishly mistook her desperation for a desire of motherhood. Smirking at my idiocy, I rubbed a thumb against her soft cheek, and she pulled my hand closer, as if even in sleep she could not let go of me.

Syl was mine now, as surely as I'd already been hers. I'd been right. There was something between us, and though we faced banishment, a fragile joy and hopefulness came to life in my chest whenever I thought of a future with her in it.

Whatever was out there, whatever was thrown at us, we'd be together at last. Mated. Bound. The idea made me giddy, and I vowed to the sleeping angel in the cell next to mine that I would find a way to protect her, to give her the life she deserved. One filled with dresses and art.

My head still ached from Carter's attack, and I leaned my sore temple on the cool metal bars. Exhausted, I drifted off, startling awake at the sound of the door.

I looked up to find Jace. His brows furrowed and his lips pressed into a tight line. Syl woke, too, and we shared a look before standing as one. Our hands joined to face him.

"Well, it's to be banishment, Ashton."

I winced at the sound of my other name. It was more foreign, more hated to me than the one I had assumed,.

"Bash. His name is Bash now." Syl's voice was firm as she stared Jace down.

"Okay, well, Bash, I'm sorry, but it's banishment." He was quiet for a moment, stuffing his hands in his pockets and looking back towards the door.

"Syl, I'm sorry, but you're being removed from the breeding program for your outburst. I'm sure it would have been forgiven if you'd been in the breeding program proper, but as someone already on an extension..." He trailed off, and I understood what he meant. Her presence in the breeding program was already granted as a favour, and she'd abused her privileges.

Worriedly, I glanced over at Syl to see how the news affected her, giving her hand a comforting squeeze. Only she looked up at me and smiled, her eyes shining. There was no hint of sadness within their clear blue depths, and I couldn't help but smile back. We'd assumed she'd be ousted, and with her no longer deemed a breeder, they'd be more likely to allow her to join me in banishment.

"It's all right, Jace. This is what we expected to happen, and with Syl released from the breeding program, she'd like to join me in banishment."

Jace gave Syl a pained look, but said nothing. He scratched his shaggy head. Licking his lips and frowning, his eyes drifted down to study our joined hands. His lips pressed into a line.

"It's not a death sentence," he blurted, snapping his mouth shut like he'd spoken out of turn.

Frowning, I waited for him to elaborate.

"You know that couple? The one who left together and ran away?" Jace asked.

Everyone knew about them and how they'd chosen each other over their loyalties to the pack, and somehow had slipped out through the borders. A guard and a breeder lost to the wilds and their certain death.

"Yes, of course."

I felt a familiar pang of guilt at their mention. I remembered watching them on the monitor. How they'd acted during the woman's breeding party. How they'd touched more than was necessary. How I'd doomed them by failing to report it.

I'd lied, of course, when they'd asked me if anything unusual had happened, but I could never lie to myself. If I'd just told somebody about how strangely they were acting, the pack would be all the stronger, and they'd still be alive.

"They're not dead."

Not dead? The possibility hadn't occurred to me, and I perked up, listening intently.

Jace sighed, his shoulders slouching forward. "There's a rumour of a pack, far north of here, where they're taking in loners and mated pairs."

Syl and I shared a look.

"What about defectives?" Syl asked.

I winced at the term, hating how Syl considered herself. Jace didn't look so happy about it, either.

"No one is defective, Syl. We all serve the pack in whatever way we can, some-"

"Spare me your pack loyalty bullshit, Jace. Everyone calls them, I mean us"—she shot me a look—"defectives."

Jace nodded slowly, his eyes filled with sadness. "Right. I have no idea if they'd take you in or not, but—Well, my brother is there, and I can't imagine him turning you away."

His brother? Interesting.

"When you're banished, you're given a week's worth of supplies. It might be enough to reach them, and if not, there's always hunting. Syl, you're fast. The swiftest in the pack, actually. You should be able to catch supper. Bash, I snuck you a few extra puffers."

Incredulously, I stared at him.

"Why would you help us like this?"

"Just—when you see my brother"—he swallowed hard—"when you see Dame, will you tell him I'm sorry?" He didn't elaborate, but I saw regret in his eyes and in the twist of his lips as he turned away.

What the fuck had happened between him and his brother?

He didn't volunteer any more information, and the tight set of his jaw kept me from asking questions. He'd done his best for us, to help us, to guide us, and I felt an urge to reciprocate.

"Jace?" He met my eyes. "Thank you, and if you ever need help from a watcher, there's this guy named Cam. His room is number eighteen, and he's the primary watcher for Pack Breeders 103C. He's a good guy. If you mention my name, say I owe you, he'll help within reason."

Jace nodded slowly. "I'm sorry I can't do more. The wilds aren't so hospitable, but if you can make it to the new pack…Well, take this." He passed a circular item through the bars, and I frowned down at it, not having any idea what it was.

The device was metal with a glass front encasing a circle with the letters N E S W set equal distance apart. A strange red arrow that moved when I turned it.

"I don't think they train watchers how to navigate, but that's a compass. It's a way to make sure you're moving in the right direction. See how the arrow moves depending on which way you point it? You want to keep the arrow just here." Jace reached through the bars and pointed to a spot between the N and the E. "Keep walking with the arrow pointed there and you'll find them."

"Thank you, again."

"It's the least I can do."

Frowning, I studied him, trying to understand what he could mean and failing. The least he could do? I wondered if this was all to do with Syl and whatever he'd meant by him owing her, or if it was something else.

"Jace, before you go. Put in my request for banishment alongside Bash, please?"

Jace swallowed like he was going to be sick, but he nodded, turning to go. With one hand on the door, he turned back to look at us.

"Banishment will take place at dawn. Good luck."

Syl met my eyes, and I found the same resolve I felt reflected in them. We would be okay so long as we were together.

We had to be.

Chapter 26

Syl and I faced the dawn, our hands clasped and her leaning into my side. Our wrists touched, the mark of our mating concealed under the warm layers and green canvas coats we'd been given to protect ourselves from the elements. On our backs, we had packs filled with more food than we could eat in a week. I suspected the excess was courtesy of Jace.

A crowd was assembled of watchers and breeders separated by social convention, with a sizeable gap running down the middle where everyone stood amongst the trees. Cam stood in the front, his bright red hair standing out amongst the others. He gave me a solemn nod, and I returned it, knowing that was as much of a goodbye as we were going to get.

Syl and I were not given an opportunity to speak, but I could tell she wanted to, just like I could tell she hadn't slept well the night before and was a bit hungry. The connection between us was a powerful thing, and I was grateful to know of her needs and wants, so I might anticipate them.

We were ushered out to the pack border by two stiff-faced guards and released into a clearing. I looked back, and the guard frowned, like even looking back wasn't allowed. He pointed a finger straight ahead towards what was surely the pack boundary. I turned to go, but Syl stayed where she stood, looking back at those assembled, her eyes shining.

"Syl, come. It's time we left."

She turned to me, and I could feel her turmoil. It was there, in the crinkling of her brow and in the set of her jaw.

"Not yet. Look at them, Bash. They're us."

I looked back and understood what she meant. Watchers huddled together in a nervous group eyeing the breeders who watched us nervously, the few women dwarfed amongst the men looking at Syl with disbelief.

Watchers and breeders, separated, and all assigned by someone who thought they knew what was best. Syl stepped forward.

"We go now, as mates. We reject this pack and the cruel roles it gave to us. This place, these roles, they do not define you. There is another way if you are brave enough to take it."

My mouth hung open. Syl had all but encouraged those present to run away, to embrace banishment rather than live under the pack's rules, and I saw more than a few shining eyes, particularly among the female breeders.

She'd only spoken the truth—our truth, her truth—but in doing so, she had gone from a banished pack member to an enemy. I turned, ushering her away, my arm slung across her shoulder protectively.

"Syl, they could hunt us down and kill us for saying such things." My whisper was harsh, and I hated it, but it came from a place of fear. Finally, we had each other, all our secrets known. We were at the start of everything, and if we died now, we would never know what it was.

"I'm sorry, Bash. I know—I just. I had to say it. The way the pack assigns people these roles, these labels, it's not the right way to live. People should be more than what they're useful for. They should be able to decide."

I squeezed her hand, drawing it to my face and kissing her knuckles.

"Yes, they should, but you don't have to be the one to say it."

She glared at me, her hand twisting and trying to escape mine, but I held it fast.

What was wrong with me? I grabbed her wrist with one hand, my other skating up her back between her and the pack she wore, turning us to press her against a tree and hold her in place while I nuzzled her soft neck.

She was pissed, rigid beneath me, and I could feel her heart pounding against my chest, but it was more than anger.

"Stop. Bash. We should get further away from the border." My hand rested at her hip, digging through the fabric and pulling her coat up so I could feel her skin. She shivered when I found it.

"This can't wait." Not after we'd been unable to connect fully between those bars, when we'd been forced to fulfill our need to consummate the mate bond without me fully seated inside of her.

Out here, we were alone. At fucking last able to press our bodies tightly to one another, to feel each other properly. Should I bite her again? I wanted to. Nuzzling her neck brought up the desire within me, the need to mark the same way I'd felt when we'd chosen each other and mated, but it felt wrong. They'd done that to us, kept us separated even as we mated, and it felt like us—defective, hated, but together. The mark we'd made on each other's wrists would always be our mate bond. Anything else would be superfluous.

Trapped in a cell, inches from her but unable to hold her properly, I'd examined the mark and noted the gap beside her incisor and how uniquely her it was.

She shivered beneath me, pulling me back to the present, and I eased the pack off her shoulders.

"We're far enough. We've waited long enough."

Her lust-filled eyes met mine, and she swallowed.

Packs dropping to the ground, I set to work on her coat and her on mine, both of us fumbling with the buttons. I barely contained myself enough not to rip it off her. She knew how to sew. She could fix it.

But she had the buttons open on my coat and switched to her own before I could try it. The air outside had turned cold, and I felt a stab of guilt when she pulled off her shirt and shivered, goosebumps rising on her arm. But then she was pulling me to her, hands bunched into my shirt, and I realized I wasn't the only one who needed this.

Eagerly, I stripped as quickly as I could, nearly tripping when I pulled off my boots, not willing to leave an article of clothing between us.

Naked, I paused to look at her and she did the same. We'd slept together enough times that we knew how well we fit together, but this was the first time with everything between us laid bare. The first time since we'd chosen this life with each other.

"Bash."

My name in her mouth was enough to break the spell, and we collided. My strength overwhelming hers as I pressed her against the tree. She was too low, and I lifted her, positioning myself so she could sink down onto my straining cock.

Crying out, she did, taking every inch into her soaking pussy like she was made for it, and she fucking was. The same way I was made for her.

"Syl." I massaged her cheeks, lifting her up and down against me, creating a friction that left us both moaning for more. She was wetness. Softness. Heat and heaven, and I sank into her, losing all sense of reality. The feel of her hot mouth moving against mine was almost too much.

How long we were out there, I didn't know.

Whether those who had assembled to see us off could hear us, I didn't care.

There was only Syl and me. In this moment, and when we came together, our roar echoed upwards to the heavens, proclaiming our union.

I kissed her gossamer hair, her face, her neck, as we came back down, as the world took shape once more.

"Bash," she whispered my name, and I understood.

She was everything to me, and I spoke her name on a breath against the hollow of her collarbone. That I could be everything to her was a dream I'd never dared to have.

We stayed like that, her in my arms and me lost to her, until the cold finally reached us, and I carefully set her down on her feet to dress.

Once we were bundled back in our gear with our packs slung across our backs, Syl gave me a shy grin, reaching out for my hand. I kept her on my left side so that the marks on our wrists, our mating mark, could sometimes brush in the most delightful of touches.

The next week became about survival. Neither of us had been trained on how to make a fire or hunt, and with it growing colder the further north we traveled, we huddled together for warmth at night. I was thankful that our packs had included mostly jerky and granola bars, nothing that would need to be cooked.

Daytime temperatures were tolerable, but watching Syl shiver her way through the night was not, and I'd never felt so useless than I did as I held my mate, trying to warm her through sheer force of will.

But by the eighth day, we reached a border and were intercepted by a brown wolf with a mask of black across his face. He shifted into a stout man with a confident bearing, short blonde hair, and a disarming smile.

"Welcome to Pack Cass. Do you seek refuge within our borders?"

Bone weary, and practically leaning on each other for support, Syl and I exchanged a cautious look and nodded. His answering smile showcased a pair of perfectly straight white teeth.

"Excellent. Pleased to meet you. My name is Arthur, but you can call me Art. Please come with me, and we'll get you warmed up in no time."

Ironic that Art should be the one to lead me home, but he did, guiding us through the trees until at last it opened up, and we saw a sprawling compound set in a valley.

The midday sun shone on people walking the streets between buildings. Mated pairs held hands, their laughing faces filled with joy, and I caught the scent of a human somewhere within the vicinity. Shocked, I followed Art into a tall grey building.

"We've got plenty of free apartments. That's the thing with starting a pack—you need people." Art laughed at his own joke, and I stopped following him, pulling Syl back to stop with me. Art came back towards us wearing a frown. "Something wrong, friend?"

"You know nothing about us, but you're willing to take us in, no questions asked?" My suspicions of this place were aroused, and I stayed alert, eyeing our guide distrustfully.

The confusion on Art's face cleared.

"Well, of course, we're going to be screening you. You're to be allowed enough time to refresh yourselves, decompress, and then all new potential pack members are interviewed by the beta himself." He laughed. "If anyone can tease apart friend from foe, it's our beta. Nothing gets past him."

I nodded, not sure I wanted to meet this beta, but we had followed Jace's directions, and this was the pack where they had led.

"This way, please?" Art led us down a hallway and up some stairs, wincing and looking back at us. "Eventually, we'll have power enough to run the elevators, but for now, all residents must use the stairs." Art opened a heavy door and ushered us into a staircase made of concrete with black metal handrails. At least this place wasn't totally perfect.

I fucking hated how I had to go slowly on the stairs, and the way Syl slowed without question, smiling encouragingly at me when I did so. She shouldn't be saddled with one such as me, and yet she was.

After three flights of stairs, Art stopped and held the door open for us. My breathing felt tight, but I smiled reassuringly at Syl, not wanting to worry her. Traveling for so long, and after the attack I'd experienced when I'd stupidly chased her into the woods and outed myself, had taken its toll and without enough time to recover. I was easily winded.

Art led us down an identical hallway to a grey door with a gold knocker, pulling a key from his pocket and opening it. The apartment within was stunning. Warm wood floors met a kitchen with all black appliances and a matching black counter. It was even furnished with a grey couch facing a flat screen TV.

"Well, here you go. If you decide to stay after meeting with the beta, this will be where you live. Of course, everyone is expected to work and—"

"Art, what about defectives? Do you allow them here?"

Art's face screwed up in confusion. "I'm not sure what you mean."

Clearing my throat, I turned to face him when I felt Syl tug on my arm. A quick glance at her, and I knew I couldn't say anything. Not now, not in this moment when we were both in need of the rest and comfort this place could provide.

"It's not important. Maybe something I'll bring up to your beta."

He nodded, giving us a parting smile and shutting the door.

Syl looked at me, and the sheer joy on her face was enough to have me grinning and forgetting my worries. She squealed, taking off to explore the apartment. I watched her go, wishing this would work, hoping they would accept two lost defectives in need of a second chance at life.

"We should unpack, right away! Come on, Bash, check out our bedroom with me."

It was starting to seem more and more likely that Syl wanted to stay here, but I was uneasy. We knew so little about these people beyond Jace's recommendation and their willingness to escort us within their borders. What would they do when they found out I was a defective?

Smiling that toothy grin of hers that showed off the gap beside her incisor, Syl emerged from a hallway off the main area to grab my arm and tug me along, laughing at my resistance.

But it was hard to accept that this place might truly be a haven for us, or even that we might rest here for a while.

Syl eased the pack off her shoulder and added it to hers on the bed, then she set to work, unzipping them and dumping the contents on the bed.

We both stood in shock at what had been buried at the bottom of our packs. Eight days of traveling in the bitter cold, making sure we made it to this place had meant we never truly got to the bottom of our bags where the nonnecessities were.

"My magazines." Syl was tearing up, and I reached out to clasp her hand, bringing it to my lips, so I could kiss her knuckles.

The pile of magazines from her dorm lay scattered across the bed, only a little worse for wear with all the travel, along with all her sketches and designs. Everything we'd assumed we'd lost when we'd headed out into the unknown.

Then there was my bag. Fuck, now I was getting teary-eyed. It had to have been Jace. Or Cam, but I couldn't see him gaining access. Whoever it was had packed my sketches of Syl and had even carefully rolled up my special project for transport.

"What's that?" Syl eyed the paper, and I didn't stop her when she lifted it and pulled off the thick elastic, holding it in a roll. She gasped, but with her back to me, I had no idea what her reaction was.

Slowly, I approached from behind her, peering over her shoulder. I'd finished it just before packing my things and intending to leave.

The painting of Syl's face was split in half. One side painted in full colour and exquisite detail. The other a rough sketch of her face in charcoal. The idea had come to me from the comics I'd completed from Reg and the dresses I'd completed for Syl.

They were two halves of the woman I loved, one simple, vulnerable, real. The sketched side of the painting cried while the other was neutral, her gaze steady, all the feeling hidden inside, but perfectly showcased by her opposite. The crying girl had been trapped inside, held in place by the pack, but I'd seen her, and it had started everything.

My hands skated up the smooth skin of Syl's arms. She shivered beneath my touch, and I felt the sensation go through my fingertips.

"Do you like it?" I whispered.

"Oh, Bash. It's beautiful. Is this how you see me?" She turned, and I found tear tracks on her face—her eyes wide, lips parted. She'd never looked more beautiful.

Happy tears.

"You're beautiful, Syl. I see *you*." I took a strand of ash-blonde hair and carefully tucked it behind her ear.

She laughed, looking up at me through her lashes.

"I think we should hang this on our wall."

Our wall. Fucking heaven.

"So, you broke into the breeding program and stayed there for almost two months with no one noticing, and you think we won't want you because sometimes your lungs fuck up and you need an easily accessible medicine?"

The beta's dark eyes were as unsettling as the scowl on his face, all of which should have been intimidating, but the effect was undone by the adorable black-haired baby he bounced on his knee. The little fellow was blowing bubbles, hanging over his father's arm, trying to capture his feet.

Fucking adorable.

"Well?"

The baby had distracted me, and I looked up to meet the fearsome beta's stare.

"You know what it's like at Pack Singer. The second they found out about my condition, I was labeled a defective."

He nodded, spiky black hair dipping almost to his eyes.

"Yeah, well, *we* are not Pack Singer. A big guy like you who's smart enough to pull off a plan like that. Shit, man. We welcome you." He smiled, and I swear it was more terrifying than the scowl he'd just been wearing. The baby started gnawing on his thumb joint, and he frowned down at the infant.

The most wonderful sound in the world reached my ears, and I looked across the room to see Syl sitting cross-legged and laughing, really fucking laughing, at something the long-haired blonde next to her said. The woman bounced a baby who looked very much like the one the beta was holding. She was Cass, the alpha. It was hard to imagine the sweet-looking blonde as a fierce leader, but I guess we'd find out.

"Sorry, Caleb's been teething lately. Not his brother, though. Guess they're not identical after all." The beta gave a chuckle, calling my attention back to him, but he gave a start when the baby in his hands gave a tiny cry. "It's okay, little guy. Daddy will get you your frozen breast milk ring as soon as we're done." The way he cooed at the child in his hand, pulling him back to sit more on his lap and tucking him in tight, was disarming.

"And mates are allowed here, no restrictions?"

The beta's eyes darkened. "No restrictions."

I nodded, relieved. Accepting us was one thing, but Syl still had the potential to produce children if they decided to reassign her to someone else.

My concerns must've been evident on my face because the beta leaned forward. "I said no restrictions. No one will part a mated pair here. I'm actually fucking thrilled to have another mated pair. There's this rumour that maybe the reason mates were banned after the pack wars didn't just have to do with divided loyalties."

I quirked my eyebrow at him. I'd never heard of such a thing.

"Mates possess a special bond that gives them an advantage in battle, a connection and the ability to anticipate each other's movements. It is a unique benefit that a pair of pack mates can never achieve, and if one pack had more of such soldiers, well, they would be putting the others at a disadvantage. Make it so no packs can have mated pairs, and the problem goes away." The beta leaned back in his chair.

"Yes, Beta, I see."

The beta snarled. "I hate being called 'The Beta' all the time. It's really fucking annoying. You can call me by my name. It's Dame."

I gasped. Jace's brother was the fucking *beta*? Not sure whether my association with Jace would solidify our place here or damage our chances, I licked my lips nervously.

"I have a message for you. It's from a man named Jace, your brother. He was the one who gave me the compass that led to Pack Cass. He wanted me to tell you he's sorry."

Dark eyes studied my face, and the beta—Dame—gave a curt nod. "Good. He should be."

"Also, I found this at the bottom of my bag." Reaching into my pocket, I pulled the plastic square free and handed it to him, the note Jace had left still attached. "I'd love to deliver it to this Tristan myself." Dame took it in hand. His eyes went wide when he opened it and looked over the disc inside. "But I don't know anyone here, and I figu—"

"Whoa, this is awesome. Tristan's been missing this one. Thanks, man." Dame grinned, holding up the copy of *Shadows of Cobalt* I'd found tucked into the bottom of my bag when I'd dumped it out. I smiled back, but my heart wasn't in it. This place, this community, it was all too much. I'd be free to be with Syl, and they would allow me to be a fighter? To protect my pack, my mate?

The idea would be laughable back home. I was a defective, a loser, assigned the role of watcher purely because I was too weak to work the fields. Only Syl had ever seen value in me, and now...

I could be happy here. I could have friends. My eyes watered as I eyed the infant on Dame's lap who had now moved onto chewing the knuckle of Dame's index finger mercilessly with his toothless maw. But, no, not a family, not me. A life, a mate, but the choice of having a family or not was taken away.

"Hey, man, you okay?"

I looked up in surprise to find Dame watching me worriedly.

"Yeah, it's just...They took so much."

Dame looked from me to his son and leaned forward.

"I know what they do to those they decide are defective, and I'm here to tell you it's reversible. Completely reversible. We have human doctors here who can do the surgery for you. It's quick and relatively painless." He grimaced.

In shock, I looked up to meet his eyes, seeing a hope of a future I'd never dreamed possible. Did I want to be a father? I didn't know. It'd never been a possibility before. I wasn't sure I did, and I didn't know if I could stand to share Syl with another person. I knew it wasn't something she wanted. But if what Dame claimed was true, we would have the choice, and that was everything.

"Dame, I think I can speak for my mate and myself when I say we'd like to join Pack Cass."

The End

About the Author

Faye writes the kind of narratives that give her strength and courage. You can expect dark themes, high stakes, true love, and fierce heroines who struggle through their broken pasts to find human connection and salvation. Her works are best described as dark fantasy with strong romantic subplots featuring non-human characters with entirely human feelings and weaknesses.

She shares her writing space with a wildly supportive husband who regularly leaves her 'cofferings' (coffee offerings), three tiny humans who provide just the right amount of distraction, and a former Egyptian street cat who warms her lap to the purrfect writing temperature.

When she's not writing, you can find her traversing the outdoors and photographing everyday moments, changing her perspective and finding the hidden beauty in ordinary life.

The best place to find out more about Faye's future projects is on her socials.

https://www.tiktok.com/@faye.knightly.writer?is_from_webapp=1&sender_device
=pc

https://www.instagram.com/faye_knightly_writer

Or check out her link tree to see everything in one place and join her newsletter for book perks!

https://linktr.ee/faye_knightly_writer